The Teller

Also by Jonathan Stone

Moving Day
The Cold Truth
The Heat of Lies
Breakthrough
Parting Shot

JONATHAN STONE

The Teller

THOMAS & MERCER

Text copyright © 2015 Jonathan Stone

Published by Thomas & Mercer, Seattle

www.apub.com

Amazon, the Amazon logo, and Thomas & Mercer are trademarks of Amazon.com, Inc., or its affiliates.

ISBN-13: 9781477828656
ISBN-10: 1477828656

Cover design by Brian Zimmerman

Library of Congress Control Number: 2014955103

Printed in the United States of America

*To my writing group
Jim P., Susan S., and George B.
and to our monthly meetings
in the Roosevelt Hotel bar.*

———————

The Teller

The banks are simply too big.

Nouriel Roubini, Professor of Economics,
NYU Stern School of Business

PART ONE

1

Always dressed the same. That same unwashed black raincoat. That same black hat. The wrinkled pants and frayed pant cuffs and scuffed-up black shoes.

The unchanging routine of someone with nothing else to do, no one else to talk to, nowhere else to go.

He shuffles into the bank branch once a week or so, comes in from the busy, chaotic commercial boulevard outside—traffic snarled, horns honking, sidewalks packed and hot—into the sudden coolness, serenity, and pristine cleanliness of the bank, with its oddly holy silence. High-ceilinged and church-like, except for the clicking of heels on the bare, buffed floor and the tapping of fingers on terminals.

He shuffles dutifully into the roped line but waits for her. Clearly, to exchange a few words. She isn't sure exactly when he started coming in, or when he started to wait for her. Other customers do, too. A couple of shy young men with eagerness in their eyes. An older woman who loves to chat. And what does it hurt her to give them each a quick, warm smile, to brighten their day a little, take their minds off the fact that the money they're depositing is already spent, that most of them can't pay their bills.

Except him, of course.

She blinked the first time she saw it. A conventional, no-frills, old-fashioned savings account with a balance of over a million dollars. Every shuffling visit, he would make a deposit. Never spending a dime of it, as far as she could tell. The balance has only grown.

Then again, there are plenty of these eccentrics around. More than a handful. An old lady in a brownstone with a dozen terriers. An irritable local landlord. The branch has its share. A number of them are Depression-trained savers, her boss Glen has pointed out before. Her mother would be like that—if she had any money. Plenty of them have big accounts. He is hardly alone.

Once, early on, after he made his deposit, she asked him if he'd like to know the balance. He frowned at her with a little irritation, shook his head no, and she never asked again.

And now he shuffles up to her teller station. His face brightens as he approaches. He stands up a little straighter, she notices. She knows these might be the only words he says aloud all day.

"Hi, Mr. Desirio." Cheerful. Her charming smile. The smile they wait in line for. (And for her other charms, too, she knows. The very charming fit of her white blouse and blue skirt, for one.) But after all, she's supposed to be friendly, charming, and welcoming to the customers.

"Hi, Elaine. How's your momma doin'?" That deep, crusty voice, clearly not used to talking. Tentative, as if startled to hear itself.

The first time, like all of her customers, he glanced at the name tag over her breast: *Elaine Kelly*. Then quickly looked elsewhere, to show her he wasn't staring.

He always asks about her mother now. He knows she is sick. Elaine let it drop once in one of their brief, clipped conversations, and now he always dutifully inquires.

"She's doin' okay, Mr. Desirio. Thanks for askin'."

He hands her a check. She pretends not to look at it, not to notice the amount.

She calls up his account. The green glowing letters read:

DESIRIO, A.M. 2339729334 1,355,567.88

She goes to deposit it, but there's a problem with her terminal. Again.

She frowns. Shakes her head. Tries again. It's frozen. *Christ. It seems to go glitchy at least once a week.* With every bank merger, there are new software programs; with every new program, new problems. A construction worker, all chest and biceps, shifts impatiently in the roped-off line, looks at his watch, then looks at her, alternately hopeful and annoyed.

"Computer's not processing it. Some problem in the system. This happens sometimes," she says apologetically. "But I'll get it in there for you, Mr. Desirio, not to worry." The serene, cool, air-conditioned branch seems so clean and crisp and orderly. But it's not; there's plenty of disorder underneath. Like everywhere, she supposes.

Desirio looks unruffled. He nods appreciatively and smiles, teeth yellow and gray. "Thank you, Elaine. Nice to see you. And please give your mother my best wishes." Formal. Proper. Always the gentleman.

"I sure will, Mr. Desirio. You stay well."

He shuffles off toward the big glass door. Rumpled black hat. Wrinkled black raincoat. Scuffed, ancient black shoes. So completely, so obviously, alone in the world.

The construction worker goes impatiently to Sam, the teller standing next to Elaine, which gives Elaine another chance to get Desirio's deposit to process. But it still won't.

"You having the same trouble?" she asks Sam, whose after-hours flamboyance and lifestyle go utterly unrevealed by his starched white shirt and perfect posture—the proper banking persona he dons each day like an amusing costume. Only his boutonniere hints at his exuberant personality, at the nature of his nightlife.

"Yes, indeed," Sam says archly, rolling his eyes with exaggerated annoyance. Punching at his own terminal irritably. "What else is new?"

The screech and crunch are unmistakable. The screaming scrape of brakes. The slam. The thunk. The hiss. The oddly delicate, tinkling scatter of glass. The reactive female scream or two. The sickening sequence of sounds that everyone somehow instantly understands.

Elaine, Sam, and all the other tellers look up at the huge plate-glass windows, to the chaotic boulevard outside.

"Jesus," says Sam. "Elaine . . . it's your friend."

There in the middle of the boulevard lies the wrinkled black raincoat, covering Desirio like a black shroud. The scuffed black shoes, twisted together as if in the middle of a dance step. The black hat on the asphalt a few yards away.

She looks back down at her screen.

DESIRIO, A. M. 2339729334 1,355,567.88

The deposit still hasn't cleared.

After five years of standing at this terminal for hours at a stretch, the program commands are all second nature now, and her next three entries happen almost instinctively. A fluid series of keystrokes. Fingers moving in an automatic, invisible blur over the keyboard, a maestro at her instrument.

Hitting "transfer."

Entering 1,300,000.

Punching up KELLY, ELAINE 3947289402M. 2,045.28.

Hitting "Transfer" again.

The computer blinks back at her a moment later: TRANSFER EXECUTED.

She doesn't even check the new amount in her account before hitting "Escape" and returning to a neutral screen. She stares at the computer, stunned by what she's just done.

"Elaine, did you hear me? It's . . . it's your friend, Elaine, the old guy," Sam repeats.

Elaine looks up now.

She appears confused, stunned, Sam can see.

"My god. No," she says.

• • •

Sirens. EMTs. The yellow police tape unspooled in just minutes, cordoning off the scene of the accident, and all of them stand just outside it. The bright, fluttering, cheap yellow cousin of the bank's red velvet ropes with Antonio Desirio lying in the middle.

Around the scene, a crowd builds. Construction workers, their helmets respectfully on their hips. Colombian and Honduran moms and kids. Black kids wearing T-shirts and baggy jeans with St. Louis and Cincinnati baseball caps, loitering insolently.

The truck driver is shaking, shuddering, moaning. He's inconsolable. The focus of the scene. A figure in a Greek tragedy. He is an Eastern European of some sort, a big unshaven guy in a work shirt, whose primitive English seems forcibly extruded through lips and larynx. "He no look. He no look," he tells the cop insistently. "He jus' walking right out. Crazy old guy . . ." He shakes his head, presses both his hands to the top of his tightly curled hair, as if not knowing what else to do with them. "Twenty years I drive," he shouts aggressively, almost belligerently at the cop. "Twenty years nothing, no problem . . ."

"Take it easy, pal. Take it easy," says the cop. "We need some information."

"Sure. Yes." The truck driver nods cooperatively, dutifully. Suddenly penitent, fearful. "I give you. I give you right now."

Elaine stands on the sidewalk in front of the bank with the other tellers—Sam, hard-edged Vicki (in her sixties, using this excuse of calamity and the unscheduled sidewalk time to stick another cigarette into her wrinkled smoker's face), pencil-thin

5

Tori, cynical LeAnne. Their formal blue skirts and white blouses stand out, as do Sam's and Glen's white shirts, blue slacks, and ties, here on the Queens sidewalk where the other silent onlookers wear T-shirts and cheap print dresses and oversize sweatshirts and sleek, spotless sneakers. The bank tellers look like another species in comparison—aliens, startled by Earth's strange proceedings, caught unexpectedly amid a sea of humanity.

Glen, with his short-sleeved dress shirt and thick-rimmed black eyeglasses, looks like a NASA engineer momentarily displaced in the unfamiliar glare of sunlight. The tellers say nothing to one another; there is nothing to say.

In just minutes, there is a white sheet covering the black coat. In a busy intersection, with children watching, the sheet is a quick, automatic, and professional response. The Wite-Out of the urban street. Angel wings fluttering down on a lost soul.

Elaine surveys the scene anxiously.

"You okay, Elaine?"

She turns. Sam is looking at her, frowning with concern. "You look all shaken up. A little freaked out."

Yes, all shaken up.

Yes, a little freaked out.

She nods that she's okay.

Elaine stands silently observing amid her fellow New Yorkers.

Like a million New Yorkers, thinking anxiously about her bank balance.

2

There are 164,000 employees of Federated Bank. Its 8,500 commercial branches, plus corporate offices, investment banking operations, trading floors, and technical centers, are flung across more than a hundred countries, and it executes, processes, and shepherds every kind of financial transaction on the planet, from mergers of global industrial titans in deals that require hundreds of bankers and lawyers, to microloans to African subsistence farmers, to anonymous credit card transactions at the rate of literally millions a second.

It is its own city. And when the chairman speaks of the bank's vision, thousands of employees chuckle. They work here. They know. Federated tries to present to the world—through its smart, elegant logo, its honed press releases, its smartly dressed executives with carefully worded responses—an impression of supreme organization and trust and control. But more honestly, it is a beast. Amorphous and amoeba-like, its essential core and services move in generally the same direction, but its edges are always frayed, misshapen, essentially uncontrollable and unpredictable.

The accounts are swept for irregularities every evening at the bank's closing. The computer programs are impressive in that regard—sophisticated, sensitive—and their algorithms are able to identify irregularities with a high level of certainty. But a computer is only half the story. A human has to see it. A human has to be assigned to look at the readouts, examine the data more closely, double-check it, trace it back, put two and two together. It requires an employee who costs money, who must devote time to the task, and must be moved from another activity to do it. It's supposed to happen at the branch level, where managers are on tight operating budgets and anxious about their P&Ls and quarterly bottom lines that will be compared with competing branches, and are reluctant to devote the adequate human resources.

It requires the cooperation, the mutual effort and teamwork, of a computer and a human. The uneasy alliance of man and machine that defines all of modern banking. The alliance that makes modern banking work . . . and makes modern banking vulnerable.

Elaine knows how the sweeps work. She's been assigned to them herself. Glen trusts her. He saw early on how she adapted to new technologies much more quickly than the older tellers, how the instructions and commands of the bank's newly integrated systems came intuitively to her, so he has always given her those kinds of extra assignments. It seems to be his form of flirtation.

And having helped Glen—assisting in integrating the branch's sweep program, making it conform to the bank's regional require-ments—she also knows what kinds of accounts are checked first, what kinds are checked only subsequently, and what kinds are checked only after primary and secondary sweeps are completed.

She knows by now, too—after five years of silently observing her bosses' frustrations, listening to cynical tellers' conversations, reading the stacks of corrections reports, and helping to institute thick sheaves of internal policy and procedural changes and changes back—that there are literally hundreds of millions of dollars in mis-takes, errors, and losses, as well as outright identity theft and fraud, absorbed by Federated and its competitors every year. (In their wildly successful credit card division, theft and fraud are grudgingly accepted as a cost of doing business.)

They are honest mistakes—clerical errors, entry errors, procedural errors, errors of all kinds—no different from the crazy charges on her phone bill, or her mom's utility bill, or an unauthorized charge on one of her cards. She has seen so many bank errors occur when old accounts are turned into new accounts, remarketed into "upgraded" accounts, or when one bank and system are merged with another, and then a third, and then merged yet again, leaving the numerous payment systems currently in place laughably complex. Where the bank should have a single system, mergers and takeovers have left it with over a dozen. Forcing the IT group—the computer geeks—to work around the clock simply fixing things, making technology repairs on the fly and jury-rigging systems until the next crisis. Her terminal's failure to process this morning was hardly an isolated error. Hardware and software act up all the time.

And then, of course, there are the losses that aren't errors at all. The bank's computers are hacked almost monthly. It isn't publicized, needless to say, and the bank is so huge that it makes good immediately on any lost customer assets—no hassle, few questions asked. It's easiest and cheapest to quickly and quietly reimburse. The bank's crime and fraud unit has over two hundred professionals running investigations around the clock. They wouldn't exist, or be so busy, if there weren't a constant flow of attacks attempted against the bank.

And it seems that every other morning, as her F train bumps and lurches and squeaks from stop to stop and she diligently absorbs the newspaper's business section—vaguely hoping that her sprightly conversancy with interest rates, foreign currencies, Fed pronouncements, and employment and housing reports will translate into a raise, or a promotion, or even just a higher notch of respect—she reads about financial crimes and investigations. New schemes. New twists on old ones. Some involving tellers every year.

Because, robbing an account? *Anyone* can do it. All the safeguards and security are *because* anyone can do it. (In the formal old days of banking, she knows, employee accounts were kept at a separate bank, but today, bank management would never give up the assets of 164,000 employees to a competitor.) Not getting *caught*, not being discovered or found out, *that* was a trick much tougher to manage. But some hackers were successful—she knew from periodic bank alerts—and they were doing it from *outside*. She was *inside*. Where every merger, every flawed system, every technological failure punched another little hole of opportunity in the employee firewalls . . .

Yet none of that even matters, Elaine thinks, as the F train lumbers and lurches above her borough and the straphangers bounce in unison, oddly somber on their twice-daily amusement park ride. Primary and secondary account sweeps, merged payment systems, IT geeks, clerical errors, hacker attacks, identity theft—none of that matters much at all given where she has put the money.

An electronic inside pocket. A digital side drawer. Hence the account number's *M* at the end.

Odds are, she has a few days undetected.

Maybe even a week or more.

By which time, presumably, she will be long gone.

She looks around at her fellow straphangers: hospital orderlies with their ID cards around their necks, security guards ending their shifts, two teenage Hispanic mothers with their babies on their laps, a bicycle messenger with his bike in the vestibule, a med student with a textbook open on her lap.

Elaine is the richest person on her subway car.

And the most terrified.

3

Arms full of groceries—milk, canned vegetables, fresh produce, a carton of eggs—Elaine arrives home, juggles the bags as she grabs the key in the flowerpot, and jiggles open the lock on the peeling red front door. The Kelly clan—the very last gasp of it now—has inhabited this Queens row house for the past seventy years. She lets herself inside, and heads down the dark, narrow hallway to the kitchen.

Elaine cooks an omelet, sets it on a tray with utensils and water, even a flower in a bud vase, and takes it up the narrow staircase to the master bedroom. As always, she hears the steady sound of the ventilator, the mechanical click and beat of the secondhand unit she found online, as she approaches. Its somber, relentless pulse is a reminder of the rule of machines in their lives. This one a dull, dutiful cousin of the sleek, silent machinery at work. It makes her feel like screaming, and yet it is reassuring. The sound means that her mother is still breathing.

Elaine enters and sits on the edge of the bed with the tray in her lap. Her mother removes her oxygen mask with a practiced flourish, always ready to whip it off.

Her mother smiles. "Laney, my Laney . . . how was your day?" The voice of cigarettes, that hoarse, tough sound that Elaine used to think was a sound of strength and sturdiness. Now that same voice stands for fragility, infirmity.

Elaine deflects the question. "How was yours?"

"You're lookin' at it," says her mother with a sardonic smile. "Same old, same old. Morning talk shows, afternoon nap, a few pages of this silly novel." She holds it up briefly. "That's why you have to tell me—tell me *anything*—about your day. Did anything happen outside this bedroom?" A thin little grin. "Pretend you just got home from third grade and I just served you milk and cookies. So, little girl, tell me about school."

Elaine stares expressionlessly at her mother for a moment.

I stole one million three hundred thousand dollars from a lonely old man.

A lonely, dead *old man.*

She breaks her gaze away, spreads the bedspread flat and neat around her mother's feet, then shrugs. "Nothing really to tell."

"Oh, but there is," says her mother. "I can see it, Laney. You seem distracted about something." She studies her. "I may be an old shut-in, but I'm your mother."

Tell me anything, share something of your day, some morsel to cheer up an old invalid, that was all she was asking, and yet Elaine still has the uncomfortable sense that her mother means more. Can see through her. It's nothing more than her own Catholic guilt, Elaine knows, hanging in the very air of this house, reduced to a whisper but still here.

"Go ahead. What happened?" As if her mother actually *knows* something did and is waiting like a priest for Elaine's confession.

"I don't want to talk about it," Elaine says.

"So there's an *it* to it," her mother replies victoriously. Shifting from priest to lawyer, parsing and pouncing. "Let's hear then."

Elaine takes a breath.

A million three.

"Remember the old man in black I told you about, Mom?"

"Who always asks about me?"

And please give your mother my best wishes, and like a dutiful daughter, Elaine had. Hoping it would give her mom a little lift, knowing someone was thinking about her, someone, anyone, outside this little room. Hoping it would make her mother feel a little better by comparison. *He has no one, Mom, but you at least have me.* She had described his rumpled appearance and the clockwork regularity of his visits to the branch. She had never mentioned the money. That was against bank rules. Rules she had so studiously and steadily obeyed. Until, suddenly, she hadn't.

"What about him?"

Elaine looks at her mother, at the ventilator. She shakes her head.

"Go ahead."

She turns away. She has backed herself into this awkward corner, into this awkward subject, and with her mother's insistence, can't get herself out.

She can't look at her mother while she says it.

"He died, Mom."

Her mother appears momentarily disoriented, annoyed. Who exactly allowed death, the forbidden, obvious subject, into the room? By what trick, what deception, did it slip its black grasping fingers in here?

Then her mother looks at her and sits up a little to play the mother role. "People die. You're anywhere long enough, Laney, and people will die on you."

"No. In front of the bank. Hit by a truck."

Death. Instantaneous on the busy boulevard. Hanging in the bedroom air for months now.

"Oh." Eunice Kelly pauses, as if in a moment of respect, then picks up her oxygen mask. She can't speak while she breathes through it, which leaves a silence for Elaine to fill. Elaine listens to the beat and pulse of the machinery delivering air to her mother, pushing it into her compromised lungs.

"Sweet old man," Elaine says. "All alone in the world. You could just tell."

Her mother holds the mask aside for a moment, listening to the machine's slight change, its pause, in its delivery of oxygen. It's the pause that will be the only sound when no one's there to draw in the air. "Well," she says. "For him at least it was quick."

No arch smile. Eyes blank and black, absent any expression. *How black Irish of you, Mother.*

Mrs. Kelly presses the mask to her face again and takes a few more breaths. She looks over the top of the mask at Elaine sourly. *You win, Elaine. I shouldn't have asked. No more talk about your day.*

After she cleans up the kitchen and takes out the trash, Elaine neatens the area around her mother's bed, checks the meters and settings on the ventilator, tucks her mother in, and turns out the light. Her mother's bedroom—the whole house—has felt strange to her these past few years. Her mother can barely leave the room now, cannot leave the house, yet it is Elaine who is hostage here. She feels like both the jailer and the jailed, captor and captive. Her mother, always exhausted, falls into sleep before Elaine is even down the hall to her own tiny bedroom. Her mother is weak. Elaine has complete charge and control of the house, of her mother. Yet her mother has all the power. Is the center, the focus of Elaine's life. Her mother can barely leave the bed, but Elaine is the one confined, unfree to leave this cramped Queens row house where she was born, the only home she's ever known.

Throughout her childhood, this street and those around it were exclusively Irish Catholic, their own little Dublin alley, complete with Irish accents overheard on the stoops and among urchin kids playing ball games in the street. Now, the neighborhood is full of Filipinos and Dominicans and Ecuadorians, Pakistanis and

Bangladeshis. She and her mother are some of the last original tenants left, as vestigial, as rare, as Elaine's freckles and red hair. The Filipino and Ecuadorian kids stare openly at her—the only redhead for blocks around. She keeps her hair pinned up responsibly and demurely during the week, brushing it out on weekends, lustrous and afire.

Other features set her apart here, too: her stern, straight nose that comes to an arrogant tip; the sea of dots marching across it and over her cream-colored cheeks. But mostly, it's that red crown of flame—so loud, challenging, and tempestuous compared to the reserved, obedient person who bears it. She's sure it's because of her hair and coloring that some of the bank customers choose her, too.

The row house is cramped but adequate, and they don't need more space. Her mother couldn't have any more children after her little sister was born. (Her runaway sister, Annelle, whom Elaine loves and hates. Gone eight years now, since Annelle turned fifteen, packed a bag, and headed for the 7 train to Manhattan.) Her parents bought the house as soon as her dad went on staff at the printer's. He died of lung cancer ten years later, when Elaine was in third grade. (There was no milk and cookies that year—her mother was hallucinating, or trying to subtly rewrite the past.) Elaine and her mother have always kept the place immaculate. Elaine mows the grass in the tiny yard, keeps the window boxes filled with annuals. She feeds her mother's cats, diligently changes their litter boxes, and vacuums frequently. Her mother has somehow accumulated ten of them by now, ancient orange tabbies and kittens that were gifts from neighbors as well as strays, curling up against throw pillows, and behind drapes, and on closet floors.

The value of the row house has risen and fallen with the changing desirability of the neighborhood over the past twenty years. When her mother had to stop working, and with just a teller's income, Elaine had had to arrange a reverse mortgage on the house. When Elaine's mother dies, Federated's real estate division will get the house, turn around, and sell it. Which is fine with Elaine. Her two responsibilities, the two themes of her life—her mother, this house—will be gone together. She has no idea how freedom will taste.

Buenos Aires. Rome. Barcelona. Hong Kong.

Her experienced fingers skitter across a keyboard again. By the light of a single desk lamp in the corner of the living room, Elaine begins to explore on their home computer.

A one-bedroom condo across from the Buenos Aires beaches: $300,000, according to the currency converter.

An apartment just off the Via Delorosa: $450,000.

A co-op in residential Madrid: $400,000.

She checks airfares, jots some notes down neatly on a scrap of paper, buries it in the bottom of her purse, then erases the computer's memory cache of the websites. Her mother can barely get out of bed, would never come down to use this computer, and wouldn't know how to check the Internet history anyway, but Elaine doesn't want to take any chances. She shuts the computer down and stares at the keyboard for a few moments in the stillness.

She touches the computer's "Return" key—abstractly, with no exact thoughts, but a sense, a feeling of . . . excitement? Tension? Regret? The key that executed the transfer, the single keystroke, the peck of the forefinger, that divides before from after. She strokes the "Return" key again, to summon up the feeling in that moment after Desirio was hit. To try to reexperience, reimagine, exactly what made her do it. What made her go outside herself, go outside everything she was, for that one strange, impulsive moment.

She had always felt such impulses, ever since she was a kid. Passing a cop on the street, she'd have the impulse to grab the gun from his belt. Sitting at a glass table or passing a huge glass window, she'd feel the impulse to break it with a rock, to put an object through it. The impulse to shout out a curse word in the middle of class. To grab a candy bar in a bodega. To run into the middle of a parade or up onstage during the middle of a play.

She was pretty sure every kid felt these impulses. Particularly good, dutiful, Catholic kids. A half-conscious wish to bust out of the life and rules that had been prescribed and ordained. A safe fantasy of challenging authority, disrupting the status quo. And they were passing impulses. Mere moments. And while she was still sometimes surprised by her own impulsive thoughts, she was mostly amused by them now.

They had shifted as she'd matured, changed along with her. The impulse to toss her work into a trash can she passes on the street. To lean across and suddenly kiss a colleague she's talking to—sometimes a man, sometimes a woman.

The impulse would surface, rise, like a fish glistening above the ceaseless, washing waves of life, and then it would recede. The ocean returning to its daily, predictable, vast self. She couldn't think of a single one of these impulses she had ever acted on. These might be the modern version, the modern analogy, of the tests of character that saints faced and stared down.

She couldn't say for sure if others had these impulses. She'd never talked about them with anyone. Didn't know if they were normal, but if they weren't, they didn't seem all that bad. It was, what . . . wanting to sweep away a blockage or barrier? Wanting to see what happened? Wanting to create a consequence? She didn't know.

No, she'd never acted on them. Not a single one.

Until today.

And this wasn't a candy bar in a bodega. (She'd never swiped one, anyway.)

This was 1.3 million dollars.

Impulse, yes, but then again, it wasn't impulsive at all. She had thought frequently about all that money, sitting in that account, unspent, never *going* to be spent—she'd thought about the strangeness of that. And she had thought about the imprisonment of her own life, trapped taking care of her mother in a Queens row house, not having enough money to pay for her mother's care, hating the banking work but unable to quit and do something else because she needs the bank's health insurance for her mother. Every time she had seen Desirio, she thought about the amount in his account. She's a teller. It's the only thing she knows about her customers, really . . . their bank accounts. She did keep the figure to herself—she was quiet about that—but it was only human to see old Desirio, bent over, shuffling in, yellowed smile, and think of it . . . Wasn't it?

She thought about it because, of *course* you think about it. You have to think about *something* standing there for hours on end, depositing payroll checks, and personal checks, and insurance reimbursement checks, and state and federal checks. As you stand there counting out cash, punching the keys by rote, all you can *do* is think. And you can't think about what you're doing. There's nothing to think about in that. So all you find yourself thinking about is how to get out of there, because if you have to stand there the rest of your life doing mostly what the ATMs around the corner can do just as well, you'll go crazy.

At some level, she had been *waiting* to do it. She just didn't *know* she had been waiting to do it. It had come from some other part of her, that surprised her, that she didn't know was there.

She knows she can't wait too long. The bank just completed an account sweep as part of a unit audit, and is due to initiate another. She knows this, but it's not so simple. Can she really leave her mother? The woman struggling to breathe in the bedroom upstairs? Certainly she can't *appear* to have left her mother; it would look too odd and heartless and suspicious. And in reality, she isn't sure she can bring herself to leave her mother anyway.

That's the problem with impulse. That's proof that it *was* impulse. That she'd have to break off now from the mother who raised her, who needs her. Can she do that? Can she do it to save herself? Maybe transferring the money was a way to make her break away. Her *true* impulse. Her true self, forcing her to give herself a chance. Her mother is going to die, after all. All Elaine's care is not going to keep her alive. So should Elaine save herself? Or be such a good, dutiful daughter that she stay with her mother too long and then be caught and sent to prison for honoring her sense of duty? Elaine turns off the desk lamp, sits silently in the dark living room. Mind buzzing but paralyzed.

What have I done?

4

In the morning, they stand at their terminals, processing customers, transacting business as always, as if nothing has happened. And really, what has? Nothing so remarkable. A customer, an elderly gentleman—inattentive, probably vision and hearing impaired—was killed while crossing the street. One of dozens of pedestrian accidents yesterday throughout the five boroughs of New York. Most don't even rate a mention in the newspaper. For local law enforcement, it's no doubt a clerical event. A New York occurrence.

Elaine doesn't dare punch up her own account. Doesn't dare to diverge from the business at hand. She feels the tension all through her.

For now, keep everything the same.

NASA Glen comes out of his office, looking as though he's stepped out of another decade with his crew cut, his glasses and his pocket protector, and strides along behind the long counter to Elaine's terminal. Her eyes flick up at him. The branch manager is only a few years older than her, a fact that Glen thinks makes his crush at least somewhat appropriate. But he's not smiling at her like he usually does.

"Elaine, phone call for you on my line."

She frowns, confused. Who would be calling her on that number? It's on the list she gave her mother for emergencies, but why wouldn't she call Elaine's cell phone first? "Sorry about this," she apologizes.

"Don't be. It's no one you know," Glen says. "Official call. Police want to talk to you."

Her heart pounds. It squeezes, hurts. Her body buzzes almost electrically beneath her. She wants to run.

How can this be? How can this be? Something I don't know. Some system I'm not aware of.

She flushes primrose and walks with doom. She follows Glen toward his office looking down at her legs to see if they will actually carry her there.

He gestures for her to take his leather desk chair and hands her the receiver. Closes the small office's glass door as he leaves her. She thinks briefly, oddly, fleetingly, that this is the first and last time she'll have an office like this to herself. Five years at the bank and she'll occupy an actual office for only a minute or two.

She can barely focus. The office is spinning. She is dizzy with fear. Surprised at how dizzy. She feels close to throwing up.

"Elaine Kelly?" says the voice. It's good-natured, deceptively friendly, a honey trap, she thinks.

"Yes . . ." she barely manages in a fluttery whisper.

Why'd you do it? What possessed you? What's wrong with you? She can feel the beginning of her new life. She can feel it starting right here, looking at Glen's old-fashioned desk blotter, at the pictures of his baby. Starting at this moment, her new existence. Her fallen life.

"Detective Nussbaum, from the One-Fourteen. Need to ask you a few questions."

What's that? The 114th Precinct? She swallows hard. "The . . . the police?" *Should I get a lawyer? Refuse to answer?* Her mind is spinning around the suddenness of the situation, unable to focus.

The detective's laugh bursts out of him. "Ain't TV, Miss Kelly. I'm no Chris Noth. I got a form here. Gotta check off the boxes, is all. You knew the deceased, Antonio Desirio?"

The understanding perches suddenly, thin and small but clear, on the edge of her consciousness. *Wait . . . this has nothing to do with his bank account.* "Knew him?" She stalls for a moment while she pulls herself together, gets ready to pay close attention, to answer carefully.

"Your supervisor said . . ."

"Well, he was a customer."

"How often he come in?"

"Once a week at most."

"You have any conversation with him?"

She thought about it for a moment. Had she? She could answer truthfully. "Not really. You know, exchanged greetings and such, but there was always a line waiting."

"What kind of banking was he doing?"

"Just . . . making deposits."

"What kind of deposits? Social security? Pension?"

She takes a breath. She knows this. She plants her feet beneath the desk for a moment. "Detective, I don't think I'm allowed to talk to you about that, am I?"

A pause.

"Good girl," says Nussbaum, ungrudging, relaxed, purely complimentary. "Absolutely correct. You're not allowed to. And social security check or golden parachute doesn't matter much now, does it? Did he wait to see you, do you think?"

She feels herself flush a little, embarrassed. "I think so, yes."

"Yeah, your supervisor thought so, too."

She catches it. A gentle little interview trick. Seeing if she answers the same way as Glen did. So was he testing her, a quick check to make sure she's being truthful?

"But a few of my customers do that," she tells him, offering up a little more information than asked for, her own little interview trick in return. "They feel more comfortable, I guess. Makes the banking, I don't know, more personal."

"Anything more you can think to tell me about him?"

I took 1.3 million dollars from him. It's in my account. I'm planning a new life with it.

"Not really."

"Then that's it."

"That's it?" Elaine sits up, surprised, relieved.

"Hey, like I said, I'm filling out a form. Just a formality. You know how they always say, 'If I get hit by a truck'? Well, this poor guy was. Hit by a truck. That's it. Thanks for your time, Miss Kelly."

"Okay, well, thank you, too, Detective . . ."

"Thank me, for what?"

It had slipped out of her, that thank-you. She understood immediately why. *Thank you for not catching me. Thank you for giving me a chance.*

"I mean, you're welcome," she says.

He laughs again. "That automatic bank teller thank-you, huh?"

"I guess."

For now, keep everything the same.

She sits at lunch, as always, in the little interior conference room where the tellers gather in two lunch shifts. Today, it's Sarah, Bob, Sam, Pam, Vicki, and herself. Elaine brings a brown bag from home. It's so much cheaper. Some of the others do, too. The rest venture out onto the boulevard and bring back fast-food chicken, or Mexican, or Indian. The TV in the corner behind them plays CNN, a background of grim mumble and drone.

"Thirty years old, still living with two roommates, brown-bagging it to work. If I behave myself, I'll get a three-thousand-dollar raise in two years, which changes absolutely nothing. What's wrong with this picture?" says Sam, taking his chicken salad sandwich out of his bag and unwrapping it.

"Your mother must be very proud," Sarah teases him.

"It's 'cause you're on the Upper East Side," Pam scolds him. She's a plain-looking mom in her forties who commutes in from the Rockaways on a series of subways. "You won't give up the bright lights and big city, Sam. That's for kids. Time to grow up."

"And what are *you* doing on the Upper East Side anyway?" Sarah asks with a broad smile, the implication clear. Why's a gay guy—a *flamboyant* gay guy—struggling to live amid the young, rich, white families and trust-funders and stratospheric rents?

Sam—flamboyant, celebratory, proud, loud, and fun—is somehow even more flamboyant in his starched white shirt and perfectly creased blue slacks. More notable, more "out," in his utter uniformity of appearance, which is such a stark contrast to his personality.

"But I'm a *banker*," he defends himself broadly, humorously. "My mother *is* proud. Her son is a banker."

"Her son works in a bank," says Pam. "Her son is not *a banker*. Big difference."

Sam looks about to defend himself again but wilts. Hunches his shoulders over his sandwich. "Some banker," he concedes. "There's, like, thirty-five dollars in my checking account. I'm constantly rotating my bills."

"Hey, who doesn't?" says Vicki in her husky smoker's voice.

"Point is, I could cross the street tomorrow and get hit by a truck. Like Elaine's friend. Any of us could. And what did we accomplish?"

Elaine goes on the alert.

"Lonely old guy like that," says Sam. "I saw him every week making his deposits. Every week the guy brought a check to the counter. Never spent a dime. You could tell."

Pam looks at her. "He had a little crush on you, didn't he, Elaine?"

Elaine shrugs.

"How 'bout it, Elaine?" says Sam. "Was Desirio loaded? You can tell us. Guy's dead after all."

"Sam!" says Pam.

"How much, Elaine?"

"Hey, you're making her uncomfortable. She's not supposed to say," says Pam.

"Ah, you'll never tell us, good Catholic girl, will you, Elaine?" Sam teases.

Elaine looks at them all. Even Pam, who is defending her, still wants to know, she can sense. They all are curious. All waiting for her response.

Elaine looks around at them. "Okay, everyone, think of an amount," she says.

They smile. She's going to make a game of it. "Okay, everyone have a number in mind?"

They all nod.

Elaine looks around at the table, regards each of them, as if about to start asking for their guesses.

Then, with a grand sweep of her hand, says, "You're all too low," and takes a bite of her sandwich.

Sam, Vicki, and Pam burst out laughing. Sarah and Bob smile.

And for the moment, she's off the hook.

Everything the same. Keep everything the same.

"Sh sh sh sh!" Sam hushes them suddenly, excitedly, looking at the TV screen in the corner, jumping for the remote to goose the sound. "Quiet down, everybody. It's the boss."

They all crane and pivot to the screen.

"Carlton Conner, CEO of Federated Bank," the newscaster intones, "spoke with a shareholder group today, defending his forty-five-million-dollar pay package in the wake of a stagnant stock price . . ."

And there he is, in file footage Elaine has seen the news organizations use before, a handsome man still blond in his early forties, coming out of his Fifth Avenue penthouse, giving a quick wave and a smile, and there, skiing, and there, on the back deck of a yacht, with his beautiful young family, two daughters and a son cavorting happily around him and his lovely, smooth-skinned wife.

". . . questioned about the stock price, he expressed confidence in prospects for next quarter. Conner's pay package represents a ten-percent raise from last year . . ."

"How come he never visits us here in the branch?" Sam asks, and the lunch table giggles appreciatively, which only encourages Sam to make some introductions, "Hi, Carl, this is Elaine . . . Elaine, meet Carl . . ."

More giggles.

"He looks good though, doesn't he?" says Pam, eyes fixed on the screen. "Tasty little watercraft, too, huh?"

"He's having us out on it, I understand," says Sam. "You didn't get your invite? Ooooh, maybe I shouldn't have said anything . . ."

Madrid. Athens. Johannesburg. Buenos Aires.

On a break, Elaine sits in front of her computer in one of the cubicles they all share. She makes sure no one is looking and searches again. She is narrowing it down as quickly as she can, trying to focus, think practically, push aside the sureality of it all—a one-bedroom apartment in Lisbon, a fourteenth-century renovated town house rental in Rome, a condo in Buenos Aires. She thinks nervously about the language barriers, but cash is the international language, she knows. She imagines the shopping, the groceries, the days, the views.

How far from the closest market? Can I walk? Is there parking if I get a car? Trying to be pragmatic, remove it from the realm of fantasy . . . put aside the fact that she is selecting a random point on the globe, choosing a future, off a computer screen in a cubicle in Queens . . .

"Hey . . ." Sam is suddenly at the door.

She disconnects immediately, automatically, from the Internet; her work screen is back up instantly.

"You having connection problems?" asks Sam.

She shrugs. "Not that I know of."

"Mind if I borrow your computer for a few minutes? Mine is misbehaving—no connectivity at all."

She gestures to her terminal graciously.

"Thanks, Elaine," says Sam. "IT tells me they'll be right over. We both know that's code for a week or two." Or several more calls to them, anyway. Sam rolls his eyes with exaggerated, overdramatic exasperation.

On her way out of the bank at the end of the day, she feels the familiar, foolish, and inevitable schoolgirl flutter that she knows she will, that she always does, as she passes Bob's cubicle. Today, she leans into it as if impulsively, as if merely breezy and friendly, with her excuse at the ready: checking on the progress of the sculpture he's been creating out of an unusual material, all their used lottery tickets.

Bob almost always joins them for lunch but rarely says a word. Amid their ritualized lunchtime grumbles and gripes, he never complains. He's quiet, seemingly self-contained. She's been curious about him from the day he was transferred here from another branch a few months ago, but nobody knows much about him since he never shoots off his mouth about himself. He's a few years older than Elaine, with a lean, taut face and gray-brown eyes that seem gently, continually amused. Despite his quiet style, Bob has been easily friendly with Elaine since the day he started. And she wishes, she wants, to be the same with him, but her inborn defensiveness and caution have prevented it. And now, because he is attractive— attractive and approachable—that defensiveness takes the form of her schoolgirl nervousness, which makes her feel incompetent and crummy and shy.

Most days she just accepts it and gives up and walks past his cubicle. But today she leans in. Today she tries. Hoping to be different.

Hoping to shed her habitual defenses and emerge. Maybe the shift in her bank account will create a shift in her, as well. Because while she is keeping everything the same, everything is about to change, and maybe she is about to change, too . . .

Behind Bob, the sculpture, with its free-form wings and tail, was gradually assuming the shape of an abstract soaring bird.

She gestures toward the sculpture. "Wow. It's getting bigger."

He smiles. "As long as we all keep losing."

She looks at that soaring bird of used lottery tickets. A beautifully simple idea. An eloquent statement of broken dreams. More eloquent than all Sam's grand complaints, than Pam's frustrated insults, than the desperation she sees in the daily parade of faces in front of her, checking their balances and account totals with confusion, disillusion, and dismay. The shorthand of art, she supposes.

She wants to say more. Wants him to say more to her. She wants to tell him her plans, that she is soaring, soaring for all of them—or is it slinking and slithering out? But she can't reveal that, of course, and because she can't reveal it, she isn't sure what to say exactly and is too embarrassed to stand there saying nothing. She senses the same suffocating reserve from him now, as well. Her awkward silence is probably the cause of it.

Come with me.

A schoolgirl fantasy, she knows, accompanying her schoolgirl shyness and incompetence.

I have money. An exotic place for us to live. Come with me.

"Well . . . see you tomorrow," Elaine says.

Tomorrow . . . my last day.

"Yeah. You, too." His gentle, friendly eyes betray that he's confused by the tone of her quick little visit. As confused as she is.

When Elaine brings the dinner tray into the master bedroom, her mother struggles to sit up against the pillows, takes off her mask, and suddenly, with surprising strength, asks, "What happens to his money?"

Elaine looks at her mother, startled. Feels suddenly off-balance. She sets the tray down quickly to avoid dropping it.

A shiver goes through her. *Why would she ask that? So suddenly, out of the blue?*

"I'm serious," says Eunice Kelly. "That old man, all alone. What happens in a case like this?"

"Goes to the government, I guess." She says it evenly. Informatively.

"A lot of money?"

"Mother."

"I'm just asking. That's all you really know about him, after all—his bank account."

"That's not your business."

"But you know, don't you?"

She looks at her mother, still visibly uncomfortable with this line of questioning. *Where is this coming from, Mother?*

Eunice Kelly shrugs defensively. "I'm lying here all day, with nothing to think about. Sorry." She grabs the morning newspaper that's folded beside her and points to a small item as she hands it to Elaine:

MAN KILLED LEAVING BANK

A man identified as Antonio Desirio, 81, was hit by a delivery truck while attempting to cross the street after exiting a Federated Bank branch on Northern Boulevard.

Elaine looks at the short article, reads it closely, word for word, searching it anxiously for hidden meanings.

She is relieved to find there are none. But that relief is followed by a weight of sadness. A life reduced to four lines. A life replayed in four curt lines in no more detail than what she already knew about him. A restatement of what she and the other tellers watched through the plate-glass window, separated from it, the event observed as if in a movie to be read about in the next day's newspaper. And now it was.

The newsprint is fluttery and insubstantial in her hand. His death chronicled toward the bottom of the page, like an afterthought, mere filler. As if an editor could as easily have chosen a joke or a recipe to fill out the column.

A news item, an obituary, and a short brutal poem, all in one. His mystery intact, confirmed and immortalized in print.

She sets the newspaper down as her mother shifts and settles into place over the dinner tray.

Her mother looks up at her, seems to drop her guard, goes softer, quieter, studying her daughter. "You know why I'm asking about him, Elaine, don't you?" Her eyes go liquid, blurry, inquisitive, imploring.

Elaine feels her heart seize.

"You know it's because . . . because I don't have any money," she says sheepishly.

They are silent a moment.

"Eighty-one," says Eunice Kelly. She shrugs. "I won't even get close to that."

Her mother is getting worse. Not steadily worse, all-of-a-sudden worse. Her breathing is now more labored, more deliberate, her movements suddenly much more difficult.

The sickness has been so consistent, so unchanging. Their home routine has been predictable, unvarying, and absolute. Elaine has thought vaguely, desperately, in the wake of her impulsive-unimpulsive act, that she must simply slip out, find a day and night nurse to replace her, now that she can afford it. A simple substitution, leaving her mother's routine and life intact. But this sudden deterioration in her mother's condition . . . it alters that vision, that version of events.

She lies in her bed, listening to the click of her mother's ventilator echo in the short hallway outside her bedroom door and staring at her bedside clock, its red second hand sweeping mutely and relentlessly. She thinks of the bank clock that hangs behind the tellers, as if at the back of their brains—simple, iconic, its second hand sweeping insistently, more metaphoric than anyone intends. In moments when the branch is very still and silent, you can actually hear the tick of its second hand.

For her, there are two clocks now ticking. One counts down the hours and minutes until the transfer is discovered. The other counts down to her mother's last breath. Two clocks, crossing each other, intertwining in a complex, uninterpretable pattern. A havoc of cross rhythm and sweeping time, where it's hard to hear anything clearly, hard to know which beat to move to.

So she lies there, shifting, unable to sleep. And a few hours later, she stands, paralyzed, in place at her terminal again. *Next customer, please. Next lifetime, please. Tick, tick, tick . . . Madrid. Buenos Aires. Johannesburg. Berlin.* A different city whispering with every second. A different Internet postcard view appearing in her mind. Nothing to ground the fantasy. Nothing to impel it one way or another. Not a city, but a city name. A point on the map. *Tick, tick, tick . . .* There's shuffling and muttering and sound in the branch lobby, but she hears the ticking nevertheless.

At lunchtime, when the bank is at its busiest, a handsome dark-haired man with an open sport coat approaches the counter with a check in hand. He gives it to her wordlessly with his deposit slip, barely looking at her. *Too bad*, she thinks in passing.

She turns over the check to make the deposit for him.

A paycheck from the City of New York.

Payee: Evan Nussbaum.

She looks up, startled, remembering the name.

Now he's smiling broadly at her. Charming. Like that actor Chris Noth.

"I can tell by your expression, Miss Kelly, you remember me."

"Detective Nussbaum."

"From the One-Fourteen. Making a deposit. Detectives do get paid . . . if you want to call it that," he jokes.

Detective Nussbaum.

Her mouth, her throat, go dry.

Relax. Relax. She is glad to have the routine of the deposit, the rote motion she executes hundreds of times a day, a hundred thousand identical motions over the past five years. All that routine is useful now.

What's he doing here? She uses one hand to steady herself against the counter, trying not to let him see.

Small talk. Normalize it. She doesn't know if she's more flustered by him being here or by his surprising good looks. He *does* look like Chris Noth. *Make small talk.*

"What brings you to the neighborhood?" she asks.

"You, Miss Kelly."

She looks up at him, stricken.

"Seriously," he says, and she watches his bright smile fade a little.

She grips the counter with both hands now, to steady herself from the instant dizziness.

"I have something I want to show you," he says. "Think you can get someone to cover for you for a few minutes?"

They borrow the little lunchtime conference room. There's a DVD player that sits on top of the TV in the corner, used occasionally to screen instructional and promotional materials to the staff. He closes the door, then pops a disk into the player, picks up the remote, and shuffles it expertly, like it's his own.

"Surveillance tapes. A compilation. Ready?"

Why is he torturing her like this? Why is he drawing it out? *Just say it. You got me. Say it. Is there a camera on the tellers and we never knew it? A camera set on our terminal screens? Or some other system we weren't told about? Just do it, you sadist. Get it over with.* She's ready to scream.

There on the surveillance tape, she sees Antonio Desirio shuffling into the branch.

Once more, the black raincoat, the scuffed black pants, the black hat are moving, alive. Once more, standing patiently in line. Once more, shuffling, broken and bent over, up to her terminal. She sees herself and is somehow shocked by it.

"Here's Desirio coming into your branch to make a deposit, just like you said."

Nussbaum shifts the disk forward with the remote. There's the same black hat and black raincoat . . . but in a different bank.

"Here he is, making a deposit at United Bank and Trust."

He shifts the disk forward once more.

"Here he is at Deutsche Bank."

Shifting forward.

"Here he is at First National."

He stops the disk. "It took me quite a while to assemble this little movie, believe me . . ." He carefully presses buttons on the remote and the TV, shutting them off. "Turns out he had accounts at all these banks. Moving money constantly through all of them. Big amounts. Changing amounts . . ." He turns to her, his smile wry and grim. "So if you thought you were special . . ."

She is shocked. Confused. "I . . . I don't get it. What . . . what is he doing? What's going on?"

"That's what we'd like to know." He looks at her. His flirtatious, winning smile is gone. "Miss Kelly, is there anything you can tell us, anything at all, that would explain what we're looking at?"

She shakes her head.

"Think back. Anything strange that he said . . ."

She bows her head, truly trying to think.

Not of something Desirio might have said, but of how quickly they were getting closer to her crime. Accidentally, inadvertently, starting to circle in on her. She is out of time. Damn it. If Desirio were just the lonely old man he had seemed to be, she would have more time. But it has just been snatched from her.

"Miss Kelly, the truck driver who hit him . . . he was so distraught and upset. But something seemed a little off to me about him, so after talking to him, that's when I started looking at the surveillance tapes. Turns out he wasn't the simple immigrant truck driver we assumed. When these tapes came to light, I went to call him. He'd given us a fake name and address. He's gone. Disappeared. We have no way to find him."

What . . . what on earth . . . ?

"Miss Kelly, Antonio Desirio was obviously not just the simple old victim that you and I thought. Something else is going on here."

Yes. Something else is going on.

Nussbaum takes out his card, hands it to her. "I know this is what they say on TV, but"—he cringes a little as he says it—"if you think of anything, anything at all, please call me."

She nods mutely.

They're already too dangerously close. How fast it happened. And maybe Nussbaum isn't so dumb or straightforward as he is playing it. He's a detective. Look what they've found already. She has to act. Give notice to Glen and go.

And her mother? Her mother would want her to live, to have a life. She had the impulse. Now she must stare unblinking into its consequences. And stay ahead of them.

5

Elaine Kelly stands in front of the international flight board at Kennedy Airport:

Madrid
Rome
Buenos Aires
Lisbon
Auckland
Shanghai
Reykjavik
Pago Pago

She watches the massive airplane tails move regally on and off the runway, bright colors glittering in the afternoon sun. Air France. Alitalia. Avianca. Qantas. Emirates.

She grips her purse closely to her chest.

She is nervous.

She looks to the Jetway at Gate 15. Watches it closely. Watches the uniformed gate agents, staring at their terminals. Her terminal sisters.

She is tight with anxiety, with expectation.

The Gate 15 Jetway is emptying the planeload from the incoming flight. The first-class passengers emerge, hurrying to waiting cars and cabs, pulling their smart black wheeled luggage behind them, followed by a swarm of coach travelers, blue-jeaned and rumpled, looking as if they've just woken up. Soon, from the back of the cabin, the last few stragglers.

Finally, Elaine sees her. Bleached blonde now, bustier, and tan, but unmistakable. And older.

Her sister Annelle.

They hug wordlessly, standing there while other passengers—while the world—slides by around them.

"Oh, Elaine," says Annelle in a voice Elaine still recognizes from the distant past. "I'm so sorry. I can't believe it. It's so . . . so *strange* that she's gone."

"I'm glad you came," says Elaine. She withholds all her other words and comments, the fury of many years alone, caring for their mother. Not for today. "My car's outside."

The old Nissan lurches forward in typical weekday traffic on the Grand Central Parkway, Elaine at the wheel.

"Who's at the house?" Annelle asks, obviously nervous about her reappearance. About how she'll be treated. What they'll say. Their mother has just died and Annelle is preoccupied by what people will say to her, think of her.

"Uncle Bob. The O'Hallorans . . . all ten thousand of them. Father Dunleavy. Some friends of hers from the library. Her bridge group. A few cat lovers, who will come in handy."

Annelle, still in her sunglasses, looks steadfastly, resolutely out the window, not at her sister. "I'm gonna stay tonight, but then I've got to get back. Can you drive me back to Kennedy in the morning?" Plotting her getaway, her escape, one more time, Elaine sees.

• • •

The huge black casket takes up one wall of the Kellys' little living room. Elaine has shifted all the furniture—the thinly stuffed chairs and antimacassars that have been worn sheer—to the edges of the room so that people can mill around the casket, visiting with her mother one last time. The undertaker has done an alarmingly good job restoring, for these few hours, the once-beautiful Eunice Kelly, coiffed and smoothed and made-up and dressed in her churchgoing best, and masking the Eunice Kelly ravaged by cancer and depleted by emphysema. She looks to be resting peacefully.

Elaine and Annelle diligently cycle the trays of hors d'oeuvres in and out of the oven, and carry them through the crowd of fifty or so, which gives Elaine a chance to exchange a few words with each of the guests. Everyone has a glass of red or white wine or a bottle of beer in hand. The guests themselves have taken firm, trusty care of opening and serving it and have been diligent in keeping it flowing. She can tell not just by the mountain of empties balanced atop the trash but by the slurring speech and decibel level as she circulates. Her extended Irish family and her mother's church acquaintances feel comfortable amid calamity. Boisterous and familiar amid death, they know their way around a funeral.

For the tenth time, she tells the story. She's sorry that it is so devoid of the drama they all obviously hunger for. "I got up in the middle of the night, went in to check on her, and she was gone."

Uncle Ed—short, stolid, with a full head of black hair even in his seventies—eagerly grabs a couple of hors d'oeuvres. "So what're you gonna do now, Elaine?"

"What do you mean?"

"With the house? You gonna stay?"

She smiles thinly. "Can't. It's not our house."

Ed frowns, and Aunt Estelle, looking stricken, gathers closer to him with incomprehension.

37

"Belongs to the bank," Elaine explains. "I got her a reverse mortgage a couple of years ago. We needed the equity for the medical bills." She shrugs. She had no choice.

Ed frowns, disappointed. "Oh, I just assumed that, you know, with you at Federated . . ."

She smiles with understanding. "Oh, you mean since I work at a bank, money's no problem? There's banking and there's *banking*, Uncle Ed. I'm a teller."

"Yes, but . . ."

"A teller," she repeats.

Ed purses his lips and is silent.

She excuses herself, and heads back into the kitchen with Annelle. They rotate another tray of hors d'oeuvres in and out of the oven.

"I'll help you pay for this," Annelle says.

Yeah, right, Elaine thinks.

"What *are* you gonna do?" Annelle says suddenly, choosing this busy moment to make it a question in passing, to ask it offhand in order to get an offhand and, therefore, authentic answer.

"What do you mean?"

"I mean, you could go anywhere. You're free. Are you going to stay at the bank?"

"You don't think I should?"

"You deserve a break, that's all. Take some time off. Go on a nice vacation. Treat yourself."

She looks at Annelle. Clenches her hands nervously at her sister's clairvoyance.

"Maybe I will."

"Have you got the money?"

1.3 million dollars.

Just did a deal at the bank.

Made it on one transaction.

Just like the bankers you read about.

"I could swing it, I guess."

"Even if you don't have the money, borrow it. Live a little."

Borrow it.

Live a little.

Elaine smiles thinly, noncommittally. She turns back to the hors-d'oeuvres and doesn't want to look anywhere else.

• • •

She lies on her bed that evening, staring at the ceiling, unable to sleep.

The transition from life to death is so quick. So unexpectedly seamless. A brutal lesson in the permeability of the two states. A lesson in their unnerving closeness, their startling kinship. Eunice Kelly's death was so long in coming, so brief in actuality—leaving Elaine no time to think, only time to plan and execute and oversee the numerous ceremonies. The transition from life to death is just a heartbeat—literally, yes, but figuratively, too.

She sits up, ambles out into the hall, leans into the guest bedroom, and sees her sister sleeping soundly. She moves silently to the master bedroom—tiptoeing out of habit, she soon realizes—and opens the door. Stares at the empty bed, the rumpled sheets stripped from it, the mattress now bare. The oxygen mask hangs off the bed rail.

Her mother is gone. The absence of the breathing, the missing mechanical pulse of the oxygen machine . . . that is more startling, in a way, than the absence of the body. She was withering away to nothing, and the emptiness of the bed is in a way nothing more than the next logical step. For two years, she was there, right there, as permanent as furniture, still the center of Elaine's universe as she has been from the moment Elaine was born, the only universe and center that Elaine has ever known. It was by biological and psychological necessity as a child, and then a permanent social condition, a human maternal epicenter and microclimate, and finally, in these past few years of sickness, central as a practical matter. And now gone. And now Elaine's options, her thoughts, spin outward, reach outward as if with centrifugal force. The center cannot hold. Without that maternal gravitational pull, the universe—her universe—is suddenly rendered random and chaotic.

She had to stay for the funeral, of course. To plan it. To supervise it. There was no one else. And to disappear before it? That would be too inexplicable, and uncharacteristic, and obvious. The gossip would be relentless, and she could foresee its clear path from some overly concerned relative to the 114th Precinct. *She just disappeared, right before her mother's funeral. We're very concerned. Could you look into it?*

Now she is supposed to stay to clean out the row house for the broker and the bank. That's part of the mortgage agreement, there in black and white. A part she is sure she can ignore, if she goes on the run.

And now her disappearance will make sense. If questioned, it will be comprehensible, explainable, accepted. Making changes. Waiting until she's fulfilled her responsibility. A fresh start.

It's time to quit the bank.

• • •

Elaine is standing at her terminal, experiencing it, thinking about it, as if it is the last time. A white box identical to a million others. Yet its infuriating failures, its numerous unexpected, exhilarating recoveries, and its continual, close partnership over hours, days, years, create a ridiculous bond. Like a carpenter's hammer, an accountant's calculator, a gravedigger's shovel, it's the tool always by your side, that lets you do your job, contribute to the workings of the world, pay for your groceries, and it asks and needs nothing in return. Through a last series of transactions on a quiet morning, she is saying her silent, silly good-bye.

Glen strides by. She is just about to say it, initiate it—*Can I talk to you?*—when he confides to her, "We just got the Freeze Order."

"What?"

But she knows immediately. *Of course. Shit. Of course.* She winces outwardly and, inwardly, feels her stomach tighten in pain.

"You know . . . on Desirio's account. Assets are officially frozen. Nothing goes in, nothing goes out. From here on in, it gets managed by the state." He shakes his head cynically. "It'll take them forever—more than a year anyway—to get to it and disburse it. Feel sorry for his heirs. If they find any, that is."

Freezing assets. Standard procedure, she knows, in any financial investigation. It wouldn't have happened, of course, if Desirio were just a lonely old man hit by a truck. But a lonely old man making circular deposits at four different banks . . . that's reason enough for the standard Freeze Order, which she'll bet came from the 114th Precinct.

She checks it herself on her own terminal. There it is, in red lettering.

A. DESIRIO. ASSETS FROZEN. NEW YORK CITY POLICE / NEW YORK DISTRICT ATTORNEY OFFICE ORDER #KORO2.

The question being, when exactly did the Freeze Order go into effect? Glen just told her about it. But Nussbaum might have put it into effect right away, as soon as he learned about the multiple banks. That would make sense. In which case, her transfer, although reflected electronically, might *not* have actually cleared. The time it took intrabank assets to clear varied slightly, between a day or two, depending on the account type, and with money going into an *M* account . . . well, she just didn't know. The Freeze Order could extend to all pending transactions, which would include hers. She realizes, with a sinking feeling, that her only chance now to track the assets, to *know* anything, is to stay at the bank. *For just another day? Maybe two? Is that insane?*

The bank clock behind her is ticking, but now the clock has an extra hand. A hand whose sweep she can't quite see. Certainly, it was now more likely that the theft would be discovered. But when? Today, tomorrow, a week, or years from now?

She keystrokes, hits "Return," keystrokes a few times more, until she finds what she is looking for. It's the simplest piece of information, the only other available data, the only useful thing her mute white terminal can tell her: *Antonio M. Desirio. 150 Hayes St., Apt 10E, Queens, NY.*

6

Elaine stands across the street from a building that is somewhere between nondescript and run-down. Ten stories tall. She looks up at it, debating . . .

If Nussbaum has taken the time to assemble those surveillance tapes and put in the Freeze Order, it seems likely he's already been to the apartment, maybe has even greased the super's palm, asking him to report back on any visitors or inquiries. *Anyone comes around asking about Desirio, you call me.* She hesitates on the sidewalk, imagining the super's words. *Hey, Detective, somebody did come by—some girl with red hair.*

She tucks her hair up under her blue knit cap.

Then again, she reasons, maybe Nussbaum hasn't been out here. Maybe he's only called the building, spoken with the super. Or maybe that duty falls to some other detective or a neighboring precinct. This isn't Nussbaum's only case, after all. And it probably isn't Nussbaum's alone, either. Who knows how they work it or how busy a New York City detective is?

The address—150 Hayes Street—isn't very far out of her way. She hadn't really decided what she would do when she got here. She can't risk asking Nussbaum more about Desirio, can't risk appearing the least bit curious about him. But she *is* curious, very curious. A lonely old man with a simple savings account? No longer. Then who was he? *What* was he?

This, too, she realizes as she stands here, is impulsive *and* premeditated. Some indeterminate mix and stew of both, just like taking the money. The money, which is now becoming something different, something else. Yes, it's sitting inert in her account, a series of blinking digits subtracted from one column and added to another, but those tiny digits are wielding an unsuspected, unruly power. She had expected those blinking digits to produce a sense of freedom—speculative, anticipatory freedom, freedom to come—but she is feeling something more immediate and direct. A freeing, a loosening in her own actions and behavior . . .

She crosses the street.

What's the harm? What's the risk? She won't say or leave her name. And no one is going to know. Her visit here doesn't matter, isn't very risky, because she's going to be overseas any minute. Any day now. It's safe at least to look.

I heard about an apartment becoming available. Can I see it?

New York City apartment hunters searched the obits like vultures. Even with how brief and vague that four-line news item was, she probably wouldn't be the first or last to inquire.

She pulls open the front door, steps tentatively into the dark lobby—a cool, musty, low space where the air itself seems to have been loitering for decades. There's a front desk, an old formal doorman's station, but no one is there. "Hello?" she says, just to be official about it, just to follow the rules, but she is relieved when no one responds.

She stands alone for another minute, looking around the old, decrepit, run-down lobby, then moves to the single elevator. She pushes the ancient buzzer, hears the hollow whoosh of the car dutifully descending to her. The door shudders and shivers itself open, like an ancient, jittering servant. She gets in and pushes "10."

When she leans out of the elevator to look down the bleakly lit tenth-floor hallway, there is a door open halfway down. As she comes tentatively closer, she can see that the cart in the hall is loaded with a few books, some papers, a few folding chairs, a couple of lamps. Obviously, this is 10E.

A uniformed Hispanic man in his fifties with, "Luis" stenciled on his shirt in script, puts a desk lamp on the cart and goes back into the apartment without seeing her.

She stands in the doorway now and sees two men. The uniformed man—obviously the super—and another man, blond haired, pale skinned, in a red tie and shirtsleeves, holding a clipboard.

"Hello?" She knocks on the doorjamb. The men both look up.

"Yes? Help you? You look for me?" says the Hispanic man. "You want to rent?"

"Well, actually, I was a friend of Mr. Desirio."

He shakes his head. "Desirio? He have no friends . . . no one come here."

The man holding the clipboard walks up to her, introduces himself. "John Ellis. With the State of New York." Clearly reveling in his officialdom. "I've been assigned to appraise the effects."

As she shakes his hand, she looks around. What a contrast to the cluttered Kelly row house. Bare wood floor, no rugs or carpeting. Nothing on the walls. A small desk under the window. A desk chair. Kitchen counter with a half-eaten coffee cake and nothing more. An old TV with rabbit ears. A monk's existence.

"Not much here," says the appraiser.

"And I never seen anyone go in or out, 'cepting Desirio. Always the gentleman," says the super.

"Can I look around?" Elaine asks.

The appraiser blinks in surprise. Looks her once up and down, his latest appraisal. His eyes narrow for a moment. He seems to be making some calculation, this one not merely numeric. Finally, he shrugs, smiles thinly. "Just for a minute. And don't touch anything."

Ellis and the super return to what they were doing—cleaning out the desk drawers, the appraiser making notes on the clipboard, then nodding to the super, who carries and slides the drawers across the floor to the cart in the hall.

She wanders from the living room into the bedroom. A single bed. A chest of drawers. She peeks into the small walk-in closet. A few shirts on hangers, collars yellowed and frayed. A couple of pairs of shoes, the soles worn through.

At the back of the closet, sharing the shelf with rolled socks and baggy underwear, shoved to the side, is a photograph of a teenaged girl. At first it startles her, makes her shudder, this bright, cheerful girl with her innocent smile. Desirio, the stooped, spittle-flecked, odd, silent miser . . . is this his perversion, his obsession, hidden away in his closet? Was young, flame-haired Elaine merely another silent obsession? A convenient object of desire reliably at her terminal every morning? But there was nothing in Desirio's courtly greetings at the bank, nothing in their weekly innocent exchanges, that suggested anything seedy, or leering, or even the least bit flirtatious. Only a loneliness about him. Nothing worse. A thin, desperate reach for a mere crumb of connection. *How's your mother, Elaine?* Nothing more.

She regards the girl in the photo. Sixteen? Seventeen? Blonde. Cute. All-American. A backyard portrait on a summer day, but the yard behind her is too blurred to make anything out. Elaine looks closer, angles the photo toward the bedroom light. No, not just cute. Lovely. Perfect skin and teeth. Surprising to find it hidden here in the apartment closet, to say the least. Elaine would think nothing of it, normally; it would lose its notability in an apartment filled with family photos or art on the walls. But there were no other photos that she could see. And no photos or frames already removed and put on the cart. Only this one.

She takes it back to the living room. "Any idea who this is?" she asks.

They shake their heads no.

"Can I take it?"

A surprising question, she is sure.

It takes both the appraiser and the super a moment to process it.

"Rather you didn't," says Ellis.

"It's got no value," says Elaine. "Isn't that what you're doing here, looking for items of value? Like that extra watch on your wrist? Is that in your report?"

Ellis stares at her. The super turns away, as if pretending not to know anything about it, to tune out whatever will now occur.

"He was a friend," Elaine says again.

Once more, Ellis narrows his eyes and seems to make some deeper appraisal against a calculus that Elaine doesn't understand, only suspects.

"Take it," he gestures dismissively, turning back to the contents of the desk. "But leave the silver frame."

• • •

She studies the photo on the subway. She lies on her bed, holds it up, stares at it some more. That innocent, authentic smile. In Desirio's sad, bare apartment, absent of sentiment—and of jewelry and valuables . . . Elaine didn't know what else had already been pilfered by the appraiser—this photograph was the one scant thread of evidence of a onetime happiness, or at least a connection to it. Evidence of a life. There in the closet . . . as a way to forget? Or as a way to remember? To hide it, protect it from the world? Or hide it from himself?

Who was it? The obvious guess was a relative. Distant? A left-over photo from some family event years ago? Or someone close to him? A photo he looked at, a person he thought about every day?

And if it is a relative, Elaine wants to know. Needs to know. Because a relative is potentially an heir. Someone who, by law or by moral obligation, should get that money. This lone photo, obviously meaningful, might very well be the person for whom Desirio intended the money. To know who she has inadvertently stolen from, that is one odd portion of her motive here. But also, maybe, it's the chance to channel the money to its rightful owner. Its rightful place. To right her wrong. Or at least know if that opportunity exists, whether or not she actually does it.

She has taken the photograph out of some mix of curiosity, and guilt, and a latent sense of responsibility. The sense that she, Elaine, may now be the only connection, the only knowing thread, between Desirio and the world. Between Desirio and justice. Curiosity, guilt, responsibility—a stew of motives. She knows only that she couldn't leave that photo in the closet.

Is she taking the money from this pretty, unknown girl? Or is she keeping it safe for her?

She doesn't know. She *wants* to know. More and more, she feels an urge, a risky compulsion, to know.

Discovering who this is, of course, could lead to an understanding of Desirio—who he was, what he was doing, what happened. It could be the only way to such an understanding. But that is something beyond Elaine's powers. Where would she even begin?

On the other hand, she has a very good idea where to begin. The right idea. The correct idea.

The detective's business card is in her purse. *"If you think of anything, anything at all . . ."*

She feels her shoulders tighten, her lips go dry. Can she really do this?

Maybe. Because the money could sit there, as Glen said, for more than a year, until the state gets to it and sorts it out.

And which money? Only the roughly fifty-five thousand dollars she left in Desirio's account? A reasonable amount for an elderly man with no income. But Nussbaum already knows that Desirio, for whatever reason, was rotating money—and large amounts of it—in and out of numerous accounts and banks. Was it possible that what she took might get lost in the shuffle of some elaborate, incomprehensible rotation of much more substantial amounts? If the transfer had actually cleared into her account before the Freeze Order, was it possible that the money might never be missed? It depended on how deeply the state auditors and examiners looked into these matters, which might be very deeply or not at all. After all, there's no paper trail, no check written, no digital instructions or path. The 1.3 million was simply in his account, and then it wasn't. An auditor might reasonably conclude it was the mysterious account holder himself—the man on the surveillance tapes—who had set it in motion, put it afloat on the sea of his financial chicanery.

And then, what about *her* account? She's been clever, very clever, so it isn't in a conventional, vanilla checking or savings account; it's somewhere it won't be automatically swept, and maybe not even noticed. Where a huge amount like that, moving in or moving out, will raise no digital red flags. Where a check issued by computer will come to her as a matter of course and no human will ever see it or be aware of it. The bottom line was, if she didn't withdraw it, didn't touch it, it might sit in there safely, indefinitely, and no one would know. If she *were* to try withdrawing it, it was far more likely to be noticed, and she'd have to do it only when she was safely out of US jurisdiction—assuming she could get at it from an ocean and several countries away.

Can she really do this? She is unquestionably increasing her risk if she does. But maybe no more than the risk that is already inherent.

She takes out the business card, stares at the number, and has one last, fleeting thought: that after years of taking care of her mother, she needs to—is trying to—take care of someone else. Someone, as it happens, unknown and unnamed. Someone other than, *anyone* other than, herself.

She dials her cell phone.

"Nussbaum, One-Fourteen."

"Detective Nussbaum, this is Elaine Kelly . . ."

"Elaine Kelly?" He pauses a beat as he tries to place the name. "Oh, sure . . . the Federated branch," he says. "How are you?"

She's right, then. He has other cases, maybe bigger and more pressing. Is busy meeting other demands from his superiors. Maybe this case has already been passed off to other detectives.

It occurs to her now that he had visited tellers at all the other banks, played the surveillance video for them, too. He obviously didn't remember which teller she was.

"You said if I thought of anything to call . . ."

"Right. And you did?"

"I have something to show you."

"I'm all eyes. Address is on the card. Come on over."

7

She expected that upon entering the 114th Precinct of the NYPD she would see a row of folding chairs filled with wild-eyed crackheads, fishnet-clad prostitutes, and dirty-haired missing-toothed homeless people holding their shopping bags and shoes together with twine. She had expected to immediately surmise who had committed what, simply by how they looked, to see every easy stereotype fulfilled and confirmed.

Obviously, that was TV. *"I'm no Chris Noth."*

Instead, while hardly as immaculate as the Northern Boulevard branch of Federated and apparently lacking any climate control at all—she moves from overheated to freezing to overheated in a checkerboard of temperature—the 114th is similarly quiet, orderly, and subdued. As for those few citizens she sees around her, she can't begin to ascertain their business or pending charges. It's all civil and somber, as church-like and respectful as the branch. Not like another bank branch exactly but not unlike one, either.

Her tentative, overly polite, "I'm here to see Detective Nussbaum," is greeted by a desk sergeant who seems either to have never heard of Nussbaum or to have temporarily misplaced him like a set of keys.

After a few minutes, she is directed back into the precinct, along ancient hallways, glancing quickly, guardedly around her as she walks. A visit to a police precinct—some would find it reassuring, would feel supersafe. For others, it would create a mild, irrational anxiety. And for someone who has just stolen over a million dollars to be striding deeper and deeper into its warren of rooms and desks and computer screens, with dozens of officers and support staff around . . .

Elaine pulls her coat tighter around her.

What am I doing? Is it self-destructive? Some unconscious wish to be caught? To be punished? The nuns humming, directing her, from the back of her brain?

Eventually she is seated in a chair next to Nussbaum's desk, which is strewn with papers and information circulars and piled high with manila folders, forms, and reports. And there is that same big, warm, genial, nonjudgmental smile, like an uncle or brother. The unkempt jet-black hair. The cherubic face.

"So whatcha got?"

She takes out the photo, shows him.

"Who's that?" he asks.

"That's what I'd like to know."

He looks at her, shakes his head, smiles. "Oh, so you meet a detective and you expect him to suddenly solve all life's mysteries? Missing Persons is down the hall."

"I found it in Desirio's apartment."

His smile drops. "What the hell were you doing in Desirio's apartment?" He looks at her. "I don't like that. I'm the detective." But he reaches out for the photograph.

"It was no big deal," she says defensively. "The state appraiser was already there."

He looks up at her for a moment, then back down to study the photograph.

"It was at the back of his bedroom closet," she tells him and can hear the eagerness in her own voice. "As far as I could tell, it's the only picture he had."

She pauses a moment, before explaining, "I was looking into renting the apartment."

"Good one," Nussbaum says, "but you're no vulture, Miss Kelly. I can tell." He puts the photograph down and looks at her, still unsmiling. She misses his smile.

"There's no way the state appraiser would be there already, Miss Kelly. It'll be weeks. Did he show you a card or a license?"

Elaine shakes her head. But the name skims the edge of her brain and brings a glimmer into her eyes. "Ellis," she says with a sense of victory in her voice. "John Ellis."

He turns to his computer. Keystroke, keystroke, "Enter," "Enter." He scans the screen. "No appraiser with that name registered with the state." There is a similar sense of victory, of *I told you so*, in his tone of voice. But with it, a frown of concern over no John Ellis listing.

He picks up the photograph again, studies it once more. He's still angry she went there, she can tell, but it's offset, apparently, by the fact that she's being truthful about it and, she guesses, because he's as interested as she is in the photograph.

He can't help himself. "We've got this new face recognition software. I'm sure you saw this, the little date on the edge here? Seven years ago now, that this photo was developed. The software can project out facial changes over those seven years—it mimics the aging process essentially—then it looks for the closest matches in our current database. Sometimes we get a hit. Mostly we don't. But it's worth a try. Let me initiate a search. I'll give you a call either way." He gets up, gestures generally toward the door. "And Miss Kelly, please don't play detective again."

8

She is back in the branch, standing at the counter—*Keep everything the same, keep everything the same*—when an elegantly dressed businessman enters around lunchtime. Even in the busy lunchtime rush, she notices him, because he is with two colleagues, it appears, and they are talking in low, polite, cultured tones, in a language that somehow seems further from English than any other she's ever heard. It sounds harsh and guttural, yet they move their mouths and facial muscles very little while speaking. It's as if they are trying to smooth it out and tone it down for the cool quiet of the bank branch. She suppresses a smile. They sound a little like movie aliens. Eastern European? Something-stan? Most noticeable of all, though, is the man's white hair—elegant and long, like an Italian count or a European industrialist.

The tourist couple she's helping are finishing up, so as luck would have it, the man approaches her terminal.

He smiles guardedly, professionally, politely. Presents her with a check to cash.

During the next minutes, the next hours, the next day, she will try to remember what shocked her more: the amount of the check or the name on it.

500,000 dollars.

Pay to the order of Antonio Desirio.

Her confusion is total. She examines, for a shocked moment, his State of New York driver's license, his Bulgarian passport. In a branch that serves the most polyglot of boroughs in the most multi-cultural of cities, she's seen plenty of such documents. She knows these are real. She can only repeat the name, expressionlessly, mean-inglessly, without comprehension. "Antonio Desirio?"

In his suave, confident accent, he says, "Yes, that is me."

Elaine stares at the address printed on the check: 150 Hayes St. Apt 10E, Queens, NY.

But I've been there. And someone like you doesn't live in a place like that.

"Perhaps I should have called ahead," he says, smoothly apolo-getic. "I'm transferring assets ahead of a purchase." His English is musical, with a singsong accent, and grammatically perfect.

Either this man knows what had been in the account and is impersonating Antonio Desirio or . . .

With a sinking, intuitive feeling, she knows. The dead man in the black coat had been impersonating this man. The real Antonio Desirio.

The formal, old-fashioned Italian name had fit the rumpled, old, black-coated gentlemen; it didn't so neatly fit this well-tailored, perfectly coiffed international businessman carrying a Bul-garian passport. But who was she to say? Who could say what his or his family's movements were across generations, across Europe, across the globe? Standing here at her terminal in a bank branch in Queens, she had to put together ten thousand faces with the most startling and unorthodox names, and she'd been fooled by the match-up many times before.

"I . . . I have to talk to my manager for a moment . . ."

"Of course," he says, assuming, she knows, that it is simply the size of the transaction that requires a higher approval.

• • •

A moment later, Glen has joined them at the counter and is looking at the check and the man's ID. By now, the man's two colleagues have gathered closer and are watching silently. There is an almost tangible uptick in tension, in import, surrounding her terminal. An elevation from the ordinariness of bank business, of daily routine transaction, to something palpably different, something they all seem to sense equally, picking it up from one another. And now that the two colleagues are standing closer, Elaine is aware of the broad shoulders inside one of their jackets. She senses them, sees them, shifting restlessly beneath the sheen of the suit's fabric.

Glen and Elaine exchange nervous glances throughout Glen's examination of the items. They both know it falls to Glen to explain.

"Sir, there's a problem. Your . . . your assets have been frozen."

There is a flash of impatience, of confusion and hostility, that ruffles the suavity of the white-haired man, who in the next moment is visibly struggling to disguise and contain it. "What . . . what does this mean?" he asks, pasting on the thinnest, briefest, most perfunctory of smiles. Maybe a smile he only utilizes in America, she thinks—in its banks.

"We thought . . . we thought you died in an accident."

The man's head, his silver mane, suddenly tilts slightly forward in resignation. His tone softens for a moment. "I had a feeling . . ." He reaches into his shirt pocket and carefully extracts and unfolds what Elaine immediately recognizes as the tiny four-line newspaper article her mother showed her. "A friend sent it to me," he says, in his guttural yet mellifluous tone. "Same name as me. I start to wonder. I have substantial assets in this account . . ." Listening to his accent, she thinks of the wildly gesturing, agitated truck driver. *"He no look! . . . Crazy old guy!"*

"But I don't understand . . . It's . . . it's the same address," Elaine blurts out. She feels her face flush red. Did she reveal too much? *Jesus. Be careful.*

The man shrugs, smiles a little at her naïveté. "He must to be claiming the same address as me."

But you don't live there. I know you don't.

"There can't be two of you . . ."

"I assure you," he informs her in a charmingly inept locution, "I am only me."

"Sir, would you . . . would you and your colleagues just have a seat over there," says Glen graciously, gesturing to the little cluster of leather couches that make up the branch's lobby lounge, "while we try to sort this out for you?"

In the file room with Elaine, Glen holds the original paperwork for both accounts, with the two signature cards, side by side. Two Antonio Desirios with the same address. "Well, there's a fuckup for you. And filed correctly, too, right next to each other." He shakes his head, amazed yet unsurprised.

But I know it's the old man in the black coat who lived there. They were cleaning out his apartment. That's who the super was describing after all—someone with a few sad possessions, someone friendless, eccentric, alone. But she can't say that to Glen, who would wonder what she was doing there. Who would look into her own account. And know how to look thoroughly.

"What are you going to do?" says Elaine.

"There's nothing I *can* do. Assets are frozen. It's already in the hands of the state. You know what it's like to try to get the state to change things quickly?" His shoulders slump. He shakes his head. "I'm just trying to look like I'm doing *something*, like I'm trying to fix things, so the guy's first impulse isn't to sue." He smiles grimly. Straight-shooting Boy Scout Glen, a little more devious and complex than she thought.

He looks around him at the fun-house collection of glass panels and angles and cubbyhole office cubes of branch banking across the globe. "Look, go to my office, use my terminal. It's got higher clearances than any other terminal in the branch. Use this pass-word." He takes the pen from his pocket protector, jots down the digits. "Open up the Desirio account. See what you can find there."

"But it's frozen. Isn't it against the law?"

"We're not hurting anything. We're just trying to figure out what happened. I'll try to get through to corporate, see what they say we should do . . ."

In Glen's office, Elaine pecks at the keyboard. The special password brings her into a whole different interface, like the surface of a new planet. She looks quickly at a year of Desirio's account activity, its steady growth. But any last transactions are too recent to be reflected in the monthly statements.

She frowns, before inspiration suddenly hits her. Maybe 150 Hayes Street was only a temporary stop, a diversion, a mask for the eventual destination of the bank statements—for either one of the Desirios, the mysterious elderly account shuffler or the man now out front. She types in *Forwarding address request?* The computer program responds with *Yes*, and gives her the date the request was made.

Jesus, There *was* a forwarding address request put in. Her instincts, her imagination, were right. Her heart is pounding instantly. She switches menus, types *Forwarding address?* Waits. She waits fifteen seconds that seem like eternity, until the response appears on her screen: *Forwarding address not found.*

How can that be? The request is in the system, but the address is not?

She can't see the distinctive flowing white hair from here, but she knows the man—Desirio—is pacing impatiently. That Glen is trying to calm him, assure him that steps are being quickly taken.

"Use this password. My terminal has higher clearances . . ."

She glances through the glass behind her once more to be sure no one is there, and calls up the account number she knows by heart: KELLY, ELAINE 3947289402M.

Types in the command *Transfer*.

The screen prompts her: *To?*

She calls up Desirio's account: DESIRIO, A. M. 2339729334

She hits "Execute transfer."

She waits—muscles clenched, breathing shallow—to see the numbers change.

Acting impulsively on a sudden chance, an exact echo, a perfect reversal of the impulsive move of taking the money days ago. As if the universe itself is providing an opening, that chorus of nuns at the back of her brain saying, *Here's your chance to make it right.* To turn back time. To leave the universe as before. She doesn't want to miss this chance.

She stares at the screen. Waiting.

Nothing happens.

And then the red lettering she has seen before, the little typographic siren with its red letters flashing insistently, the typographic alarm: *Account frozen.*

Nothing going out, nothing going in.

The universe is not so easily placated.

She took one million three hundred thousand dollars, and she can't give it back.

Back in the bank's lobby, when she shakes her head mournfully at hopeful, expectant Glen—*Nothing, sorry*—Desirio sees the grim, somber expression pass between them and reacts predictably.

His voice rising, his English plenty clear and pointed, and plenty knowledgeable.

"Financial malpractice."

"Let me speak to the regional manager."

"You'll hear from my lawyers."

"What precinct is it? I'm going over there now."

"Grounds for a lawsuit."

The conventional, predictable, daily business of the branch pauses. Customers look over, on guard for any escalation. Elaine is surprised by such volatility lurking beneath the surface of his elegance.

Edwin, the branch's uniformed rent-a-guard, comes over to stand alertly, tensely, at the edge of the proceedings, not wanting to get involved and not knowing what to do, but figuring everyone should know he is there. Edwin is a sweet-natured retiree willing to stand in the branch's lobby for $9.75 an hour, Elaine knows, doing even less than a teller. Like a uniformed paper cutout that only happens to be flesh and blood. Neither Desirio nor his colleagues even look over at him. He has no effect.

"Please, sir," Glen begs. "We'll rectify the situation. Please just be a little patient . . ."

In a moment, Glen is on the phone in his office. Elaine can see him through the series of glass partitions, pacing as he speaks into the receiver.

He returns to the lobby a minute later. "I got through to the DA's office. It's . . . it's going to be a process. You'll just have to be patient . . ." he repeats, a mantra to himself as well as his customer.

The silver-haired Desirio shakes his head, eyes the general incompetence around him as if for the last time, and strides out, clearly furious, fuming, but doing his utmost to keep that fury in check.

His colleague—the one with the broad shoulders—lingers behind for a moment, looking around the lobby. Inspecting it, registering it, seeming to take mental notes before following Desirio out, departing as if reluctant and regretful to leave it in such a pristine, orderly state.

The bank seems to return to its previous state, to its accustomed business and mood, in the wake of their exit.

But not for Elaine Kelly.

9

Night, Elaine stands across the street from 150 Hayes once again.

She crosses to the old sandstone building entry again.

The super—in his same tan uniform with curlicue "Luis" sewn across its breast pocket—is at the front desk this time.

"I'm here about the apartment," she says, truthfully enough, approaching the desk while the super's head is down, buried in paperwork.

"Apartment?" The super looks up.

"10E? Remember me? Friend of Desirio's?"

He puts on his glasses, looks her over.

"Is it still available? Can I go take a look at it?"

"10E is rented to Antonio Desirio."

"Yes, but . . . he died."

"I'm sorry, miss. Is rented to Antonio Desirio. Has rented it very long time. Excellent tenant, many years. Very good with the payment." He fidgets with the glasses on his nose. "When he will move in? Dunno. Best kind of tenant, yes?" He says it all in a kind of nervous rush while attending to the paperwork in front of him, being careful not to look at her.

She leans toward him. "You know I saw you days ago, cleaning out 10E. You know Desirio died. You remember me from the other night." She ticks off the facts as if daring him to refute them.

"Is rented to Desirio, miss. So sorry. No available."

"Who's paying you to say that? What's going on here?"

He doesn't look up, pretends she's not there. Which only confirms the deception. *What's going on here?*

It's as if she was never there before, saw nothing the other night. As if an old man in a black raincoat never got hit by a truck.

She wants to leap across the desk, force some answers out of that arrogant tan uniform. So easily bought off for a few bucks, like a hundred thousand building supers in New York. *How much is he paying you?*

But she stops herself. It's her, too. She, too, let money determine the script. She, too, let cash shut her up, make her go silent.

Her cell phone rings. In the midst of her frustration, she answers immediately, without thinking or looking.

"Hello?"

"Miss Kelly?"

She knows the warm voice immediately.

A twinge of anxiety shoots through her. Here she is, standing precisely where he asked her not to go.

"Nussbaum, at the One-Fourteen. I kinda have something on that photo. It's a little involved, something I've gotta kinda walk you through, that you'd have to come down here for . . . I know it's late, but . . ."

"No problem. I'm on my way."

She hangs up, looks silently at the super. Dangles her phone between them. "That was Detective Nussbaum, from the 114th Precinct," she says, alert to any telltale reaction from behind the desk. "Ever met him?"

The super stares purposefully, blankly, down at his paperwork. "Yeah, I thought so," she says before turning to leave.

If the detective did grease the super's palm for information, then he's definitely been outbid.

10

This time of evening, the precinct is a lively match for her imagination. Two streetwalkers argue loudly and inconclusively with three patrolmen; a couple of junkies stare at the walls and at their feet; a teenaged runaway looks around, jumpy and terrified. Tones of irritation, frustration, aggression, are amplified in the overly echoing hallways and the arched stucco ceilings. Fractured lives are framed by the wildly colorful, cracked Art Deco tile.

And standing amid it all, waiting demurely, politely, in prim peacoat, is the smooth criminal whose offense, in dollar terms, far outweighs all those she sees around her. An unrecognized master thief. And these lives in disruption around her, the strange late hour, the harsh echoes of voices in distress through the precinct house—she feels a resulting sense of dislocation and unreality, and yet she feels oddly, conversely, at home. Like she belongs here. Every minute that the money remains undiscovered makes it seem a little more like it could simply stay that way. Tucked away, as if in an old, unopened desk drawer, and the longer it sits still and undisturbed in the dark, the more that becomes its natural home. Or is that a fairy tale she is telling herself, to bear the insanity, the crazy self-destructive impulse, of her being back here in the 114th Precinct?

A minute later, Nussbaum is walking her past the tightly packed offices, then through some squeaky-hinged wooden double doors, into a back section of the precinct house, and in another minute, the precinct house is transformed. Seated, slouched, hunched in front of an array of computers, electronic control panels, and ancillary screens, young technicians of both genders are working away in T-shirts and jeans.

Nussbaum glances over at her. "I know . . . Not what you expect, from the sorry-ass front of the house. This is where we actually get something done." He gestures to four or five people leaning toward their screens. Colored, spiked hair. A couple of nose and lip piercings. "Our search specialists can input hair color, eye color, age, ethnicity, and have categorized over two hundred shapes of noses and cheeks and chins," he says with more than a hint of pride. "Our missing-persons database includes all states' driver's licenses, all US passports, and every high school yearbook in America." Nussbaum smiles. "Facebook portraits, Myspace photos, we're very into social networking . . ."

"And?" She can't wait anymore.

"Nothing," he says.

Confusion. "Nothing?"

"Which to me is a good sign."

She furrows her brow. "How is that good?"

"Because it says she disappeared off the face of the earth."

More confusion. "How is *that* good?" But she also notices that she's feeling comfortable enough with him to be a little flippant.

"When you showed me that photo, I figured it was some favorite niece. But if there's no trace of that person—no *trace*, Miss Kelly—that tells me to get involved. Because nobody disappears off the face of the earth without a little shove."

"That's what you brought me here to tell me?" She is deflated, annoyed, frustrated. *All this computing power, all this technology, and a pretty little blonde girl remains a total mystery? Then why did you bring me back here?*

"No. Something else . . ." and he gestures her to follow him back toward his desk.

Seated across from Elaine, he takes the girl's photo out of an envelope and holds it up, close to her. "This particular brand of photo printing paper, turns out, was used by only two pharmacy chains in the late nineties. This photo—see here?—was printed in July. Our lab guys tell me that based on the rate of decay of chemicals in the paper it would have been July ninety-seven or ninety-eight."

He is looking hard, focusing, at the back of the photo, as if studying it for the first time himself. "I went to those pharmacies' credit card transactions of July ninety-seven and ninety-eight and cross-referenced them against the billing address of one-fifty Hayes Street. I ran it against the name Desirio, against all the Desirios in the five boroughs, the tristate area, then national. The card companies store it all on disk, which police can request."

She feels her excitement rising. Nussbaum is clearly smart, careful, dogged. "And . . . ?" she asks him hopefully.

"It was a lot of man-hours, a lot of resources . . ." he says. "And it might even have worked. If the guy's name was Desirio." His irritation is sudden, sharp.

She starts to feel uncomfortable. "I don't understand. If you have nothing . . . why'd you call me down here?"

"I wanted to see you, Miss Kelly," Nussbaum says. But there is no flirtation in it. He looks at her flatly, expressionlessly. A purposeful blankness on his usually expressive face.

She looks at him, confused, off-balance.

"I wanted to see you when I asked you," he says, somberly, annoyed, "why you didn't call me when a man named Antonio Desirio, with ID to prove it, showed up at your bank?" He looks at her. "I asked you to call me with anything, *anything at all*, and you didn't call to tell me *that*?" And then he looks at her harder. "Why?"

The implication is obvious. *Are you hiding something from me?*

Shit. Her ally. Unfailingly good-natured. Showing her the surveillance tapes, taking her into his confidence. Helping with the photo only because she asked. And now she's alienated him, inadvertently burned the bridge. Created not only a rift but outright suspicion. Shit.

Why *didn't* she call him? But she knows immediately. Because she doesn't really believe or accept that the slick-looking silver-haired man at the counter is Antonio Desirio. In her mind, Mr. Desirio is still her black-coated customer. In her mind, she was trying to stay with her original plan, keep some semblance of it, stop it from veering any further out of control. At some level, she couldn't seem to accept the shifting reality, the shifting footing, in that confusing moment in the bank branch.

And fear. Abject, paralyzing, overwhelming fear. Closing in on her, suffocating her. She didn't call him because a mysterious and short-fused man came in to retrieve his 1.3 million dollars, which is sitting in an account belonging to Elaine Kelly, and it is all she can think about or focus on.

And then she watches a remarkable thing happen.

She sees Nussbaum smile at her gently.

He sighs. "I could see that you were excited about the photo paper. You thought maybe I had an answer. I can see you want an answer as much as I do."

"I wanted to see your face . . ."

And her face had revealed her—revealed a part of her, at least. Revealed enough of her, but not too much.

He *is* smart, careful, committed. She can see it clearly. She also sees what Nussbaum doesn't say: *I can tell it didn't occur to you. You didn't even realize it would relate. Or else you were frightened. Frightened by what you just witnessed in the bank.*

He knows, after all, that she showed up with the photo, so he knows she wants his help. She's proved herself. And he accepts it.

She isn't used to such acceptance. To so quickly being granted the benefit of the doubt. Maybe it's a trick on the part of a big-city detective. Creating anger and hostility, then instant forgiveness. Building trust. Maybe he's his own good cop and bad cop all in one. Or maybe this is her own paranoid reading of it, amid all her other paranoia.

She's been aware of the gold ring on his finger for some time. She can't pinpoint when she first noticed it, but as he showed her the photo just now, carefully explained the paper quality and degradation, she noted how the ring had lost its shine, and she speculates that it's from thousands of dishes washed, and probably children's chaotic soapy baths, and building shelves, and taking out trash, and changing diapers. Although there are no pictures on his desk, no direct evidence to support her supposition, except for who he is, how he happens to seem—settled, satisfied, accepting of his own life. And here he is, willingly, naturally, extending that spirit of acceptance to her. His willingness to continue on with her, to believe her, earns him that gold ring, as far as she's concerned. He's comfortable around her and doesn't have that hungry, hunting regard of her that emits in waves from other men, which would emit, she knows, from virtually any other testosterone-fueled New York City detective. Yet, he *does* have that hungry, hunting look as far as the photograph goes. Focusing not at the girl, but at the girl's fate.

Settled and comfortable and not about to search the Internet for a far-flung city to escape his life, to start it over.

In that spirit of acceptance, he goes on as if nothing has happened, and their odd, casual, undeclared partnership continues.

"Miss Kelly, we still don't know who this is, but we do know something bad happened to her. And we don't know if your Desirio, or whoever Mr. Black Raincoat really is, wanted to avenge it or, in fact, caused it. We can only speculate he was thinking about her, that she was on his mind."

He leans back, catching her up on another detail as if she is a colleague, part of the team. "Just so you know, my partner and I went over and flashed our badges at the super and rattled his cage, but he was sticking to his story. That it was always Desirio who rented the place, that he never moved in, that the super was just cleaning up after a sublet. I mentioned your appraiser, John Ellis. Super said he didn't know what I was talking about."

Elaine feels a knot of rage in her at this outright denial of what she had seen there, of the conversation, of what had occurred in 10E. "Jesus, I can't believe this . . ."

"Guy is outright lying to a New York City police detective. Only two reasons you do that, in a situation like this. He's either being paid enough for that story that it's worth the risk of lying. Or he's scared, totally terrified, and whoever he's lying for is a lot more threatening than I am. Either way, it's someone making him do this. Whoever you saw in that apartment with him, probably. We made him show us the apartment, by the way. Empty. Rented, but empty."

He starts to lead her out to the front of the precinct.

"And what about that truck driver, Detective? Anything more?"

Nussbaum shakes his head. "I wish now we could have held him on something, but we had nothing to keep him on. We had to let him go. Disappeared into the woodwork, too. Into the night. You really stumbled on to something, Miss Kelly."

As they are walking out to the waiting area, Elaine hears raised voices from behind a frosted-glass office partition and suddenly stops. Because one of the voices is so distinctive, so recognizable from earlier in her day. Its hard-edged English is spoken in an oddly mellifluous, practiced delivery, its hostility barely contained in its struggling civility. She freezes. Reaches out her slender, keyboarding fingers to Nussbaum's rolled-up sleeve and bare forearm, to gently, silently stop him, too.

He looks at her. *What is it?*

She gestures toward the office. "That's Desirio," she whispers.

It's the precinct captain's office, she learns when Nussbaum silently, instructionally points to the silver nameplate on the door: "Captain Edward Hanratty."

On the other side of the partition is a lively, contentious meeting. She can tell by the number of different voices and what they're saying, and by the shadows of forms moving behind the frosted glass, there are clearly at least four players, maybe more. Desirio, Hanratty, and judging by the jargon one of the men is using, a lawyer who is presumably representing Desirio, and some kind of police lawyer, as well.

"We don't know who opened the matching account and don't much care," says a lawyerly voice—self-assured, arrogant, with an undercurrent of self-righteousness and irritation. "We do know our client has substantial assets at Federated and has a legal right to transfer them to a safer and more orderly institution." Pointed, sarcastic, as if personally offended. "And if the state has made a mistake in freezing those assets because the bank mistook someone's identity, that is the state's problem, not ours." Enjoying his righteous indignation to the fullest. Celebrating it.

A quieter voice speaks next, contrite, penitent, trying to restore calm and smooth ruffled feathers, but obviously someone of some authority. "Look, we'll release the assets. The order will take twenty-four hours or so to clear. There's a few hoops to jump through, and I will jump them for you, okay? You have the state's *deepest* apologies." Said, however, with unmistakable sarcasm. Not deeply apologetic in the least. Rather, deeply annoyed.

And then that distinctive voice again. That startling combination of rough and smooth. "Banks are very big. A mistake can happen. But a mistake cannot happen twice. Do you understand?"

Jesus, was he threatening the police officials in the room? It was couched in such a way that she couldn't be sure.

There is movement, a shifting of bodies, in the shadows beyond the frosted glass, signaling the end of the meeting. Nussbaum silently gestures Elaine away from Hanratty's office, and toward the precinct door.

She wants to discuss what they overheard. Ask Nussbaum if he can place that accent, if the police lawyer is just stalling for time. Ask him if he heard the threat the same way she did. But Nussbaum is hustling her down the hall, as if to avoid any chance encounter between Desirio and Elaine. As if Nussbaum knows, by instinct or experience, the risk of a guy like Desirio recognizing her from the bank, a coincidence that might set him off in some unmanageable way.

The fascinating, rough-smooth voice still echoes in her head . . .

11

In Elaine's tense, unsettled existence, the broker is like a creature from another planet: bubbly and cheerful standing there in her bright-red outfit in the center of the gloomy, shadowy Kelly town house like a tropical bird chirping in a dark, rusted cage. "Got a buyer all lined up. Ready to go. We can close in fifteen days, if you can pull it off. Think you can be out by then?"

Elaine reflects that it's probably the only moment of unbridled enthusiasm witnessed inside this house in years. The broker's mood seems so alarmingly contrary to the surroundings, to the situation.

Elaine looks around at the objects, at the furniture, coolly assessing it all. In the last few months, she has felt that these paperback books, teacups, figurines, and trinkets are the embodiment, the last signs, of a life. Today, she feels not a drop of that sentiment. It's not her house; it's her mother's. And it's simply her mother's collected junk, which she must now dispose of to meet the terms of the mortgage agreement. The reverse mortgage is very specific about the holder's obligations to the real estate brokerage that the bank assigns to the sale. You must cooperate fully. It is the bank's property, not yours. You have certain rights as a resident, but you don't have the rights of an owner, or even a renter. You're something else. A kind of modern serf. A squatter in your own home. The home you grew up in . . . "Yes, I can be out," she assures the broker. She doesn't know how she'll do it, but she'll do it. She wants to be out. To be done with it. Start fresh. Whether it's with nothing or with 1.3 million dollars.

The broker bubbles anew. "Great, great, I'll let the buyer know. Thank you, dear."

Thank you, because they both know Elaine doesn't *have* to clean it out. There's no leverage, no penalty behind the mortgage-agreement language. After all, the house isn't hers. The bank can pay someone to deal with it. She can just walk away. Disappear. But she won't. She'll honor the agreement because the escrow account needs to stay in perfect order.

In case there's a little money in it at the end . . .

You know, a rounding error or something . . .

Once again, she is alone in the row house. Looking more closely at all her mother's objects, her mother's accumulated junk. It only has sentimental value. She'll have to get a Dumpster.

Elaine sits on the bed in her bedroom. Puts her purse on her lap. Ceremonially opens it, reaches into it, withdraws the ticket.

Lisbon. Athens. Johannesburg. Rio de Janeiro.

She's narrowed it to those four but has not been able to decide, so it's an open ticket for now. *"Yes, we can certainly issue an open ticket. It costs you more, but yes, we can."* The travel agent on the phone probably thinks she is chasing a boyfriend, their relationship still unclear. Flighty. The definition of flighty, it occurs to her. The plan refuses to form clearly. The paralysis is too great. That's why she has said yes to the broker, yes to the fifteen days. To break the paralysis. To make herself act. An impulse has put her into this situation, a single momentary impulse, and now she can't seem to summon a second impulse to follow it through.

She takes out her passport, tucked next to the ticket in her purse. Ordered and delivered by mail. It's pristine. Virgin. Not a stamp on it. She cracks its spine as she would a new book and regards the redhead in the tiny photo, who appears stunned, unsure, not ready for the flash of light from the upbeat Pakistani snapping the photo at the little Queens camera store. A doe in the headlights. Not ready for the flash . . . or its bright, sudden promise of mobility, exploration, freedom.

Of course, it's a completely different plan now. At first, the ticket meant starting a new life with 1.3 million dollars: an apartment with a view, purchased with cash; wonderful, if anonymous, meals out; a comfortable, but watchful, expatriate existence. Now, since the Freeze Order, forensic eyes will eventually fall on the Desirio account, and since she can't move or spend the money at this point, the ticket simply means escape. Getting a head start so that she'll be gone, hidden, difficult to trace or retrieve when they discover the theft. Now she'll be going destitute. Without a dime. The ticket purchase has pretty much wiped out her regular account. It will now be an existence of youth hostels, church basements, the sympathy of priests and nuns, and soup kitchens. Finding some illegal, low-paying work, if she's lucky. Yes, the ticket still stands for a new life, but not at all the new life she'd been thinking of. In fact, pretty much its opposite.

Alone in the low bedroom light, she holds the ticket. A single piece of printed paper amid all the piled documents, the folders, the records, the collected magazines and books, the written past and witness and testament to the life in the row house. All worthless, all nothing, except for this little slip of paper that she slides nervously in and out of her purse, unsure where to keep it, what to do with it, what to think about it, where to go with it. In every sense. She's never been out of the country. She's rarely been out of the borough. The places are only fantasies, as unreal and as flat to her as the screens she sees them on, a series of page views on the Internet, and yet, her future, her only choice, her only chance. *Do I just disappear? Go tonight, get on the plane?* So easy. So incomprehensible.

First her mother's death, then the funeral arrangements, then the Freeze Order, then the broker for the row house. Everything is conspiring to keep Elaine here. Including her own conflicted morality, perfectly captured, ensnared, unsettled, by a mysterious photograph of a brightly smiling unidentified sixteen-year-old girl in an unidentifiable backyard. As if that girl is a version of her—or rather, she is a version of that girl—on the cusp of dreams, of an independent life, and yet some force or swirl of forces materializes from outside her, from within her, to keep those dreams, that imagined life, just out of reach.

She was going to leave, thanks to the money. Now she is going to leave, broke and with little choice, anticipating that the money will inevitably be discovered. Leaving with nothing. Starting over. Circumstance keeps pivoting on her. Keeps pivoting, displacing, shifting her fate.

12

"Elaine," Glen instructs, "please liquidate Mr. Desirio's account and consolidate all funds in a bank check." Once again, unctuous and ashamed, he looks to Desirio. "We're so sorry this happened. We appreciate your patience in this matter. Again, our sincerest apologies . . ."

Antonio Desirio brushes off the apology, not because it is unnecessary but because he wants nothing more to do with this short-sleeved powerless functionary. Doesn't want to see him again. Wants to forget his name, and probably already has.

Desirio and the two other men—the same ones from his previous visit—have just swept into the branch once more, purposeful, unsmiling, triumphant. Glen is already in the center of the lobby to greet them. There must have been a preliminary phone call—the DA's office notifying the bank. Glen looks relieved, in the belief that this will all be over soon.

As Desirio and Glen approach Elaine's window, she wonders if he remembers, even dimly, that she is the teller from before. It's possible he does, faintly, and also possible he has no recollection. Glen is alongside him to escort him, to make sure everything goes right. Glen hands her a slip of paper with the account number on it. She knows it by heart, of course: *Desirio, A. M. 2339729334.*

She also knows by heart the command keys to close out an account. Types them in sequence. The command appears on-screen: *Liquidate all funds.*

She inserts the blank cashier's check into the networked printer behind her. It stutters the numerals and prints quickly and efficiently.

She looks at the check, cross-references it with the balance on-screen, nods to indicate that it matches, and hands the check to the elegant Mr. Desirio.

Glen breathes a sigh of relief, steals a look at Elaine to catch a glimpse of her shared relief. She can only smile back at him reassuringly.

Elaine watches Desirio closely now as he looks down at the check. She watches his face flush with rage. He looks up—not at Glen, but at her.

"What is this?" He can barely sputter it out.

She looks terrified. She *is* terrified. "It's . . . your balance."

"Fifty-five thousand, five hundred dollars?"

She looks at the screen, looks back at him. "Yes, sir."

Desirio suddenly, unexpectedly, does something not normally tolerated in the branch, but that Glen and Elaine feel powerless to stop or alter.

He roughly swings the monitor around to see it himself. "Where? Where does it say?"

Edwin the rent-a-guard moves a few steps toward the counter, uncertainly.

Desirio's two associates step in, too—smoothly, practiced, and unafraid, Elaine notices—seemingly more at ease now than they were a few moments before.

Elaine obediently points. Glen looks in.

55,567.88, the number says next to his name.

Desirio stares at the monitor. His rage narrows down, leaving him expressionless. Like a predator just before striking its prey, it occurs to her.

He goes silent.

He stares at the screen.

Then at Elaine.

As if he notices her for the first time.

He says, with a sudden preternatural calm, "Well . . . another error."

Glen stutters. At a loss. A bad dream he can't seem to awaken from. "Mr. Desirio, if . . . if you can just show us paper statements, deposit slips, anything at all, I'm sure we can get to the bottom of this. Now that it's unfrozen, we can start looking . . ."

But Desirio does not seem to hear him. He is still looking at Elaine.

Another error.

And Elaine realizes what Desirio must be thinking: *One error too many. One error too many to be mere error.*

"Elaine. Elaine Kelly, is it?" he says, reading the name off the badge on her white blouse.

Elaine nods mutely.

He smiles slowly, making a show of generosity. "Well, thank you for your help, Elaine." And again, with his reassuring calm—as if to calm and reassure them all—directing it now at her, "Yes, I'm sure we'll get to the bottom of this."

He shoves his sunglasses onto his nose, pivots, and exits the bank into the sunlight, his two bulky silent colleagues in tow, obedient dogs swallowing their growls, muzzling their bites, sensing, perhaps, that they will soon be unleashed.

"Glen, I'm giving my notice."

Impulse? Not if it's self-preservation. Not if it's life or death.

"You're what?!"

"Giving notice. I'm leaving the bank."

Glen falls back in his chair. Looks up at her. Takes a breath. "Elaine. Now, look. I saw how Desirio stared at you. But, Elaine . . . that's the heat of the moment. It's computers. Computer systems.

We'll get it worked out. And, well, it's money. Money makes people crazy." He takes a deep breath. And another. "We'll get it worked out. He knows we will. You saw how he got a lot calmer almost immediately. And it's not your fault; it's not anyone's—"

Elaine shakes her head vigorously to stop him. "No, it's not that . . ."

"Is it the accident? That could rattle anyone."

"It's . . . it's everything, Glen." Quieter. Pretending frankness. Pretending trust. "My mom's death. Selling the house. It's just . . . the right time for a change, I guess."

Desirio knows. He looked at me and just knows. And he is going to kill me. I have to leave or I'm going to die.

Glen looks at her for a moment now, too. Regards her closely. Seems to sense her resolve and folds further into his leather chair with acceptance. "Everyone is going to miss you, Elaine. Everyone loves our Elaine. You know that, don't you?" Then his eyes light up. "Hey, let me throw you a party. I know a really hip place . . ."

"No." She cuts him off uncharacteristically. Her first act of defiance, of independence as an ex-employee. "I'm leaving, Glen. Really. As in, now."

She tries to wipe away his stunned, hurt look as she turns, to concentrate on what she has to do.

• • •

As she hurriedly tosses her few personal items into a cardboard moving box—pictures of her mom and their cats, a hairbrush and mirror, a light cardigan kept on the back of her chair—Bob, the lottery-ticket sculptor, appears at her desk. He leans in toward her and whispers, "I know why you're leaving."

The words stop her. The words, and their tone. Matter-of-fact, casual, friendly . . . but pointed, meaningful. She looks at her hands, paused midair above the cardboard carton, then forces them to continue packing.

"You do, huh?" she says, throwing more items in. A couple of paperback books on finding romance, on finance, on financial self-improvement.

"Our Sam's quite a snoop, you know."

She pauses again in her packing. Sam, flamboyant Sam, had borrowed her terminal several times when there were computer problems.

She keeps packing the cardboard carton. A little slower. Listening.

"He loved telling me all the exotic destinations you were looking at. He thought it was funny that quiet, above-it-all Elaine turns out to be a deluded dreamer just like the rest of us. But I know you're not a dreamer, Elaine."

She pauses completely. She looks up at him.

"What happened this morning with the Desirio account . . . suddenly I knew," he says.

Elaine stares at him.

In her deep, fearful, anxious dreams of being discovered, it has always been the disappointed, weary face of Nussbaum before her. Or the shocked face of Glen. Or the pained, shamed face of her mother. Or the nameless faces of unrecognizable police and bank authorities flowing vaguely around her. It has never been Bob. The face at the beginning of the end.

Bob. In fact, the only person here she feels any real connection with. The person she's always felt a sense of promise about. It figures, doesn't it, in its inescapable, paradoxical way, that it's him? When, and to whom, and how precisely, is he going to turn her in?

But no. If he's telling her all this, maybe he's not going to turn her in. If he's telling her all this, maybe he has something else planned.

"If you saw what happened this morning, then you saw the look in that man's eyes," says Elaine. Honest, direct. *I'm trusting you, Bob.*

"I saw what you saw," Bob says. Just as honest. *You can trust me.*

She shares it quietly, half-stunned by her own words, by her own instincts and perceptions. "If I stay here, they'll kill me. Like they killed the old man. Whoever he was . . ."

"I'll help you," says Bob. He looks around them, at the high walls, the cubicles, the other tellers, at all of it, as if assessing it, then looks back at her with an admission. "That's why I came over here."

She is suddenly anxious, suddenly unnerved at having revealed so much so easily. "And what's your help going to cost me?"

He smiles. "Take my help, Elaine. Take someone's help for once." His smile remains easy, natural. "This would be a very good time to start."

He's right. She knows it. Feels it. "I have an overseas flight booked for tomorrow night. I have to disappear until then."

"Stay at my place. Believe me, they'll never find you there." He stoops down to the desk and jots a phone number and address on a slip of paper. She folds and pockets it. Silent, fluid teamwork, she notices.

"I know you know the account sweeps," Bob says quietly. "The timing. The system. I know you help Glen with all that. What I don't know is why you didn't just go—"

Her cell phone rings. She looks at the number.

Shit.

What now?

She answers it. Feels she has to. Feels she has no choice. She can't *seem* to disappear before she actually *does* disappear. She can't create interest, questions, suspicion.

Keep everything the same. Keep everything the same.

"Nussbaum here. Got something really interesting to show you," he says. "Any way you can get down here? Lunch break tomorrow or something?"

She stares at her small box of belongings. Five years of work and just a few cheap items and photos to show for it. "I . . . I can come right now."

Learn about the photo, the girl, the black-coated man, then leave the photo and girl and black-coated man behind her forever.

Elaine Kelly slips out of the Federated branch silently, with no formal good-byes. Only a quick, firm, hidden, wordless squeeze of Bob's hand with her own.

13

They are standing in front of an old television set on a cart rolled up next to Nussbaum's desk. He is replaying the surveillance tapes of "Desirio" going into various branches.

"Real name, Arthur Holden. Occupation, bank teller."

"No." She hears herself utter the word from somewhere far off.

"Thought you'd like that. Bank teller for forty years. Couple years ago quit his job over some undefined personal issue not described in his file. Twenty bucks says it relates to that photo."

A bank teller. Standing there in some silent, sterile branch just like hers, hour after hour, week after week, year after year. A member of the same somber fraternity of wandering minds, window-gazing eyes, brooding powerlessness, flattening routine, and richly imaginative escape. Standing on a similar square of linoleum at some nearly identical branch, watching the same plastic clock above him, a mildly humming overlord. Her psychic kin. And he never said a word. Never shared it. Did he not want her to know anything about him? Or did he not want her to see her own lonely future?

Nussbaum holds up a thick manila folder, shakes it like a maraca, wiggles it as if just to hear its sound. "Helped introduce computer programs, software upgrades . . . apparently really knew his stuff. I *know* he was pretty good with computers, 'cause he hid himself so well that it took us this long to find out who he really was. And from what we're only starting to piece together here, he managed to create a bunch of identities, open a bunch of accounts, moving money continually, *and* making it grow. We might be talking millions here, Elaine."

"I thought he was eccentric. I didn't think he was a . . . a . . ."

"A thief?" says Nussbaum.

She looks back, repeats the word, hears it hang in the air. "A thief."

Nussbaum drops the folder on his desk again and sits heavily after it. "Well, it's not so simple. Here's the thing . . . All his money is coming from other accounts, right? And yet, at these branches he's going in and out of, there's no related complaints from any depositors." Nussbaum's eyebrows lift and seem to let new light into his eyes. "Which tells me one of two things: he's either pilfering from people so rich and sloppy in their finances they don't even know or he's taking from people who can't say anything that would have the authorities looking into it. And the neighborhoods we're taking about, it ain't rich people."

"He's stealing from criminals." The suave, silver-haired Antonio Desirio looms up richly, fully, in her mind's eye.

"Miss Kelly, let me educate you a little about the one thriving recession-proof neighborhood business that the average citizen of Queens never really wraps their head around. There is so much money in the drug trade out here, it's hard to even comprehend, impossible to keep track of. It's a whole separate economy. With two kinds of people operating in it: the kind who are completely careless with money and the kind who count every dime. And drug money, because there's so much of it, usually makes its way into other enterprises, both legal and illegal. Like prostitution . . . white slavery . . ." He holds up his copy of the photo of the girl, glances at it, then turns it over as if to avoid looking at it or thinking about it too closely.

"Let's say Arthur Holden was taking money from their accounts," says Nussbaum, "and one of them finally figured it out, got real pissed off, and knocked him off, figuring they'd find wads of bills in his mattress or behind a wall in his apartment. They'd never think he was keeping it in various *other* banks. Where they couldn't get at it. But there's some *reason* Holden is doing this, right? I mean, it's apparently not to enhance his lifestyle . . ."

As he pauses for a moment to let them ruminate on that reason, she jumps in with further cause for rumination. "Detective Nussbaum, I quit the bank."

"You what?" But she knows he heard her perfectly well, because he leans back, clasps his hands behind his neck, studies her.

"Why would you go and do that, Elaine?" Is it a simple question, merely curious, or is there more arcing behind it? More pointed interest, more intent, outright suspicion slowly forming, gathering. "To a guy like me, sure seemed like a nice, cushy place to work . . ."

She shrugs noncommittally.

Nussbaum smiles grimly. "First Arthur Holden quits, then you. And here I thought everyone wanted to be a banker."

14

A few minutes after midnight, she stands across from 150 Hayes Street once more. Looks up at the apartment, raising her eyes to 10E as if searching for an answer, seeking resolution or understanding from on high, as if 10E's windows are stained glass, holy, as if imploring the sky and stars themselves to help her.

She doesn't know what she's doing here or what she hopes to accomplish. It just seems to her that this is the right place to be. That whatever is wrong, whatever is going on, involves that apartment somehow. Cleaned out by an appraiser who wasn't an appraiser and a super who disavows and denies the activity entirely. Emptying it for some reason.

But she is here for a subtler reason, too. It's the last known address of Arthur Holden. As if she hopes to pick up the trail of his death, to pick up the scent of his routine, of where he would or should be. This is crazy, she knows, but also knows that it feels right to be here. For some sense of closure? Some sense of ending? Or is it just the beginning? She has no idea.

She'd been quickly packing her bags for tomorrow's flight, trying to reduce the future of her life to just a few pounds of essentials, watching anxiously out the window for any unusual traffic or movement. In the utterly familiar and routine silence of the street outside, she started to realize she was probably overreacting after all—seeing a momentary rage in a man's eyes and expanding it to a death threat, largely because of her humming, ever-present guilt and fear about what she'd done. She'd gone out for a cup of coffee, to give her energy to keep packing, to take a break, to escape the suffocating row house and its memories, and—impulsively? planned?—has found herself here once again.

She stands here, she is sure, for the last time. And in a way, for the first time, knowing now that it is where Arthur Holden lived. Knowing now that Arthur Holden was a bank teller. Led a bank teller's existence for most of his life until . . . something happened. Something that he set in motion? Something that he fell victim to? Some inextricable mix of the two? She feels a kinship with him acutely, almost physically.

"Now that we've got a name, we'll search the girl's photo again," Nussbaum said to her earlier. "It'll take a few days; I can't make it a priority. After all, no one's officially looking for her or filled out a missing-persons report, no relative or guardian, which is what New York law requires. We don't really know enough. It's just your nosiness and my cooperation," Nussbaum said. "Just you and me and a big dose of curiosity. I'll call you." And then that sudden warm smile. Casual and natural, tender and trustworthy. A smile that, in different circumstances, could keep a girl from fleeing overseas.

Now she stands out here at midnight, looking up at the window of empty 10E, wanting it, wishing it, willing it to tell her more, to reveal something, settle something, let her flee while carrying some answers along with her bags as she moves on with her secret life.

And then, 10E's light flicks on and flicks off.

Just for a moment.

Like a signal, a quick blink of code across a harbor. A signal to someone else? Or a signal to her?

The super said no one was living in that apartment.

Could it be the super, or a janitor, retrieving something? Checking something? A little odd at this hour, but explainable.

And while she stands still looking a minute later, a figure emerges from the entrance of 150 Hayes and into the night. A large figure. Filling the doorway as he exits, standing there a moment, taking a cigarette, casually surveying the street up and down, something vaguely recognizable in his bulk and slouch . . .

In a moment, she has it.

Like a signal. A signal to her . . .

The truck driver. The protesting, pleading driver of the truck that hit Arthur Holden.

Who has managed to disappear on the NYPD.

Who, according to Nussbaum, isn't so clean after all.

He heads right, walking down the street.

She has no choice. Without thinking—and thinking everything—her mind and body buzzing with anxiety, intent, fear, nervous energy, she falls in behind him.

Confused, alert, determined.

She is not about to let him disappear again.

15

Dark streets. An unpredictable route. She is careful to hang far back, but not so far as to lose him. It helps that he is big, substantial, and that his red baseball jacket catches the ambient street light even at night. An easy animal to track. But a bad one to tangle with, no doubt.

At one point, he turns and looks behind him. Because he senses something? Elaine's heart claws at her chest. If she were on the same side of the street, she'd have to keep walking directly toward him so not to arouse any suspicion, and if he were stopped for more than a few seconds, she would have to walk by him. Luckily, shrewdly, she is on the opposite side of the street and can keep walking without it being a problem. Even casually looking over.

He continues on quickly, satisfied he is alone.

He stops in front of an all-night Greek diner—Christina's—and surveys around him once before stepping into the warm light and busyness inside.

She stands in the shadows across the street. When he enters the diner, she crosses the street toward it, comes up to its entrance, and pauses.

On the one hand, the truck driver doesn't know who she is or what she looks like. He would never remember her face from the thick crowd gathering in the accident's aftermath. She would be safe.

On the other hand, she can see—through the narrow window beside the diner's door—the truck driver sliding into a red booth. And can see who is sitting in the booth across from him.

Antonio Desirio.

Casual leather jacket, gray turtleneck—less international businessman, more neighborhood night owl.

She freezes.

He would almost certainly recognize her. *Elaine Kelly, is it?*

She drifts back into the shadows to catch her breath.

If you think of anything, anything at all, call me.

The card is still in her purse. *Evan Nussbaum, Det. 114th Precinct, City of New York.*

It would be one quick phone call, one quick urgently whispered sentence—*the truck driver and Desirio are sitting together in a diner*—as if each of them carries an electric charge and their union produces instant ignition, and Nussbaum would be here immediately.

But she has stolen 1.3 million dollars. Not spent a dime of it, no, but moved it, transferred it, and therefore stolen it . . . and therefore can hardly risk more contact with a detective of the New York Police Department.

A moment later, the big truck driver and Desirio are up out of the booth and heading toward the door. And at the same time, clearly choreographed—obviously summoned by cell phone—a big silver sedan pulls up to the door of the diner and Desirio and the truck driver look both ways before ducking purposefully, wordlessly, into the back of it.

Shit.

As the sedan pulls away and stops in a moment at a red light, Elaine steps out of the shadows, raises her hand high above her head, waves it around irrationally, frantically. As if to halt the silver sedan purely on the strength of her authority, through the power of her righteousness, for the obviousness of the vehicle's illicitness.

But the frantically waving hand is, in fact, searching for a tell-tale flank of yellow in the night. Still watching the sedan's receding glint of silver, while desperately seeking the glint of yellow, waving with frantic energy as if to a long-lost friend . . .

There! Thank god!

The cab pulls to the curb. She jumps in. Like jumping into a movie, filming on the mean streets of Queens.

Leaning forward toward the cab driver, pointing out his windshield, "Follow that silver car." *I said that? I actually said that?* And then, gulping, quieter, more tentative, apologetic, "Not too close."

Why is she doing this? What does she hope to discover? This should be Nussbaum following them, not her. Maybe make an anonymous call to the detective? But he would know who the information came from. Or maybe a call in a few days, from safely overseas? Somehow get the information to him, leave an anonymous tip? But he knows that he and Elaine are the only two people interested in this. Looking into it, he'll realize the information came from her. And wonder why. And look deeper.

The familiar streets fly by. The streets she knows, has grown up in, transformed now by the tension. *Not too close. Not too far.* She wants to shield the cab driver—a Punjab Indian—from her anxiety, but she doesn't want him to screw up. Wants to direct him but holds her tongue. He seems to silently, dutifully understand the urgency. No questions asked. Alert. Concentrating. Good man.

The silver sedan begins to slow, making her heart pound faster.

And then pounding faster still, stuttering with speed, when she realizes . . .

She draws her breath in, so loudly, so shocked, that the cabbie looks back in the mirror at her to make sure she is all right.

The silver sedan has slowed nearly to a stop in front of them, to crawl into a parking space.

Across the street from the Kelly family row house.

"Jesus." She slides down in the back of the cab, below the window line. "Just keep driving past them. Don't slow down. Don't look. Just keep driving past them."

Jesus.

The simple thought presses down on her like a weight on her back.

Desirio knows.

16

The Indian cabbie drops her on a street corner at one thirty in the morning in an industrial-looking neighborhood in lower Manhattan. She doesn't give him the exact address, doesn't want the cabbie able to say where it is, whether voluntarily or cowering in the face of a threat.

It clearly distresses the cabbie to drop her here, in the middle of nowhere. Particularly after the stress of the fare—the unexplained task and urgency of following the silver car, and her shocked response as the sedan they were following pulled in to park. "Here? You want . . . here?"

"Yes, this is fine."

"No, I . . . I can't to drop you here, miss. Is . . . is not right."

"You have to. I'm sorry."

He shakes his head. He is very distraught about it.

"I'll be fine." She hands him the fare with a twenty-dollar tip. "That's . . . that's all I have."

"Miss, please, maybe a coffee shop we find for you—"

"Take it," she cuts him off, jumps out of the cab. Waits for it to pull away, then walks alertly, quickly, through the empty, industrial night, the one and a half blocks to her destination.

She looks up at a run-down loft building—cracked facade, chipped tile, peeling paint—as she dials her cell phone.

"Hello?" she hears.

"It's me. Elaine. I'm downstairs."

"I'm the fourth floor. Come on up."

In a moment the door buzzes. She pushes hard to open the heavy industrial door whose hinges are bent, and begins to climb the wooden stairs—irregular, dented, a hundred years old.

Bob meets her in the stairwell, halfway up. A friendly, familiar smile. So obviously more relaxed, more himself, in jeans and a T-shirt. And maybe as a result, more handsome, she notices. He's leaner looking, once out of those formless gray flannels and the loose-fitting white button-down oxford. And more than anything . . . here.

After she has washed her face in the bathroom sink, taken a few deep breaths to calm down, she sits on a worn-out couch in the living room and looks around her. It's a run-down industrial space with cement floors and exposed brick walls. HVAC pipes hang from, and run across, the high ceilings. And sculptures, all around her. Metal and wood. Some small and intricate, some large and formidable. More than a dozen of them. She understands Bob's double life immediately. Because she has largely been leading—or has always led—one of her own? In a moment she finds a glass of white wine in her hand. Cool and sweet. She swallows half of it in one gulp.

"I didn't know you made anything besides lottery sculptures."

"My little secret. My other life," he says. "And apparently I'm not the only one with a secret life."

She studies one of the sculptures. A polished wood core, floating waist high, sleek reflective metal legs protruding from it, outstretched, as if reaching, running. His soaring lottery-ticket bird, his running, leaping creature—all seem to be in motion, in flight.

Toward a dream, or away from a nightmare? Or is the sense of flight only her unique interpretation? Would someone else see only shapes and materials, no movement at all?

"Well, your secret life is inspirational. Mine is terrifying."

He says nothing. Letting her say whatever she wants and needs to, or stay silent, if she chooses. Giving her space. She studies him. Catches herself examining him like another sculpture, moving softly in socks around the loft. Leanness, tautness, hunger in his face and limbs.

She sets down the glass of wine he poured her. He fills it again. "They're sitting across the street from our house in Queens, waiting for me." She shakes her head in disbelief at what she's seen. A life not her own. "Bob, they're going to kill me." She lets the words hang there, like a strange piece of sculpture themselves, to examine in puzzlement, in wonder. She doesn't dare look up at him. Doesn't want to see any confirmation written in his face.

For a moment, he gives no response. Maybe because he knows she's right.

Then, with logic, "Not before they try to get their money back. That's what they want." He tilts his head quizzically. "You've got that going for you, right?"

Now she looks up at him through her gloom, and realizes it's true. But it, unfortunately, doesn't matter.

"I can't just give it back, Bob. They won't just take it and leave it at that. They'll think I know more about them than I really do. Or that I helped move the accounts around. That I know too much. They'll want to protect themselves." She shakes her head. It is so clear to her. So immovable and unchangeable. Fate written in stone.

"Couldn't you ask that detective for help?"

She shakes her head. "How?" She looks at Bob. "I'd have to tell him what I've done. He'd have to charge me. He'd have no choice."

Bob shrugs. Tops off her glass of wine once more. "Maybe not."

She looks at him. "What do you mean?

"Maybe he doesn't want to see you in jail. Maybe he's got ways to work around it." He smiles thinly. "Sexual attraction can make people morally flexible, you know."

She looks at him doubtfully.

"Elaine, you really think he had to come over to the branch to update you on the investigation? To show you those tapes?" He smiles again. "He wanted to meet you. I could see it from across the room." His smile lingers, confusing to her, unclear.

So when she'd first called Nussbaum, and he said, "Oh, yes, sure, from the Federated branch," had she misinterpreted completely, and it was simply a form of flirtation, a version of a high school game that had gone right past her? *Of course I remember you, silly girl.* Or was there no game at all to it and he was simply confirming, for her, that he knew exactly who she was.

The moment is suddenly loaded for her. For just as she realizes Bob may be right about Nussbaum, as she recognizes the force and evidence and logic of it, she also senses, with equal surprise, Bob's own interest, his own attraction, obliquely revealed by the sudden appearance of the good-looking detective at the bank. *"Sexual attraction can make people morally flexible, you know."* Watching her from across the bank. Hiding her now, protecting her. It was a level of interest she'd been sure ran only from her toward him. She doesn't know what to do with the moment so she chooses to ignore it, to push it away.

Nussbaum had seemed pretty sure it was drug money. Would that soften it for Nussbaum? Make him consider helping her without applying the consequences too firmly to her? Maybe make some kind of deal?

Drug money and Arthur Holden, bank teller. An unlikely, volatile chemistry. She thinks again about her sense of connection to him and wonders: Did that truck catch him unawares? Or did Arthur Holden experience what she is experiencing now? Did he know they were on to him? That he was a marked man?

She looks at Bob with a new, sudden focus and force and commitment. "That old man . . . he was doing it all for some reason . . . some good reason . . ."

He frowns a little. He doesn't know what she's talking about, she hasn't explained. He listens patiently, waiting for her to.

". . . And maybe I should be picking up where he left off . . . seeing it through."

"Seeing what through? You're losing me . . ."

"I don't know exactly," Elaine says disconsolately, ghostly, unconnected. "That's the thing. I just don't know." Despite—or because of—the silver sedan sitting across from the Kelly row house, she feels a new, raw, free-floating sense of purpose and mission, but it is surrounded by a paralyzing fear. She wants to act; she's afraid to act.

Her wineglass is empty now. Both of them notice it at once, like seeing a mistake. He pours her another. Is that three? Four? With his diligent refills, she's lost track. But she is finally feeling the wall of her terror and guardedness give way, loosen and crumble, and she feels the hazy flow of the river of wine, its thick mist of relaxation, and it is through that mist that his questions float toward her.

"Elaine, one thing I still don't understand," says Bob, carefully. "If you did this, moved this money, and you know the bank systems, why didn't you take off? Why'd you only do it . . . I don't know . . . *halfway*?"

She is silent.

"I mean, the fact that you were still there, still coming to work, made me think I was wrong. Then I thought, no, that's the cleverest way to do it. Take it and go on like nothing's happened."

She grimaces. "I'm not that clever." The wine, oddly, seems to allow her to focus, to make it suddenly clear to herself: *I didn't take off because too much happened too fast.* Identities, assumptions, everything shifted on her. Which paralyzed her. A Christian suddenly facing a lion. And instead of running, she stands there, frozen.

They don't really know each other, she and Bob. This is the first time they've talked. What odd circumstances for their first chance at a connection. What a subject, for their first real chance to communicate. And yet the oddness of it, the untestedness of it, seems to pave the way for a frankness between the two of them. Unpracticed in social deceptions around a subject like this, they go down the path of the truth.

"You knew you were doing it . . . ?" he asks, as if to make sure. To let her off the hook, to wiggle out of it, if she doesn't truly understand.

"Yes, I knew. But I did it, because . . ." She is looking for some way, any way, to finish the thought.

He finishes it for her, with a simple shrug. "Because you thought you could get away with it."

Yet, he says it, she notices, without judgment attached, as a simple statement of fact. She's never heard that phrase uttered and meant that way. In her upbringing, it was always a phrase of accusation and condemnation.

Elaine takes another gulp of wine. Shakes her head. "I knew I was doing it. But still, it was . . . an accident."

"You mean . . . the truck?"

"No, I mean . . . me. What I did."

His eyes go wide at the statement. She thinks she sees him suppress a smile. "An accident," he says, nodding as if he understands perfectly.

"I mean . . . the terminal didn't process the deposit and then . . . it just happened."

Like a locked door that suddenly opens a crack. So you slip in. And in the next instant it closes behind you and you can't get back out.

An accident of the machines, of the system, conspiring to let her do it. Giving her the chance.

"So many people commit crimes," she says. She hears herself saying it, her voice soft, drifting on the tide of the wine. Yet, at the same time, the alcohol is focusing her thoughts. "You read about them every day. Rip-offs, scams, insurance fraud, insider trading. Even my bank, committing its own legal ones—credit card penalty fees, giving liar loans . . ."

There are crimes in the news all the time, she reminds him now, and with help from the merlot, her recitation flowing, spreading, like a liquid spilled on the floor. Indicted lawyers, executives and union leaders, corrupt judges and elected officials, a constant media parade of white-collar criminals. And these, of course, are only the ones who are caught. Some percentage aren't. Maybe a small percentage. She bets it's more than that. An insistent, ever-present, pulsing undercurrent of crime. Of untruth. Pulsing real and pulsing close. Every day, dozens of employees are fired from Federated—for fraud, for theft, for misrepresenting themselves on resumes, fabricating their pasts . . .

These were the thoughts that pressed at the periphery of her consciousness, that she weighed only theoretically, when the old man with the black hat entered after he exited. Thoughts she had allowed in, but not confronted, barely voiced to herself. And here she is making the points to Bob, to hear how it sounds aloud, to see how it's received.

He smiles. Smiling, she knows, at her trying to justify it. Soften it. It must be clear to him she's been thinking about this. Brooding about it. "Of course, that's the Catholic in you," he says.

"Meaning?"

"Evil is all around you. A world soaked in evil." He shrugs. "Maybe that's what let you figure, what's the big deal if you dip your toe in it as it flows by? Taste your little morsel. I mean, if everyone else is doing it, right?" He rubs a palm over one of his sculptures, as if literally gathering perception, perspective, from his art.

"It doesn't forgive it," she says flatly, resolutely.

"No, it doesn't forgive it." He pauses to consider. "But it puts it in a context."

The context of what she reads and hears about every day. The context of a world cutting corners, where morality is up for grabs. A context of reality.

In a little L-shaped corner of the loft, there is a rudimentary office, and Bob instantly transforms it into a sleeping alcove by rolling out a cot from the closet and tossing a blanket over a low rafter to create privacy for Elaine.

Hailing the yellow cab so suddenly, changing so quickly from pursuer to pursued, Elaine has nothing with her but her purse, of course, so Bob tosses her an oversize T-shirt and a pair of gym shorts.

She sits on the cot and slips her hands under the sheet and blanket he has spread across it and tucked in with bachelor-like adeptness. Having her hands beneath the sheet gives her a moment of comfort, a sense of security.

She is suddenly completely exhausted, can barely keep her eyes open. And amid that utter exhaustion, she feels . . . protected. She knows that's absurd, knows that it's the multiple glasses of wine that are producing the sensation, knows he can't protect her, that no one can, but the feeling washes over her like a wave—thick, forceful—and she lets it.

She is experiencing, however tenuous, a moment of release, and support, after all the tension of the last few days. She knows he is trying to relax her, to distract her, to take her mind off it. Music plays in the loft—an indistinct Europop that seems to have no source, seems to emanate from the woodwork itself. She sees that he is making sure her wineglass is never empty. Her words are slurred now, she notices, everything is slowed down, and she is relieved that his own words are slurred, too, that it's not embarrassing, that she's not alone in this.

She's grateful for the momentary relief from the overwhelming reality, hanging over her like a black sky—broad, dark, inescapable, implacable. She has stitched it together vaguely in her mind, and the fragile stitching seems to hold. The silver sedan in front of her house—she can never go back there—but in her purse is her ticket, her wallet, her credit cards, her phone, her license, and her passport, and the account numbers are in her head. She can go like this. Just like this.

She feels her body going pleasantly limp, and she is unable to stop it. It occurs to her that the greater the stress, the greater the relief—a formulation she would never have had the chance to test so powerfully and directly before now.

She realizes that the whole evening here in Bob's loft has been a gradual process of slowing down, calming down. One long process of relief. She looks up at Bob, smiles for that. Whether he's right about Nussbaum hardly matters right now. It is Bob who is providing an island in the torrent of events, a port in a storm. She looks into his eyes, centered, present, swimming in calm.

Come with me. The thought comes back to her.

You're a lifesaver, Bob. Maybe literally. Come with me. But something stops her from saying it, saying anything like it. Some habitual boundary in her, which frustrates her, which she is only too aware of, which she wishes weren't there. Some self-protective, alert, rigid piece of her—which, she suspects, is the *real* cause of her impulsiveness—this innately protective, cautious, rule-bound personality so deep in her that it tethers her. And her impulsiveness is pulling against it, rebelling.

He chooses that moment to lean forward and kiss her. She feels the salty-sweet taste of his lips on hers, an unfamiliar taste, like some startling new fruit from a vendor's cart in some foreign land—Buenos Aires, Johannesburg, Lisbon, Athens—and for a moment she feels, deep in her chest and lungs, a powerful sensation of opening up, and then a powerful clamping down a moment later.

As if he senses it—or senses something—he leans back, looks at her.

She shifts uncomfortably. Suddenly sets the wineglass down firmly, as if surprised it has been in her hand.

She tries to deflect the moment graciously. "Bob, you know what I've been through."

"It's your bank account," he says with a coy smile. "It turns me on." He is not letting go of the flirtatiousness. He is not deterred. He is trying to hang on to it.

"Bob . . . I quit my job today, my mother just died, a strange car is sitting outside my house . . . this isn't the night for us . . ." She looks at him imploringly, a lawyer who's made a compelling, inarguable summation and is just waiting for the judge and jury to take it in. The wine gives her fluency she wouldn't otherwise have.

The summation works. He stops suddenly; a shift registers in his eyes. His coy smile goes gentler, and then from gentle to sad. He nods with understanding. Scoops up the two wineglasses. "Okay," he says. "You rest. Try to sleep." His disappointment is palpable. It penetrates her. But that note of understanding penetrates her more. As he looks her over again, surveys her shape as if for one last time before he stands up, she feels the sympathy from him, a gentle wave of it. Not merely hearing what she says but taking in what she means and feels. Watching him walk back to the kitchen with the wine and the glasses, she feels an acute sense of regret. *Your bank account . . . it turns me on*, he'd teased. *Your understanding, Bob . . . it turns me on.*

An hour and a half later, Elaine turns restlessly on the cot. The room is dark, practically black.

She can't sleep. She is exhausted but manages to close her eyes only to open them a moment later, uselessly alert. What she'd said to Bob was all true—she's just quit her job, her mother has just died, a strange car is sitting outside her house, a swirl of upheaval—but her conclusion might be exactly wrong, she senses, because in a life so unmoored, maybe she needs to connect to something, to someone, if only for a moment. Hide out for a moment from the dire, insistent, swirling present. Hide not only from the car across the street but from herself. And when he scooped up the wineglasses, headed toward the kitchen, she felt that moment retreating, slipping away.

Come with me. The vague, foolish fantasy returns to her in the dark. But with it comes its more practical, obverse side: *Better yet, I'll go with you. Disappear with you in the here and now.* And why not in a sculptor's downtown loft, with a man she trusts, who is sheltering her, harboring her from harm? What better moment or reason could there be?

At the alcove's partition, a figure is silhouetted in the low light.

Elaine sits up startled.

"Just me," says Bob quietly.

His voice is reassuring. A reassurance she hasn't felt since . . . she can't think when.

"Can I come in?"

She pauses.

And then nods yes.

A nod she knows means more than simply, *Yes, come in. Sit here on the cot, reassure me.*

And by his own pause, and his slow measured steps into the alcove, she knows that he understands her nod's greater meaning.

And soon he is kissing her breasts through the T-shirt, pressing his lips to her nipples, to her mouth, pressing himself to her, pulling back only to look at her, take her in . . .

She starts to feel dizzy, as if the warm spin of the alcohol has returned to her, but this spinning is sharper somehow, without the wine's dulling effect.

She is losing her self-awareness, slowly losing herself in the feel of him, in the feel of his arms, in the breadth of his chest, in the pulse of his breath growing quicker, his kisses more insistent. She finds her focus and alertness giving way, falling away to join him, to catch him, match him, a little behind him but almost there—an ecstatic struggle against him and yet a struggle to be with him. What an odd sensation, and she finds herself starting to smile in anticipation. *So this is how it feels . . .*

Suddenly, he stops.

He stares luridly, almost dazedly, down at her.

Pausing, it seems, to take her in. To drink in the vision of her, swallow it whole one last time, before going any further.

As he does, a small trickle of blood and saliva drops from his mouth onto her T-shirt.

In a single motion, he is swept off her like debris.

There, behind him, is the truck driver.

Holding up a needle and syringe.

She feels the night tightening around her . . .

Bob's body lands with a thud on the floor next to her.

The truck driver checks the syringe.

Having plunged it into Bob's, neck apparently, a moment ago.

Another man is standing in the dark a couple of yards behind the truck driver. When he steps forward, it draws the cord of night even tighter. The currents of connection create a jolt.

It is John Ellis—the "appraiser" from Arthur Holden's apartment.

They must have entered the room unnoticed in the rising passion. Watched it. Used it. Bob and Elaine melting into each other, the world beyond them receding. Elaine's senses giving way, Bob's urgency—they had worked together to let the two men enter unnoticed.

Professionals. The thought goes through her instantly, easily, like liquid. Their silent teamwork tells her. Criminality at a certain level is fluent, expert, practiced, confident. She feels it, knows it.

Both men now stare down at Elaine, who is wearing only panties and the loose T-shirt, the fabric up around her neck and shoulders in the precoital excitement, her pale breasts exposed.

She jerks the T-shirt down to cover herself, scrambles up off the cot to make a mad bolt for the window, for the door, for anywhere . . .

They catch her arms and push her back onto the cot.

The truck driver holds the same needle to her throat. He has a knee up on the cot. He concentrates closely on the needle's position, floating it over Elaine's neck.

Elaine looks down at it—its thin steel shaft, its tip an inch from her throat.

"You saw what it did to your boyfriend." The warning from Ellis is delivered flatly, clear, inarguable, and effective. It freezes her.

The truck driver and Ellis speak to each other briefly in a guttural, aggressive, violent-sounding Eastern European language—surely the same language she heard Desirio murmur smoothly to his colleagues in the bank, but here, it sounds frank and harsh, rude and unbound. Despite his bland Midwestern looks, Ellis seems to speak it as fluently as the truck driver.

She can tell, by their blatant assessment of her, looking her up and down, and by the quick crass laugh from the truck driver, that part of the discussion is of her assets, her body, and—by where their eyes travel and linger—her red hair. But that seems to be wrapped inside a quick, efficient, businesslike discussion, and the word goes through her head again like a train roaring past: *professionals.* She can further sense, by the tones of voice in the exchange, that Ellis is in charge.

"Get up," Ellis suddenly instructs her in English.

She gets up off the cot.

He thrusts the gym shorts at her. Picks her street clothes up off the floor, tosses them onto the cot's bedsheets, then gathers the bedsheets and pillow into a bundle. "For prints and DNA," he says. "Not ours. Yours. You were never here."

She watches Ellis and the big truck driver begin to systematically attack the apartment. To quickly, violently pull out drawers, to topple items from the closet shelves, to shatter dishes in the sink . . .

"Bad neighborhood. Lot of burglaries," Ellis explains. Instructional. Almost professorial.

And then the truck driver—after methodically tucking the syringe into a black leather kit and sliding it into his black jacket pocket—heads into the kitchen, and emerges with a carving knife.

Elaine flinches, steps back as the truck driver passes by her without even looking, crouches over Bob's corpse, and begins to stab the knife into it deeply, repeatedly, and with undisguised relish. Unable to suppress a smile at the inanity—or the satisfaction—of the work.

"Lot of meth addicts in this neighborhood. They go crazy," Ellis explains further, in the same cool, calm, dispassionately informative Midwestern voice.

She looks at the corpse, jumping with each blow . . .

She feels herself beginning to retch . . .

"Don't you dare," Ellis warns her, a flare of anger in his tone, the first hint of anger he has shown so far. And it stops her. She doesn't dare.

They hustle her down the dark stairs in her T-shirt and gym shorts. The truck driver bashes the door lock violently with a metal bar as they pass it on their way out. "Meth heads," Ellis repeats. "Extremely violent." Adding, "Nobody will know the lock was broken *afterward*."

They keep Elaine between them as they pull her out into the night.

17

It's the silver sedan that she had followed earlier. That had parked across the street from the Kelly row house.

Now she is in its backseat. The huge truck driver sits next to her. A needle is once more against her neck, threatening. Ellis has just slid across from the driver's seat to the front passenger seat, and is up on his knees, facing them. To Elaine, it's obvious: he's ready to help handle her, for whatever is coming.

"I gave you that girl's photo to get you out of my hair," says Ellis. "A little keepsake so you'd go away happy." He squints his eyes as if freshly annoyed. "I guess you were planning on going away happier than anyone guessed." *He knows. He knows everything.* "We figure if you're still around, then our money is still around." He shrugs at the irrefutable logic of that. "It *is* our money, as you know by now. Time to give it back." And she realizes instinctively, at a level below consciousness, why she is still alive and Bob is dead. It's a thin thread of difference: She has the money, and she's the only one who can give it back. Bob is not a thief, and she is, and that's why she's alive.

Time to give it back. And now the moment that Elaine has dreaded . . . the admission. The confession she hoped never to have to make to someone like Desirio or Ellis. "I can't."

"You can't?" Ellis looks more dumbfounded than angry.

"It . . . it has to do with the account . . ."

"Try me." And Ellis even settles back a little in the passenger seat, to indicate that he is listening . . . for now.

Focused on the needle pointing at her—a thin silver glittering venomous snake—she explains it in a terrified rush. "My mom had no money, but I had my job so we qualified for a reverse mortgage on our house"—heart pounding, eyes on the syringe—"and all mortgages come with an escrow account, for taxes and insurance . . ."

"I know what an escrow account is," he cuts in sharply, irritably. But he signals the truck driver to lower the syringe for a moment. He wants to follow this. To try, anyway.

Elaine takes a breath. "There's never any money in a reverse mortgage's escrow account . . . People with reverse mortgages don't *have* any money. So banks don't bother sweeping them . . ."

She can see he's listening.

"Some of the big banks are getting out of the reverse mortgage business, transferring the accounts and paperwork to those staying in. The transition's not orderly, different systems and record keeping, it's prone to errors . . ."

The explanation spills out of her. To show she's not hiding anything from him? To show her own criminal cleverness, to prove her value? Or because she senses this may be her last chance, her only chance, to ever tell anyone?

"With any real estate purchase or sale, a huge amount can pass through the escrow account. Just a normal part of the transaction." She looks at Ellis, takes a breath, cuts to the bottom line. "That's where the money is sitting. When the bank gets our house, I get what's left in the escrow account. A check is issued and mailed to the account holder automatically, by computer, to zero out the account. Whether it's ten dollars, or a million"—continuing to look at him—"or more."

The reverse mortgage. Financial instrument of the cashless, elderly poor. And Elaine has turned it around. Hiding cash behind the financial facade of poverty. Tucking it into an automated function of countless real estate transfers.

Ellis is silent. She can tell he is reluctantly impressed. "So you get at the money when the house sells."

"The broker's already got a buyer," Elaine tells him truthfully.

He shakes his head. "My employer won't wait for a real estate closing in Queens." He wrinkles his face with a general disdain for the borough.

He looks Elaine in the eyes. Studying her face frankly for a moment. There's a slight and sudden aliveness in his own eyes, which Elaine understands as quiet amazement. "Our regular clientele is always trying to skin us for a grand or two." He shakes his head. "Not a million plus . . ."

He looks now, just as frankly, from her face to the rest of her. At her T-shirt. At the body under it. At her red hair. The Appraiser again appraising the value of the merchandise. Again, hiding the merchandise from the authorities. She tries to pull the T-shirt down around her. She is shivering in the night.

He checks out the windows cautiously but continues to talk to her. "You're a lucky girl, Elaine Kelly."

Lucky? A lonely old man has completely fooled me. Killers have grabbed me. A lethal needle is at my throat. A few foolish keystrokes have turned my existence upside down. Lucky?

"A very lucky girl, believe me," he says, surveying her body once more, then looking hard into her eyes. "You see, Banker Girl, since you took out this, uh, unapproved loan," he says with a mean twinkle of amusement, "we're going to let you service your own debt . . . until such time as you are able to return our assets in full." Giving a slight smile at his own drift into legalese.

Elaine is silent.

"It's good you quit your job, Elaine Kelly." Using her first and last name again . . . to keep her at a distance? Keep her a name and not a person? "This way, your bank friends will hardly notice . . . just figure you took off for parts unknown"—a thin little smile— "just shrug and say that you kind of . . . disappeared." The last word is a reverent half whisper.

A cue for the truck driver next to her, whose shoulder turned away protectively to fill another syringe from the kit, as if drawing the word *disappeared* itself up into the narrow cylinder, along with the pale-blue liquid.

Elaine starts to squirm and scream.

Ellis reaches back from the front seat to help hold her down.

The truck driver administers the shot, a stab into her shoulder. *Professionals.*

It is her last thought, falling apart, fracturing in her head.

In a few seconds, Elaine feels her mind and body go loose together, a synchronous collapse. Consciousness gives way beneath her, and she passes out before the silver sedan even pulls out into the street and the night.

PART TWO

18

Her memories of her father *are no longer visual. They have receded into something more primal—a touch, a scent, a presence without visual representation or confirmation. The smell of ink when he came into the house in the evening. His sweet wine breath. Her skinny body surrounded hugely, completely, in an enfolding hug. The sense of him hovers vaguely when she opens the morning newspaper to a lingering scent of ink. For years, the black-and-white family picture of him occupied its sacred place on a doily on the couch's side table, and then her mother removed it one day, couldn't bear the relentlessness of memory's burrowing pain, and for Elaine, its disappearance was like him dying again. Reducing him further to only scents, sensations, evanescent half-formed images. For years he has been a ghost, a shadow, confined to the deepest recesses of her memory, inaccessible. And yet he comes alive now vividly, and she is riding his shoulders, holding his hand as if he is a guard or guide, and then he lets her go. And she knows, even within this strangely vivid, expansive dream, that his presence is metaphoric, standing for everything she doesn't have, everything that hasn't happened, everything she longs for, the intangible that is just beyond her. He stands for failure and hardship, yet at the same time, for all the promise beyond failure and hardship. His image, her understanding, are so strangely heightened, kaleidoscopic. As he enfolds his skinny little girl hugely in one last hug.*

• • •

Elaine Kelly awakens.

Somewhere on the planet.

Maybe in the same city.

Certainly to a new world.

Like a newborn, about to greet its new existence.

And as befits the newborn experience, she awakens naked in the darkness . . . but in a cold, unforgiving womb.

She is still extremely dizzy, woozy, unsteady, from the powerful narcotic, whatever it is. But through the wooziness—despite it, within it—she feels raw elation, because she is alive. Whatever they shot into Bob wasn't what they shot into her. Elation, and accompanying guilt, the image of Bob on the floor now hanging immense, inescapable in the surrounding blackness.

The darkness is absolute, thick, voracious. She presses tentatively into the inky black, tests it, feeling the walls around her. They give away nothing. She is aware of the beat of her own breath. "Hello?" Nothing. "Hello?" Her inquiry is so civilized at first. Laughably polite. But it grows louder, more desperate, till her last hellos are bellowed at the top of her lungs. The word falls muffled. The walls are clearly ready for her terror. Fully expecting it. Unmoved by her screams.

She feels around her. There is nothing here but the bare mattress she is on. No bedding. Presumably nothing on the walls or floor. Darkness so black and complete that she wonders—feels compelled to check once with her fingers—if her eyes are open or not. She feels along the walls looking for a door, only because she was put in here somehow. Her fingertips find the seam in the wall, and she finds the hinges, too, cool to the touch, but the door has no handle.

The dizziness remains. The darkness gives her no perspective, no visual clues with which to shake it off. It seems to be a permanent state, a kind of vertigo that has leached into her completely, a physical dizziness that has given way to a cerebral, interior dizziness, too. The dizziness and disorientation of not knowing where she is in the world—a block away or somewhere halfway around the globe—not knowing what day it is, what hour, how long she's been out before coming to. Time and space are suspended, reduced to her naked body and this black box, this benighted cell that contains her like a wrapped gift for some unimaginable recipient and celebration.

There are 164,000 employees at the bank where she worked. She's the only one starting unemployment like this.

And yet, the thought beating at the back of her head, amid this confusion and emptiness and blackness—and maybe the very notion that allows her to bear it—is the nun's refrain, stern and unbending, tapping at her insistently: *I deserve it.* The universe seeking balance for the theft. *I deserve it.* And now, like any good Catholic, you must survive the punishment to learn from it.

Buenos Aires. São Paolo. Johannesburg. Madrid. The images of those cities—their skylines at sunset, their bustling boulevards, the exotic faces of their citizens caught in candid turns—float in front of her, illuminate and occupy the darkness as if in mocking accompaniment. This black imprisonment is so literally the opposite, so apt a punishment, that it leads her to freshly suspect a higher force, a higher justice at work. Those cities a dream of escape. And this imprisonment, this nightmare of actuality, the very opposite of escape. The cities are flung far across the globe and the imagination, and these walls—so close, tangible, impenetrable—are resistant to imagining what lies beyond them. Her mind is still slurry, liquid, drifty, but this primal opposition between freedom and imprisonment, between *out there* and *in here*, this she is able to process.

Eventually, there are voices just outside the door. Muffled, male. She leaps to the door, presses her ear against it. They stop. Taunting her. Tantalizing her with their sudden silence.

And then the door opens.

The womb's seal is broken.

The sudden light overwhelms her, is too much for her eyes. She holds up her hand to shield her eyes from it, then has to close them—the brightness is too painful—but in a moment she forces one eye open to try to see something. Only vague, blurry shapes. Two looming shadows stand over her, their smells, their foul breaths, the male heat coming off them, and then the sudden, unexpected prick of the needle again in her shoulder, the pinch, the spread of nausea, the same collapse of her thinking, and everything goes dizzy and black once more.

The door opens again.

The light blinds her again.

The door closes almost instantly. She is alone again.

They dangle the tantalizing tease of companionship, the tease of connection, the teasing promise of humanity—in whatever form—and then they snatch it away.

But in the recurrent blackness, she is aware of the scent by the door.

She reaches through the blackness for it.

A bowl of soup.

She is hardly even aware of herself devouring it. She is hardly aware of it, yet the soup is all she knows.

She awakens thrashing, disoriented. Disorientation would seem to be the point. She is aware of her intense dreaming, yet she can't remember what the dreams are. Can't imagine them. And she is sleeping what . . . seconds? Minutes? Days? The nausea is constant, low-grade, always there, like a virus or sickness that you live with. Some of the nausea is obviously a side effect of the narcotic. But is some of it the darkness, enforced, unnatural, and some of it the situation itself?

When she next awakens, it's to music pulsing beneath the floor. Percussion. Bass. A rumble that buzzes beneath her. She has the sense of inhabiting herself, of some piece of her old self responding to the music. Some vestige that is preserved. But some new self too—unfamiliar, an intruder into her former being.

She presses her ear to the bare floor beside the mattress. The music becomes fuller. It pulses now, tickles a little, running through her naked body as she presses herself flat against the hard floor. And she can also hear the very edges of human voices—some male, some female. Party sounds. Gleeful screams. Laughter. Raucousness. Individual words are discernible here and there, but not enough to pick up any useful information. Who? Where? Why?

Hearing the strains of music, she feels like dancing. Like writhing. Like showing off. Like her body is being instructed, encouraged to do it, without the intercession or inclusion of her mind. Like mainlining elation. Like the drug is just a feeling. Just energy. Just excitement. What is this that they're giving her? Are they keeping her in here to get the dose just right?

She is naked. Imprisoned in a room. Starving. Forgotten. Alone. Terrified. And yet she hears the music and feels like dancing.

And then she recognizes it, is able to analyze and describe to herself exactly what the feeling is: it is her occasional feeling of "impulse." That rare, surprising urge from childhood to speak out, break glass, grab the cop's gun, now somehow extended by the drug into a long-lasting chemical effect, a way of being in which the impulsiveness is stretched out, humming steadily in her, as if pharmacologically time released. That was it. A built-in, chemically unleashed, long-lasting disinhibition. The ability to watch yourself do something, behave in a way you'd never have behaved before, and to observe it, amazed, and still participate, still partake. She's aware of it, observes its urges, vows vigilance.

Professionals. The word comes back to her. And doesn't it make sense that their pharmacological sophistication has made a leap, too? That it is far ahead of what she might have thought? From those submerged in the netherworld of sex and drugs, an unsurprising expertise . . .

Voices outside her door again.

She jumps off the mattress to press her ear against it.

Male voices. At least two.

And then from one of them a phrase that cuts through the thick door and her pharmaceutical fog: ". . . *she's a virgin.*"

What?!

She shudders.

Feels like retching.

Looks down at her nakedness—invisible in the dark, only available to her sense of touch—and feels a fresh wave of nausea, imagining them in here, inspecting.

"Yeah, sure," says the second voice. Annoyed. Skeptical. Dismissive. And somehow authoritative.

The first voice again. "When we saw what we had, we called you." The voice is sardonic, jaded, yet boyishly proud and dutiful. "Rescued her just in time, I understand." Dangling the word once more teasingly, tantalizingly: "A virgin." Like a sly sideshow barker making promises outside the tent flap.

The second voice, guarded now. "We shall see."

The door opens.

Onto a new world?

Onto her new life?

A man enters. A low, blue-colored light snaps on above her, bathes the room and her naked body in blue.

The door closes behind him. The light goes dimmer.

As her eyes adjust, the man takes off his clothes unceremoniously.

Elaine is terrified. Panicked. Frozen in place. She looks away. The room is spinning. The world beyond, everything she knows, spinning . . .

She turns toward him to plead. Recognizes him as he comes closer . . . puts his hands on her bare shoulders. Chilly, forceful . . .

She thinks of the grainy CNN file footage. Of the television blaring in the lunchroom corner. Casting the yacht and gleaming wife and sparkling children in an unreal televised blue.

And here he is, cast blue and unreal, too, his hands beginning to press against her, exploring . . .

Carlton Conner.

The chairman of Federated Bank.

There are 164,000 Federated employees.

Very few of them ever meet the chairman.

Fewer still get to really know him.

With a key, he opens a closet that is flush against one wall, unrevealed in her previous search along the walls in the dark. He steps into the closet, emerges holding a bullwhip, a studded restraining mask, some leather straps, and a leather halter, then some more spiked and studded leather straps.

Elaine's whole body shudders involuntarily. She looks down at it, surprised by its shuddering. Her own body, and not hers at all.

"Understand English?" he asks.

Elaine nods.

As he hands the whip to her and straps the studded restraining mask on himself, "Good. Then do it exactly the way I tell you."

"She's a virgin."

The voice said it with pride, like bagging a particularly elusive species of big game.

Catholic school through twelfth grade. A day student at community college, on campus only for classes. Long hours of bank training in a focused, fast-tracked program. Hurrying home to her mother. Only her oldest friends for a stolen hour of companionship here or there. Thirty percent of college women remained virgins through college, she'd read, trying to reassure herself. Twenty percent of women were still virgins before marriage. Was she simply one of them? A mere statistic, like any other number on the bank's computer screens?

But, of course, she sensed it was more than that, the reasons ran deeper. Was it some paralyzing respect for the hardworking, saintly, missing Catholic father ever present in the parlor photo? For the saintly, mortally ill Catholic mother ever present in the master bedroom? How subtly, how completely, had those presences shaped her? Because she knew—saw and felt, after all—the looks she drew from men and women, the glances and the stares of interest or resentment. Red hair like a beacon, marking the untapped resources beneath, leading to a murky, inaccessible reservoir of desire. Because it went both ways, was circular: she was ambushed by her own feelings, was revealed to herself by her own glance or stare at a tanned construction worker's arm swinging a hammer, or a certain chest beneath a shirt, or a certain smile.

And her impulsiveness . . . was her odd, unpredictable impulsiveness caused by some subversion or twisting of a young woman's natural sexual impulses, thanks to the oppressive combination of her dead father, dying mother, and Catholic background? Was her impulsiveness a kind of leaking out, a symptom, her body and psyche protesting the relentless constraint? She didn't know, couldn't stand far enough apart from her own psychology to say.

These were the questions that had circled in her incessantly, that beat at the back of her brain, half-formed, advancing and retreating, vague questions she had asked herself over the years.

"She's a virgin." Because the right circumstances, the right moment, the right person, hadn't come along? Was that the simple, comprehensible truth? Or a lie she told herself for deeper reasons layered with her background, psychology, her unique makeup as a person?

And then, suddenly, there she was in an artist's downtown loft, with a man who was protecting her, and the wine was plentiful, and her aloneness and fear were too much, and all the arguments with herself fell momentarily away, and she felt herself relaxing, disappearing, into his arms, his chest, his body. And the universe cruelly intervened. As if sending her one final, stern, cruel, mocking message.

"She's a virgin."

And there is a part of her—a rational, functional, intact piece of her operating alongside her terror—that knows it is the fact of her virginity that is perhaps now keeping her alive.

"She's a virgin."

Scarcity creates value. A law of markets.

The value of her virginity . . . it may be her salvation. Just as her Catholic upbringing, as her Catholic god, would have it.

It is her fury at this, the contemplation of this, these final measures of her virginity's silent history and tethered memories, that let her displace her thoughts, displace herself, as she follows his instructions and compounds and adapts and amplifies them in the way she senses he wants. It is this displacement that lets her initiate and follow, give and take, push and yield, to the exacting degree that he seems to minutely require. Is it a lifetime of obedience and duty that gives her a sensitivity, a natural feel for obedience's nuances? Or is it a lifetime of obedience and duty that creates an unthinking habit of them, that lets her "perform" them without thinking, while keeping her real self hidden, even from herself?

She watches herself as if through a lens, down a tunnel, far away yet participatory, both performer and audience, on center stage and hidden deep in the theatre's darkness—two places at once, severed from herself. Watches the movie unspool in blue before her . . . Watches her own hands slipping into the studded gloves, as if they were always waiting to, meant to, fit into gloves like that. *As if always meant to.*

She watches her white haunches glide through and drink in the low blue light, as she slides her legs into the tight, studded stockings.

And the props in her hands—weighty, strange, consequential—allow her conversely to float, to exist outside her own body, beyond herself, the blue light reinforcing the otherworldliness, her body fairly buzzing with strangeness . . .

Watches him slip himself into her—the reverse, the negative, the mirror action somehow—of her fingers pushed snugly into a studded glove, of her leg slid into a stocking. *As if always meant to.*

So much happening at once, a compression of subject and object and vision and sensation. That must be part of the excitement for them, she thinks, witnessing that. So much that would usually be parceled out minutely over months of courtship, over languorous hours of a special or magical night, here compressed into pure, efficient function. Not emotionless, exactly, just a different color of emotions, emotion in a darker register . . .

"She's a virgin."

But no more.

19

From his desk at the 114th Precinct, Detective Evan Nussbaum tries the cell phone number one more time. Once again, it rings and rings. Nothing. No answer. Frowning, frustrated, he snaps his cell phone closed.

"Whassup?" asks Dominguez, his partner, from the facing desk.

Nussbaum shrugs, shakes his head. "Nothing really. That woman who brought in the picture? She just left her teller job. Like, just up and left. Kid was pretty rattled, I guess. Saw the truck hit the old guy, and then the guy didn't even turn out to be who he said. Just trying to check on her, but she's not picking up."

Dominguez, whose big, black shaved head is somewhere between a bowling ball and an overripe eggplant, knifes the eggplant carefully to reveal a little smile of perfect white teeth. "Pretty."

"What?" Nussbaum looks up.

"Pretty girl." Smiling still. "Real pretty."

"So?"

"That why she find you so helpful?"

Nussbaum regards him evenly. *Fuck off, Dominguez.* The thoughtless, knee-jerk obscenity was the standard station house response to just about anything. The reigning verbal currency of this adrenaline-soaked conclave of alpha males, and some impressively alpha females, too. But he resists the urge to say it. Not that he's above it. He's not. But he's thinking for a moment, giving consideration to Dominguez's observation. She is undeniably remarkable looking—flaming-red hair, great legs, magazine-model body every inch. He is thinking about the fact that Dominguez is half-right. Her looks are, he realizes now, exactly why he's so concerned that she's not picking up the phone.

He makes no further comment to his partner, looks back down to his paperwork and plays it close to the vest, which he is known for, admired and resented for in equal parts across the 114th.

Woo and Knots cross the scuffed brown linoleum floor just then, a sense of purpose in their step. "What ya got?" Nussbaum asks, knowing it is at least partly—maybe mostly—to change the subject.

"Burglary slay in a loft downtown," Woo says. "Cut and dry . . . Oops. No pun intended." Nobody laughs, but he earns a couple of smiles.

"Just like old times," declares Knots, who's been a detective thirty-five years. "These young banker types move into a rough neighborhood figuring to flip it for a big profit. Market changes, neighborhood doesn't, and they're stuck there." Knots's big forehead wrinkles with rumination. "Not even much rough neighborhood left anymore."

"What'd they take?" Nussbaum asks.

"Who knows? Place was tossed pretty good."

"Downtown? How'd the One-Fourteen get it?" Dominguez asks.

"Not sure. I think the vic was employed out here."

• • •

It is the shock of his body, its smells, its feel, its soft, white appearance, and yet surprising dormant strength and muscle and sinew. It is her abject terror at the suddenness of the surroundings, the completeness of the displacement, and at how quickly the circumscribed little world that is the only world she has ever known has been utterly and instantly pulled out from under her, turned inside out. It is her sense of duty, obedience to instructions, to her mother's needs, to her job, to others—the theme of her life. It is her enormous guilt at what she has done, at what she has taken, and so the appropriate expiation of guilt is punishment, and this is condign punishment. It is her fury—fury at what has happened to her, fury at herself, at her own foolishness, fury at the world, at its unfairness.

It is all this that is behind the force of the whip against him where he wants it, behind her angry stance over him, behind the perfect modulation of rage, behind the cries of subjugation, behind her adept adoption of the sadistic rituals. Shock, terror, duty, obedience, guilt, fury—the conscious and semiconscious and unconscious elements deep in her mix together inextricably, the stew of them just right, apparently, for the task at hand.

Lying exhausted on the mattress, she overhears another of the male conversations outside the door. The same two voices, heard as if through a haze. A coda.

"I want to take her with me."

"Sorry, she's ours."

"I'll pay you. Whatever you want."

"You know that's not how it works . . ."

"Look," the first voice cuts the second off impatiently, "she's . . . she's just what I want . . ." This last part is said with urgency, arcing with feeling, with desperation.

She's . . . just what I want . . . Which is what, precisely? Her inexperience? Her green eyes? Her red hair? Her scent? Exoticism? Or the Irish girl next door?

Not her virginity. That novelty is now gone.

The pharmaceutical haze, its melted reality, heightens the memory of it, sharpens it, mutes it, allows it . . .

She feels the whip as it lands against his body, feels it as acutely as if it is landing against her own, and yet, she doesn't know exactly what she feels.

20

Elaine is wrapped in a light-blue robe in a dark room with low light, knees drawn up, curled into herself in the corner of a once-luxurious divan.

The opposite of escape.

Stark realizations have cut knifelike through the narcotic haze of the last several hours, the last day.

Once you take their money, you enter their world.

A world where the men are killed and the women are enslaved. A primitive world of primitive retribution. A parallel world with its own rules, operating alongside the world she has always known. She thinks again of Bob, who—whatever else she might think or say—had stepped in and tried to save her. If the administrative rules of the bank, with their pages of manuals and updates and amendments, seemed burdensome, these rules—unwritten, simpler—are far more constrictive.

The opposite of escape.

The cause and effect are stark, primitive, too.

Their money got taken. Then, got stuck.

So she was taken. And now, is stuck.

The opposite of Johannesburg. The opposite of Lisbon.

The opposite of freedom.

It is as if she has stepped into the photograph somehow, been lured into its alternate universe by the young pretty girl, into its dark, inverse Wonderland, and there is no escape.

She pulls the light-blue robe tighter around her, futilely. It offers little comfort, little illusion of protection. Like cheap blue gift wrap, it occurs to her. A sloppy, careless wrapping job, hiding the product—a product of arms, legs, torso, freckles, red hair, fingers, toes, orifices, a product of apparently significant but negotiable value.

A dark-haired, low-voiced beauty is on a matching divan opposite Elaine, speaking to her, she now realizes, but not looking at her. Smoking a cigarette. Thumbing through a magazine. Barely even glancing up as she talks.

"Client Seven likes you," she says to Elaine. The cigarette glows in the dark for a moment. "You can use the same routine another time or two, but then you'll have to up the ante. They get bored fast."

Backroom advice from one prostitute to another.

Elaine starts to weep.

The woman glances up at her. Regards her more closely now, but remains distant, unfeeling, cut off. "You feel like you've died," observes the woman. "That's how they want it to feel. But you've survived. You *would* have died, if you hadn't done it. I promise you. These people don't compromise."

Elaine continues weeping. She can't stop. It is seeing this woman . . . She is a glimpse of Elaine's future.

The weeping is unleashed, and it feels good, necessary, because she feels it as a connection to the previous world, to the lost world, to herself. Time, place, everything has been upended. The hours and minutes and clocks that were the backbone of her banking world, that paced her days, vanished, replaced by a timeless drifting, replaced by time's opposite. The weeping is a lifeline to the known. She needs it. She weeps copiously. Unstoppable, disconsolate. It is all she can do, all she has of her own, this weeping. But she notices, nevertheless, that the woman is untroubled, unsurprised by it.

No longer looking at her, staring at the wall, the jaded, flat-toned woman continues to talk, junkie-like. "Look, I don't know your name. No names in here, like I'm sure they told you. Don't know where you're from, if you're rich or poor, sane or crazy. I only know you did something to them, or they think you did—and you've got those looks and that body—and that's why you're here." The woman's flat voice has been robbed of connection, wrung of feeling, and floats dead in the dead air around them. But she's smart enough, distilling the situation into a few short and inarguable observations. Yet, she doesn't seem to care much about conveying meaning. Her words seem mostly to be mere accompaniment to herself—a cold comfort, a cold reminder to her carved-out self that she is even alive.

No names—yes, they had told Elaine. Warned her. Here, you're a number only. A time slot. An appointment. Numbers only. Protective for their keepers, a subtle dehumanizing effect as if to soften, to cast into doubt, the reality of it. As if it is a dream. As if it is not really happening to *them*. Not to their real selves. As if, perhaps, it is not happening at all. A world of numbers, like a weird, dark, mocking inverse of a brightly lit bank branch. And like a bank branch, it's a locus of pure commerce. A locus of exchange. *Withdrawals. Deposits. Transfer slips. Riders.* The standard crude innuendos and jokes in passing—*I'd like to manage her assets. I'll take his deposit anytime*—snickered almost daily by Sam, Vicky, the other tellers, had just become bluntly real. The crudest joke of all . . .

Elaine now looks closely at the other woman. And maybe it is the experience of Carlton Conner above her, naked on her, breathing on her, that opens her to the possibility. Or the sudden reappearance of the truck driver and John Ellis, materializing together out of the darkness above her on Bob's cot. Or the notion of being lured into the photograph, into its out-of-focus backyard, by the smiling girl. Or seeing her own future in this woman. All of it like a circle of rope drawing tighter around her, trapping her. But a *circle*. All the elements, all the fibers, pulling closer to one another.

She experiences it as a click. Like the click of a camera's shutter capturing the moment. The click of a lock's tumbler falling before opening a door. A click that divides before and after.

She studies the woman a moment more. Tries to remain calm in the face of the possibility. There is a way to test it. *No names.* Meaning, not their own names. But other names? She leans forward and utters one. A name she has been hanging on to desperately.

"Arthur Holden."

The woman looks up, startled. The name seems to penetrate, shake her from her junkie fog.

She focuses, narrows her eyes at Elaine. Looks at her with disdain, annoyance, hostility. "What?! What is that supposed to mean?" And Elaine has the sense the woman is now beginning to deflect or bury or deny any meaning in the name.

So Elaine simply says the name again and nothing further. To get the maximum effect from it. To summon its full talismanic power. "Arthur Holden."

The woman shifts, reaches anxiously, irritably, for another cigarette in her purse. "Arthur Holden what?"

"Your picture was the only personal thing in his apartment. I can see it's you." *I looked at your photo on the subway. Lying on my bed. At the police station. Unless I've gone crazy, I know. I may have gone crazy, but I still know.* Elaine looks at her, stares as if making sure. "Your hair is darker," Elaine says matter-of-factly. "But it's you."

Hey, Detective Nussbaum, I found her. Got lost myself to do it, but I found her. Elaine is staring into hard years, into transformation, into nightmare eyes. But it's her.

The woman stares silently, balefully at her.

Now it is Elaine who is purposefully oblique, careful, reserved. But she leans forward intensely, acutely aware of the sharp limits of time and opportunity in this conversation. "I don't know who you are to him, or who he is to you, but I know there's some reason your picture was there."

The woman shudders.

And then, softly, in another voice from another life, a previous world left long behind, she asks, "Where is he?"

Elaine takes a breath, exhales, listens to the words. "He's dead."

The woman's eyes fill. A rush of tears long foreign to those hard eyes, Elaine thinks.

The silence hangs in the dayroom.

"How?"

Elaine pauses. She's unsure whether to say . . .

"Tell me!" The woman unleashes it, harsh, furious.

Elaine does not measure her response but is prompt, obedient. "Hit by a truck crossing the street. But . . . it was no accident."

The woman leaps up off the divan. She is shaking. She reaches down to her purse, tears it open, pulls out a crack pipe—charmless utilitarian hardware, a stubby black stem and bowl—and stuffs it with a thumbnail-size crystal from a baggie.

"Go on," she says to Elaine.

Elaine stares.

"More!" she demands.

More pain? More affliction?

"He'd been moving around their drug money. Taking it from their bank accounts and hiding it in other bank accounts." She looks at the woman preparing a practiced hit of crack. "No one knows exactly why."

The woman lights a match, draws hard from the pipe stem. The match flickers with the work of it. Tough, practical, she asks, "How do you know all this?"

"I saw the truck hit him. I worked in a bank where he used to come in."

The woman asks no more questions.

She sets down the pipe. Stares ahead.

She hangs her head. Her shoulders begin to shake and shudder uncontrollably. It looks to Elaine like some kind of seizure at first, some unnerving but perhaps common effect of the drug, before she realizes . . . the woman is weeping. First it was Elaine; now it's this woman's turn to weep.

"Why didn't he just forget about me . . . ?"

On a sea of wet eyes and silent tears, she whispers something to herself. Something private that Elaine can't hear. Half-muttered and mumbled, hidden in the high. A confession? A prayer?

Who is he to her? Elaine's banker calculations spin efficiently and intuitively, but don't get her anywhere. He's too old to be her father, too young to be her grandfather. Nothing so linear fits the woman's reaction. Something subtler. Uncle? Neighbor? Family friend? Elaine is desperate to press the puzzle piece into place.

But at the same time, Elaine knows. Realizes it simply, profoundly, as the residue, the pointed punctuation, of the past few hours, of the past day. Not knowing who it is, Elaine knows *exactly* who he is.

He is the last person to care about this woman. The last person who wondered where she was. The last person who cared whether she was alive.

And now that person is gone, and the woman is finally, truly alone. *Truly alone.*

Arthur Holden.

Eunice Kelly.

Their images conflate, cavort in a passing, half-formed visitation . . .

Grandfather, uncle, cousin, friend, invalid mother—it doesn't really matter.

It's their status as the last person who cared that matters most. And the question is, does it matter anymore?

21

In the genial morning bedlam of the Nussbaum household—lively, loud, warm, young, chaotic—it is even more chaotic than usual.

In the Syosset ranch's small kitchen and playroom, all three kids are running around, hanging on their dad as he tries to gobble his own breakfast while helping to shovel breakfast into the three of them, then force them into not just clothes but, this morning, their best clothes to make them and keep them clean and presentable, if only for an hour or two, while also putting on his own ironed oxford shirt, tie, and jacket.

Amid all this, he is dialing a number, watching it ring. Still, no answer.

His wife Leah brings him a juice and ruffles his hair. "Who you trying to reach?" she asks him.

Nussbaum waves it away. "Ah, it's nothing. Just work."

"Must be important. Since you can't seem to let it go even in this mayhem."

Nussbaum is about to wave it away again, send it further out into the sea of his distant concerns, but instead, impulsively, he shares it. As he steps back from the tale to tell it, he sees its oddness, its absurdity. "Well, first, this woman was a witness to an accident.

Then, a day later, she brings me a missing-persons complaint." He smiles ironically. "And now? *She's* the missing person."

"Wow. A three-peat," says Leah. Then, looking at Evan for a moment, one eyebrow arches purposefully for comic effect. "Good way to stay in a handsome detective's inbox." She brushes a black bang out of his eyes, as if to help him see it for himself. Smiles teasingly at her handsome husband.

He smiles obligingly back. "No, no, honey, this isn't a cop junkie. This woman's a banker, a worker bee, good kid. And in the middle of all this she suddenly quits her job. Out of the blue." He grabs little Leo, swings him up onto his shoulders, heads for Leo's changing table. "There's something going on here, honey, and I just don't know what it is."

• • •

The five Nussbaums—beautifully dressed, miraculously neat, quiet, and orderly, faces clean and hair combed—are pressed together into a twelfth-row pew for the Yom Kippur high-holiday morning service. Little Leo is on Nussbaum's lap.

The rabbi intones authoritatively from the bema. "For the sin we have committed before thee for hard-heartedness . . ."

The congregation responds in unison: "Pardon us, forgive us, grant us atonement . . ."

"For the sin we have committed before thee for obstinacy . . ."

"Pardon us, forgive us, grant us atonement . . ." The walls of the old shul vibrate, unaccustomed to the congregation's strength in numbers—hundreds of two-day Jews, the temporarily devout.

The litany of call and response continues.

For the sin we have committed against you by omission . . .

For the sin we have committed against you for neglecting our duties . . .

For the sin we have committed against you for tolerating injustice . . .

Amid which Evan Nussbaum leans over to his wife.

"I've gotta go."

She looks momentarily annoyed, and then softens with acceptance. "She's got you, doesn't she?"

He nods.

"Hope she's worth it."

"Me, too. I'll make it up to you."

He takes two-year-old Leo off his lap, puts him in Leah's, and quietly slides out of the pew.

On the street outside the synagogue, Nussbaum dials his cell phone. "Hey, Knots, that banker in that loft last night . . . just out of curiosity, know what bank he worked for?"

"Yeah. Federated." And then a cackle of laughter. "But don't they all?"

"No, I mean, what branch?"

"Northern Boulevard."

Evan Nussbaum's eyes go wide.

22

White slavery. In millennial Manhattan.

Is it possible?

Of course.

Highly unlikely, in fact, that it *wouldn't* exist.

New York has everything.

Every customer service. Every consumer opportunity. This is where the best gravitate. This is where the best set up shop. So it operates seamlessly, no doubt. Run by the most experienced in the world. People who have opened the show out of town, perfected it overseas. Systematized it, worked out the kinks (worked *in* the kinks), learned the ropes of real estate rental, real estate law, false identities, forms of payment, and tax issues in urban venues across the globe before bringing it here.

New York. The best of everything.

One of the very qualities that draws her toward its towers, rising impossibly amid the morning mists when glimpsed across the strip of glistening river from the crowded boulevards of Queens. Facing *west* toward Mecca. One of the very qualities that makes her proud, that she brags about, that she longs to be a part of.

Well, now she is.

Professionals. The word whispers at her again. White slavery, the drug trade, even murder—these had presumably evolved just as banking had. She has experienced, and now seen—passing by a doorway, at the end of the hallway—two small, dark-complexioned men, Indian or Pakistani or Sri Lankan, with syringes and prescription bottles. Rogue doctors or medical students, patrolling the herd to ensure docility and compliance and participation.

Professionals. Sharpening their business practices. Competing more aggressively. Using technology more ingeniously, more pervasively. Becoming more focused. Working harder, smarter, more profitably. Her heart sinks. The realization crushes her.

Elaine and the woman, and now several others in various states of undress, are sitting in the small dayroom. An old TV is droning in the corner, and there is a tray of fresh sandwiches on the coffee table between the divans.

Elaine can't help but think of the bank's lunchroom.

A few of the women, lean, lanky, hungry-looking blondes and brunettes, speak to one another in an Eastern European language—sharp, harsh diphthongs and consonants, strong insouciant vowels. She'd bet it's John Ellis's and the truck driver's language, but she can't be sure. The girls' speech is sometimes languid, sometimes angry. Its harshness, the lurch and attack contained in the delivery of its heavy phrases, succeeds in isolating Elaine even further, if that's possible. It cloaks her in an extra wrapping of aloneness in which she remains singular, separate, even in the huddled and intimate life that she's sharing with them.

By now, she's seen some other women, too. Passing wordlessly by a doorway, eyes on nothing. Some Mediterranean looking. A couple obviously Nordic.

Barcelona.

Stockholm.

Moscow.

Prague.

She wanted to see the world.

The world came to her.

White slavery. The term, she realizes vaguely—her thinking still slurring against the slow, lingering chemical swirl and haze—is an insult to the centuries of black slaves, as if their servitude is common, expected, and hers is special, shocking. On the other hand, "white" whitewashes the activity, robs it of meaning, makes the term pale next to its actuality. *White slavery.* The phrase is like a wall of white—smooth, impenetrable, incomprehensible, to a mind and body existing outside it. As she once was.

The dayroom around her is weighted, specific yet still dreamlike. A dream she is forced to inhabit, from which she cannot awaken.

When she glances up at the TV, which is tuned to CNN, she sees the same file footage of Carlton Conner: striding from his Fifth Avenue apartment to his chauffeured limousine; on the sun-drenched back deck of his yacht. There's new file footage of him schussing down the mountain at a Colorado ski resort. She gets up as if in a trance and moves closer to the television set.

"Federated Bank gave guidance on its fourth quarter today," the CNN anchor intones. "And things are looking up for charismatic chairman Carlton Conner, shown here skiing with family and friends. Net operating results are improving, and his pay package may soon face less criticism . . ."

Elaine goes over to sit down next to the woman, who has paid no attention to the television.

"All that money . . ." Elaine says, as if simply continuing the conversation from before. "Arthur wasn't taking it for no reason."

The woman is silent, trying not to listen.

But Elaine is quietly undeterred. "You don't move money in and out of lots of accounts for no reason. You've got something in mind . . ."

The woman is still silent, but Elaine can tell she is listening.

Elaine speaks low, so the other women can't hear. "He wanted you to have it . . . to buy your freedom . . ."

"You don't know that," the woman hisses suddenly, accusingly, angrily.

"No, I don't," Elaine says calmly.

The woman turns to face her. Speaks low, as well, keeping it between the two of them. "What you did was simple. You took money. You can give it back. For me . . . it's more complicated." But she offers up none of those complications. And doesn't seem like she's about to.

"I don't know what happened or why you won't tell me," Elaine says, "but I just know he wanted you to have that money." She looks at her earnestly. "And if we help each other, I can get it for you."

It's a version of the brief, strained, start-and-stop conversation they've been having for days now. A quick, urgent exchange when there's an incidental moment of privacy in which Elaine pushes herself through the pharmacological haze, reaching out through the fog to this woman, this photograph. Still unnamed. But Elaine can't risk breaking the rules and won't risk asking her to, either.

The woman regards her, shakes her head. "You don't understand how good you have it, do you?"

Elaine looks back at her, stupefied. *Good?!*

"You don't get it," the woman says. "Why do you think you sit up here with nothing to do, watching TV? When the rest of us are working?"

She'd just thought she wasn't chosen. That no one wanted her.

"He's bought out all your time . . . Client Seven."

What?

"He doesn't want anyone else with you. He's paying for all your hours. For you to sit here eating sandwiches," the woman says, her tone resentful, puzzled. "What have you got?"

Red hair? Green eyes?

Virginity, which now translates to exclusivity?

No experience at all. The best qualification for the job?

Lucky, Elaine thinks sardonically. *I'm . . . lucky. I have it . . . good.*

"You'll say anything," the woman says to her dismissively, cynical and defeated but still weighing it, Elaine can tell. Somewhere in there, hearing what Elaine has said. Hiding her attentiveness behind her hard exterior. Maybe trying to hide it from Elaine. But is she trying to hide it from herself?

Elaine processes the resentment. At first, sees it as a setback. How can she get anywhere with the woman if this hostility is simmering?

But in a moment, she is glad for it. Because the resentment, the annoyance at Elaine's perceived special status, at her youth and freshness, means that, somewhere in there, on some level, this woman still cares. Still wants. And if she still *wants*, then at some level she *wants out.*

Elaine stares around the room. The lean, restless, bored, hungry Eastern European contingent has thinned out a little—some went back to work in rooms down the hall, others to side rooms for a few hours of daytime sleep before the busy night. Some can come and go, she has noticed, seem to have unspoken privileges. Others, like her, cannot leave. She is not yet able to get the patterns of the place. That's one of the disorientations they rely on. No discernible pattern, no plan. It's odd that this is a den of desire, because desire is what they take from you. Desire is what evaporates and turns out to have been so fragile that it needs to be manufactured by the med students' injections.

It has shocked her to accept so quickly that there is no escape. To adapt so quickly: Is it a character flaw or an adaptive mechanism for this new, harsh environment? The escape she longed for, fantasized about so vividly, now abandoned, tucked away, folded neatly into a bottom drawer. Although she has begun to sense—in the harsh light of these stripped-down, extreme circumstances—that escape wasn't what her fantasy of travel was really about. That wasn't what was at the heart of it. She senses now that it wasn't just a longing for escape from her responsibilities, her sick mother, her constrained, changeless working life. The fantasy of an exotic city, a fresh, anonymous start, had been a signal, a symptom, of something more profound. That she has been more deeply, more vastly imprisoned. Held captive by her own way of seeing, of thinking, of being. Imprisoned by all she has known. Had the obsession with escape that she had nurtured, her half-conscious, steadily growing preoccupation with far-flung exotic cities been an attempt to escape something not so easily fled or left behind? It was something she did not see in herself, *could* not see in herself, until it got focused, until she has had no choice but to confront it fully, here in these rooms, in this literal imprisonment.

This woman will be—has already become—Elaine's project. Something to safely focus on beyond herself, so as to achieve forward motion, to cling to a thread of motivation and hope. The woman's photo led her here; the woman herself must lead her out. There is a symmetry that she must honor, that fate is directing her to. If you can make your way in, you can make your way out. That's basic physics. If she can just bring the woman's thinking—and keep her own thinking—to that level. Because this woman's escape will also be her escape. Whether together or by proxy.

Because doing for others—a lifetime of doing for others—may be the only way she can do for herself.

"You'll say anything."

"Yes, I'll say anything. I'll do anything," Elaine openly admits, hopeful, fighting, newly intent on escape, fully focused on staying alive.

23

Nussbaum and Dominguez wander the deceased's loft carefully, examining the murder scene. The victim's body is long gone, but the police tape is still up across the doorway, draped like bunting—a celebration of calamity—around the apartment.

Nussbaum is staring down at the cot. He wipes a finger across the cot's surface.

"No dust," Nussbaum says. "No clothes tossed on it. Why's a single guy, artist type living alone, got a clean cot in the middle of the living room, do you think?" He looks at Dominguez, barely suppresses a roll of the eyes that this wasn't reported by Woo and Knots, and moves on to extend the chain of evidence. "See these tracks in the area rug? So he just pulled the cot over here, maybe a day or two ago. See the clear spot on that closet wall? That's where the cot was stored. He just took it out. Just." He looks, shakes his head that this wasn't in the report. "Am I right?"

Dominguez looks carefully and seems to decide, independently, that there's no other possible conclusion. "When you're right, you're right."

"Now the question is, what am I right about?" Nussbaum looks around at the tossed and tumbled shelves and drawers, their contents spilled chaotically across the floor, and then turns back to the bare cot in the middle of the alcove. "All that broken glass in the sink? Well, there were two wineglass stems. So the victim was likely entertaining someone. The cot's put out politely for a guest . . . a guest our host doesn't expect to share a bed with. Like, let's just say, a fellow employee from the bank branch where he works"—the same bank branch, Nussbaum had noticed in the report, where he first interviewed Elaine Kelly, the same branch where she had been employed before suddenly quitting—"who suddenly shows up on his doorstep." He squints again into the chaos of books, and magazines, and clothing, and kitchenware tossed across the floor. "So with such a polite host, why's there no bedding on or around that cot? Not even a pillow?"

Dominguez swallows. Bedding is used to wrap up bodies. Even meth freaks know to do that.

Nussbaum knows what a fellow cop is thinking. Shakes his head. "Take one dead body and leave the other? Makes no sense. And the blood profile only matched the vic." Nussbaum is trying to reassure himself that it's not her blood. That she's still alive.

"You think she was here." Dominguez's little ironic smile. "Your friend."

"Yeah. I think she was here," he says brooding morosely, intensely. Then anxious, irritable. "And where the hell is she now?"

· · ·

Nussbaum slides onto a long wooden bench (a bench almost identical to his high-holiday seating) in the twelfth row of Courtroom 23, daypart 504, of New York Civil Court, to observe civil hearing 3101, *Desirio v. State of New York*.

Like a fan arriving late to a game, he makes a quick assessment of the players in their positions on the field. Three lawyers surround Desirio. On the other side, the state has two. Desirio's lawyers are expensively dressed—nearly, but not quite, as expensively as Desirio.

Nussbaum had the 114th intern staff put a Google watch on the name Antonio Desirio, and the name had popped up suddenly in a pro forma courtroom hearing. He went to the State of New York website, and found the preparatory filings. He wasn't able to follow the argument perfectly, but apparently, in the process of releasing the funds, some other discrepancies in Desirio's state residency, or incorrect registration, or the number of accounts and their inter-relationship, violated statutes or was not necessarily or clearly in accord with state banking regulations. The kind of thing that would never have surfaced or been flagged had one of Desirio's accounts not been frozen and then thawed. But some diligent nerdy assistant DA had noticed, and here they were.

Nussbaum observes the court proceedings. Desirio's lead lawyer is in the midst of addressing the broader financial issues that have apparently developed. Nussbaum can't help but notice that, *Jesus*, this is a lot of legal firepower over some simple savings accounts.

"Your Honor, let the record show these assets are the rightful property of Antonio Desirio, my client, an international business-man who was victimized in this regard by Arthur Holden, now deceased. In either the state's zeal or the bank computers' overpro-grammed automation, the erroneous Freeze Order extended to all my client's assets across multiple linked accounts. We ask that all these assets be unfrozen immediately and that the error be expunged from the record."

The judge looks over his bifocals with a frown. "Why the acute concern about the record, Counselor?" Nussbaum hears the cynical edge, the knowing little bite, in the judge's question.

Desirio's lead lawyer ignores the question, instead handing a pile of documentation to the judge.

"I'll sort through this as expeditiously as possible," the judge prom-ises. "Does the state have any countermanding argument to make?"

"No, Your Honor. Opposing counsel has represented it fairly, if overdramatically. Because of the extensive flow of assets and the bank's automated computer programs, the freeze extended to all the Desirio accounts, unbeknownst to the state. Assets for all the accounts should be unfrozen forthwith, pending your examination of presented documentation."

So now the state is aware of the size of the assets, the number of accounts, and any irregularities.

In the twelfth row, Detective Nussbaum allows himself a smile, and a small moment of tribute to the dead teller in the black overcoat.

Nice work, Arthur.

In the hallway outside the courtroom, Nussbaum approaches the Assistant DA—a clean-cut type who looks just out of Fordham Law—and flashes his badge.

"Hey, Counselor. Detective Nussbaum, One-Fourteen. I'm investigating a missing persons."

"Missing persons?" The ADA is confused. "So what brings you here?"

Nussbaum shrugs. "Long and involved." *I don't want to take up your time. Not yet, anyway.* "Hey, look, I wonder if it'd be okay to take a quick look at the list of Desirio's accounts."

"Definitely not. Privileged. Sorry."

There were over a hundred ADAs. You never knew which type you would get. He drew this type. But then again, maybe this is the one who stumbled on the Desirio account irregularities. The one who was looking closely enough, working late enough, had enough math chops to catch something, see that something was up. Nussbaum remains unruffled. Tries a different tack.

"Then how 'bout this . . . can you just tell me how many bank accounts were at issue when Desirio first made his complaint?"

The lawyer looks suspiciously—or else curiously—at Nussbaum.

"That's eventually public record, right?" asks Nussbaum. "The original complaint?"

The lawyer takes another beat looking at Nussbaum but opens his thick legal files, and in a moment is counting—carefully mouthing it, kindergartner-like—from a sheet of paper.

He looks at Nussbaum. "Twelve."

"And how many are listed in today's complaint?" Nussbaum asks.

The lawyer flips quickly through the sheaf of paper. Nods his head counting—as if he's moved up to first or second grade—and looks up at Nussbaum with interest piqued. "Eleven."

"How 'bout that," says Nussbaum. "Thanks, Counselor."

He doesn't know what the lawyer will make of the discrepancy, but he knows what *he* makes of it. That for the twelfth account, Desirio thought he had a better way to recover it.

24

Elaine Kelly lies on a chaise lounge by a rooftop pool. The pool water shimmers, reflects its wavy hallucinogenic sheen on the white stuccoed walls around her. Above her, the night sky is alive with the skittering beams of helicopters, the blinking of distant aircraft, the winking strings of bridges beyond. Manhattan twinkles in the night all around her, stupendous and regal, close and alive.

Its towers had always loomed like a distant dream whenever she would enter or leave the bank branch in Queens or when she would look out the upstairs bathroom window of their row house. Gleaming Oz, shrouded in the mists. Rising up through the morning fog, many days quite literally. Aspiration, rendered in brick-and-mortar and bold architectural gestures. And now, tonight's new perspective on the same city is unimaginably different.

She stares out at the lit-up buildings. It looks for a brief moment—even to herself—as though she is living a life she dreamed about and angled for.

But, of course, she is not. This is, in fact, a mocking opposite. She is naked. A prisoner in a seraglio. A sex worker in a brothel. She could be in a fleabag hotel in a port city in Thailand or on a humid mattress in some booming, unpronounceable industrial burg deep in mainland China. She happens to be in Manhattan.

Arthur Holden's granddaughter/grandniece/neighbor/friend/ nightly torment/recurrent dream lies naked on the chaise next to her. Her seraglio sister. She, too, looks out at the twinkling city spread around them.

"From up here, at least you can figure out where you are. Most times, you never know exactly. They keep us moving. Exciting for the clients. Safer for our bosses. Disorienting for us. Just how they want it." She looks at Elaine. "Play along or you're done for. Simple as that." A prostitute's practical advice. One to another, teaching the ropes. But there is a hint of something sisterly in it, too. A seed of connection that Elaine has been cultivating gently, often silently, by a simple, companionable presence. Tapping carefully against the woman's hard, protective shell. Looking for any softness in it, any give.

She guesses the building is twenty stories or so. Indistinguishable from hundreds of others. Purposely unremarkable, she is sure.

The chill of the air on Elaine's nakedness and the compensating domed heat lamp over her create a strange dance of hot and cold, of chill and sweat, that narrows her attention to the elemental, like meat being kept at a temperature for serving, sweet white flanks, nipples plumped in the cold, waiting . . .

She sees how they do it. Taking everything away, all interaction, all connection, their clothing, their jewelry, their physical identities, reducing them to bodies, to skin and limbs and breasts and vaginas and nothing more. Their bodies become the only thing of value, their only currency . . .

"You know who he is, don't you?" Elaine asks.

"He's Client Seven. Don't tell me more than that."

She doesn't want to know anything. Or tell Elaine anything. Self-protective in some way that Elaine has no choice but to respect for the moment, as a necessary path of survival. Okay, but . . .

"What do I call you?"

The woman says nothing. *No names in here.* Those are the rules.

"We're . . . we're about to be . . . together. Please . . ." Elaine searches the woman's face softly but openly, for some vestige, any trace, of the happy teenager in the bright, blurry backyard of the picture.

The woman turns away.

"Anything. You choose it . . ."

"*You* choose it," says the woman irritably.

Elaine is about to. *Anne . . . Allison . . . Andrea . . .*

"Olivia," the woman says suddenly, under her breath.

Elaine looks over. *Really?* Or is the name another protective piece of artifice, a layer of buffer, of bluff?

The woman glances back at her. *Yes, really.* Elaine can tell by the quick, pained look on the woman's face before she turns away again. The pain of the personal. A door forced ajar to let in a sliver of the past.

Olivia.

"For you to know, all right? Not for any of them. Ever."

A quick, murmured declaration of identity. Reclaiming it. Stealing it back. A start, thinks Elaine. The start, the thread of connection, she's been waiting for.

And then a further moment of surrender, of a return of humanness. "Liv for short."

Liv for short?

No, thinks Elaine.

Liv for longer.

And now Carlton Conner stands over them at the poolside. Naked, too. Reveling in the moment: the situation, the surroundings, the power, the fantasy. The pool light twists and dances and warps across his naked body, as if he is some ancient painted warrior.

"Odd, isn't it?" he says in that smooth, unplaceable, professional voice of natural and perverse command. "How you're my prisoners . . . yet . . . I'm yours." It's all the more insulting, the more provoking, for being a thoughtless cliché. He expects no response to his observation so waits for none. His tone shifts suddenly, to the instructive, the prescriptive. "Do it exactly the way I want and I'll put in a good word for both of you . . ." Arch, cynical, deadpan.

Client Seven, watching out for their interests.

Conner struts away, and Elaine turns purposefully away from the cocky, confident roll of his naked backside. In a moment, as if in its wake, the hulking, shaved-headed guard known as Kimbo, silhouetted in the pool light, gestures for them both to follow.

"He's ready," says Liv, barely above a glum whisper.

"The question is, are you?" says Elaine.

25

The realtor, in a tailored powder-blue suit and sporting bleached blonde hair, stands on the stoop of the Kelly row house, ringing the doorbell, frustrated. There's no answer.

Until finally, surprisingly, a man opens the door. Smiles pleasantly. "Yes?"

The realtor looks confused, concerned, by the man's sudden appearance. "Is . . . is Elaine here? I tried her at work. They said she's no longer with them . . ."

"No, Elaine's not here," says the man. His accent is Midwestern, the realtor would guess, flat and calm. "I'm cat-sitting. She said you'd be coming and that I'm supposed to show you in."

Ah, okay. It's planned, thinks the realtor, thought through. They're expecting her. The realtor is somewhat reassured. In these grief situations, you never knew if the parties were really paying attention to the real estate issues. You never knew if they really heard you or were just too distracted and preoccupied. "Where's Elaine?" she asks the man.

"Oh, just taking a little break, you know, with her mom and all."

The realtor nods with understanding. Clearly the cat sitter knows the story. "When is she back?"

"She said just a couple of days," he tells her reassuringly.

"Okay. Well, will you have her call me?"

"Of course."

John Ellis smiles and, as if with great and habitual respect for property that is not his, gently shuts and bolts the door.

Sitting at her desk, he sorts through Elaine's mail as casually as if it were his own. He combs through the contents of Elaine's purse—the purse that he kept—open now on the desk, as well.

In a moment, he comes across an envelope in the desk that says, "Federated Bank."

"Ah, there we go," he tells the cats. "Now we're getting somewhere."

He opens the envelope, looks at the statement.

"Huh." Nothing there. Just as she had explained to him, terrified. Not in her regular account. Not generating a regular statement.

Pretty little bitch knew what she was doing, he thinks to himself.

He takes the lampshade off the lamp to shed a little more light on the subject and goes to work. Practiced. Systematic. Efficient. Professional.

26

The dream resumes. The recurring dream from which Elaine cannot seem to awaken. Saying it is a dream makes it easier. And conversely, it is easy to say it is a dream, to believe it is a dream. The unreality of it, the disconnection of it, helps. Elaine wonders in passing if they—her unseen keepers—share the sense that it's a dream. The pills they give her—now pills, not shots—that they carefully watch her swallow, no doubt allow and encourage that perception.

Elaine and Liv are dressed in black leather thong bikini bottoms, black fishnet stockings, and high heels.

Conner is tied to the bedposts. He has a hood on him and can see out the eyeholes.

Liv and Elaine exchange glances.

Glances at the edge of a precipice, looking down, about to jump. Or not. But the enemy is coming up from behind. *You have to jump. You have to.*

In the penthouse foyer, Kimbo rubs his smooth, brown head with his massive hand. Slouching idly, he turns the pages of a gun magazine and listens to his iPod, the volume cranked up high. He finds the sounds emanating from the bedroom too arousing, wants too much to jump in there with them, knock them around, join the party, give it to them. It's too much for him to take, so he keeps the iPod loud, loses himself in hip-hop, street sounds that originate twenty stories below and a hundred blocks north of here, where the sounds, the people are real . . .

Billy Boy, the second guard, sits leaning against the wall. He, too, has his iPod cranked up, 'cause the little he can hear he finds sick, disturbing, and he can tell Kimbo is turned on by it, and he finds that even more disturbing . . .

Liv is on top of Conner, straddling him, her naked breasts hovering above him, creating an ample, teasing, nearly smothering distraction.

She tops off the CEO's excitement by suddenly stuffing a bandanna in Conner's mouth. He moans, even more gratified by this new degradation. He rattles his cuffed wrists against the bed frame in a jangling of pleasure. His animal satisfaction pervades the room.

While Conner pants and moans with the intensity of the pleasure, Elaine slips over to the pile of Conner's clothing.

She takes his cell phone out of his shirt pocket. The latest, fanciest model, befitting the chairman. Its GPS has probably been disabled so that no one would ever find out Conner is here. Its video function is clearly marked with a button on the side.

Elaine is pretty quick with technology. Picks it up fast. That's why Glen took her on to help set up the branch's systems. Sometimes she's too quick—at her own keyboard on an impulsive morning, for instance. Now, here, she's just quick enough.

Elaine shoots a video clip around the sex room. A master shot.

Zooms in for close-ups of his clothes, shirt monograms, and designer labels.

Turns the phone's camera on herself, then back to Conner and Liv.

When Conner is just moments from ejaculating, Liv, still on top of him, pulls his black hood up, revealing to the camera for several seconds the sweaty, ravenous, insatiate face of the Federated Bank CEO.

Conner sees the phone pointed at him. Sees the pulsing white video light in the dimly lit room for only an instant before Liv pulls the hood back down over Conner's face, spinning the eyeholes enough so he can't see, and stuffing the bandanna a little farther into his mouth, while Elaine quickly punches in two e-mail addresses, inserts the video file, and hits "Send."

It will make quite a graphic, explicit, and unmistakable twenty-second piece of blackmail.

Standing at her terminal at the bank several mornings ago, Elaine Kelly pressed a few keys on a computer to try to salvage her life.

It had done the opposite. Ruined it.

Here she is, pressing buttons, trying to salvage it again.

How will it turn out this time?

Conner's confused grunts of protest are muffled by the bandanna as he realizes what is happening and struggles to push Liv off him.

But Elaine and Liv are quick. And have multiple advantages: Liv's weight on top of Conner, the twisted hood blocking his vision, and two against one.

They shift and force one of Conner's shoulders up.

Uncuff that wrist from the bedpost.

Cuff it immediately to his other wrist still on the other bedpost.

Conner yelps from the pain of such a sharp angle. Curls his body instinctively, helplessly, to accommodate the shoulder position.

They release the other wrist from the bedpost.

Strength tied to surprise, the darkness of the room, the weakness of Conner's arms behind his back. All working in their favor.

Conner's wrists are now cuffed behind him.

He squirms violently against the cuffs and tries to spit out the bandanna.

Liv leans forward and whispers to his hood, "That little piece of entertainment is now sitting safely in an e-mail, ready to make its way via YouTube to the *Journal*, and the *Times*, and the world. So calm down and think before I take off your hood and bandanna."

Elaine gingerly hands Liv Conner's cell phone—a ticking time bomb, a detonator.

"You yell for help, and I hit 'Send,'" Liv explains to him, "and that video heads somewhere we *can't* control it. You follow?"

She's competent. Assertive. As if she's waited for months, years, a stolen lifetime, Elaine thinks, to turn the tables. A personality buried beneath drugs and imprisonment, a turnaround as quick, as surprising, as the events now unfolding around it.

Conner goes quiet. The horizontal, thrashing, hooded figure lies suddenly motionless. It's obvious that beneath the hood, the CEO is doing some serious strategic thinking.

Elaine removes his hood.

Leaves the bandanna in his mouth.

Liv, still straddling him, holds the cell phone high above his head, her finger still poised on the "Send" button. A simple visual confirmation to greet the CEO, his first postcoital vision.

Reaching out two fingers surgically, as if retrieving something from a drain, Elaine removes the bandanna from Conner's mouth.

A snarling whisper. "How could you do this? What's wrong with you?!"

What's wrong with you.

Elaine blinks at the statement in disbelief.

And there in the sex room, the CEO quickly emerges. Cuts to the bottom line. "What do you want?"

"First, we want you to get us out of here."

He looks at the two of them like they're crazy. "How the hell am I going to do that?"

What, do we have to do everything for you, Carlton?

The door to the sex room opens. Kimbo and Billy Boy pull out their ear buds alertly.

The two whores are standing there in their black leather bikini bottoms and fishnet stockings. *Holy shit.* The client stands between them in women's underwear, cuffed, leashed, hooded.

Whoa.

Kimbo swallows.

The whores start to lead the client toward the staircase of the duplex.

Kimbo stands up from the desk.

"We're going up to the pool," announces the client.

Like it's nothing. Normal. Just a nice little swim.

"Everything okay?" Kimbo asks.

"Perfect, in fact." From the hood's mouth hole, a little white man smile.

Kimbo nods his understanding, big and slow. He is stunned by what he sees but tries to take it in stride.

Hey, it's what the client wants. It's a client business. He's seen a lot stranger. He knows what's going on in there. His job is not to stop the fun. It's to—*what's the word?*—facilitate it.

Elaine and Liv guide the handcuffed, hooded Conner up the duplex steps, through the sliding doors, and out to the rooftop pool.

It happens in a blur, as discussed, as planned—and all new, unplannable, too. Elaine quickly pulls a plastic patio table up against the farthest section of the surrounding stucco wall and tosses one of the plastic pool chairs on top of it—a makeshift way to scale the wall.

Carlton Conner starts to put it together. "No way . . ."

Liv displays his cell phone. "You've got no choice."

"Jesus, don't you understand what you're dealing with? If they think I helped you, they'll kill me, too. They'll kill us all. That video won't matter to any of us. If we go over that wall, we're dead."

"We have nothing to lose," says Liv. "You have everything. Let's go."

The unexpected. The utterly unpredictable. The impossible. The unthinkable. That was their only way to escape, Elaine realized over the previous days. That was their only sliver of a chance. And that was why, when she'd seen the pool wall—looked out over it and beyond it—she talked Liv into it and through it, quietly, urgently, as they lay on the chaises in naked privacy. And something—maybe in the closeness, the concreteness of the plan, of seeing it literally in front of her, of having Elaine whisper her through it—had convinced Liv, and she finally, sharply, nodded yes.

And the brief, hushed, rushed, and tentative half conversations leading up to it played their part. Elaine coaxing, assuring, begging, crying, and finally eliciting some latent thread of human connection. Returning Liv to herself, to some reflection, some distant version, of the girl in the photo. Elaine is glad to have studied the photo so obsessively. Because in some sense, all she has done is hold the photo up in front of Liv—admiring its swirl of color, reanimating its spirit, recapturing its promise—for Liv to see.

And when she had finally said her name, Elaine took that as her verbal signature. Her nod. Her readiness. Her yes.

Back at the desk, Kimbo cocks his head, drops the gun magazine on the chair, and smiles a dirty little smile before standing up and stepping silently, carefully down the hall toward the penthouse stairs up to the pool.

He shouldn't look, but he has to. He can't stop himself. They're whores, but they're babes.

And hey, he has to check. It's his job to be sure everything's okay. Or the penthouse version of okay, anyway.

They guide, push, and pull the handcuffed, leashed, hooded, stumbling Conner up onto the plastic table, onto the plastic pool chair, and over the stucco wall.

As Elaine goes over the wall behind Conner and Liv, she reaches back and pulls the flimsy plastic chair over the wall with her.

Lets it drop onto the gravel on the other side. So there's no easy way to follow them. Buying a precious minute or two . . .

Kimbo looks both ways through the sliding doors.

Where the fuck they go?

Hey!

He sees—*Jesus!*—an ass, a wiggling, bikinied ass, just above the white stucco wall, before it disappears behind it. *Jesus!*

He rips open the sliding door.

"Hey!" he screams. "Hey!"

He runs to the wall.

Jumps up to see over it.

Pulls out his gun.

By the time he can drag another pool chair over to the wall, by the time he stands on it to look over the wall, there's nothing but darkness. He has no shot.

Fuck.

On the other side of the stucco wall there's rough asphalt roofing and a minefield of HVAC components.

Liv and Elaine are hustling Conner through it.

Scampering through the dark, twenty stories up in Manhattan at night, Elaine is surprised by the strange gusts of wind, by the clutter and chaos of the roof's surface, by the hum of the rooftop machinery. An alien environment. Suitable for ductwork, cables, piping, bolts. Unsuitable for humans. Even the oxygen smells, tastes wrong, feels thin.

In a moment, they're at the roof's far edge.

Nothing but a low wall, only shin-high.

And the city below, which she will not look at.

She was sure there'd be a door, a stairway, a marked exit, some route down, that she couldn't see in the sunset but that they'd stumble upon in the dark. But so far, there's nothing. Nothing she can find in the dark, at least. She'd counted on residential building codes, fire laws. The exit is somewhere. Has to be. But she can't see where and there's no time to go back searching for it. *Shit. Shit. Shit.*

The unexpected.

She looks across to the next roof.

The unthinkable.

She couldn't see it in the red Manhattan sunset when she stood at the stucco wall, and if she had seen it, she probably would have dismissed it. *Unthinkable.*

A jump of eight feet across or so, it turns out.

Plus another eight feet down to the landing they'd need to hit.

In pure distance, pure physics, with adrenaline pumping . . .

Maybe . . .

Probably . . .

But a lot more unnerving, the task substantially altered, by being twenty stories up.

The breeze whistles weirdly through the pipes and ductwork, as if issuing a whispered, sinister warning. The breeze unsettles her, threatens her balance. A breeze that seems created by and confined to this rooftop like an occupying ghost.

Elaine can't bring herself to look at the street twenty stories below. There's only the low wall in front of her bare feet.

But for a moment, impulsively, she glances down.

Immediately, she's sorry. Immediately, she's dizzy. Feels her mouth go completely dry and her legs go rubbery, untrustworthy.

The dizziness is not just in her head but all through her. Like a warning set off in her entire body. *Don't do this.*

Elaine looks behind them, to see if anyone is following. She catches Kimbo's shaved head bouncing up from the other side of the stucco wall like a ball, trying to get a glimpse of them, then disappearing.

"Congratulations," Conner calls out above the breeze and machinery, seeing the shaved head, too. "You've just gotten us all killed."

Meaning, as she looks across and down, one way or another.

27

The cat sitter has settled in comfortably.

Sipping tea, nibbling a sandwich, Ellis is methodically going through the drawers in Elaine's desk.

Her desktop computer is on in front of him. She's conveniently left it on sleep for him. Why not? No one else in the house except her.

He takes stacks of papers out of the drawers, sifts through them—bank statements, account numbers, tax returns. He smiles on finding Elaine's social security card.

While he holds it up and examines it, his cell phone rings.

"No, nothing yet," he tells the caller at the other end. "A lot to look through. But don't worry, I'll find it," he says with confidence.

Hangs up. Looks at the social security card again. Smiles.

There's a chime of an arriving e-mail on Elaine's computer.

Ellis squints at the screen, clicks to open the e-mail.

Carlton Conner has sent a video to Elaine.

Carlton Conner?

Huh.

Small world.

Ellis clicks open the video.

Holy fucking shit.

Ellis leans forward, watching, then dances around the desk gleefully, then leans forward to watch some more.

For many viewers, it would be among the most disconcerting twenty seconds of video they've ever seen.

For Ellis, it's perhaps the most beautiful.

He doesn't know what to do. Keep watching it or keep dancing around the desk in victory. He breaks into a huge unguarded smile.

A million three is about to work its clever digital way from Elaine Kelly's account into his own. But now, with a bonus. A bonus of leverage, of protection. A bonus as if in congratulations on his plan, the icing on the cake. Like some power beyond him wants his plan to work.

Smart move, Elaine girl, shooting that video, sending it home for safekeeping.

But hey, not smart enough.

28

She had stood obediently, immovably in one spot at the counter of a bank branch, for hours, days, years.

Now, she has just a few chaotic seconds to choose—to leap—between life and death.

Elaine Kelly, who had always dressed formally, perfectly, crisply, in the bank.

Now virtually naked.

Like a superhero against the city's night sky. *Look, up in the sky, it's Banker Girl! No, it's Crazy Girl.*

Elaine Kelly, who has obeyed every rule.

Now, breaking every rule, she is certain.

Except the rule of survival.

Maybe she's about to break that one, too, in a broken heap on the narrow strip of pavement between the buildings, far, far, far below.

There are 164,000 employees of Federated Bank. Not a single one of them finds themselves on the ledge of a twenty-story building at two in the morning. She's pretty sure of that.

Well, one other.

The bank's chairman.

A few more precious seconds to adjust to the raw height and dizzying edge . . .

To take in the reality of the next building's landing . . .

And the deep, narrow canyon between the buildings . . .

On the neighboring roof, she can see some greenery, a tenant vegetable garden, and therefore, a way into the building.

A midtown Eden for their near-nakedness.

Her mind is running fast, making rough, quick, intuitive calculations. Her thoughts are skittering between the obtruding points of data . . .

How much spring, how much energy . . . ?

Where's the shaved-head guard?

Should she look again for the rooftop door?

No time left . . .

Just eight feet over and eight feet down . . .

But the main calculation is not feet and inches, but a calculus of power . . .

Calculating correctly a man who commands 164,000 workers, who risks sadomasochistic ritual and release, a man for whom power is everything, in his being, in his bones . . .

And if the cell phone threatens that power, what will he do to get it back?

Leap tall buildings in a single bound?

Reach for it across the Manhattan sky?

She can measure its value to him, her ultimate negotiating leverage, literally in horizontal and vertical feet.

He needs that phone.

And with that intuition, and the pharmaceuticals cycling through her, and the uncontrollable flood of adrenaline at that rooftop edge, Elaine suddenly grabs the phone from Liv.

"Me first," Elaine says. "Conner next. You, right behind him." Her eyes narrow and she adds, "Don't leave me alone with him."

"Me first."

To show them they can do it. That it can be done.

She feels displacement—the same strange sense of displacement she's felt these past few days. A displacement she knows is adaptive, protective, and a byproduct of the drugs in her bloodstream.

Elaine looks. Takes a breath.

And leaps.

For a moment—a strange moment that can never be duplicated, a moment that she will turn away from, too hard to even relive or reimagine—the street is twenty stories below her.

And her life is beside her.

And her fear coats her, runs freezing along her limbs.

For a moment, she is in midair. In flight—in both senses—above the city of her vague but fondest dreams. Incomprehensibly, briefly, in air above the metropolis. It is impossible. But it is happening.

She must have passed out from the fear, because in another moment, she finds herself on the next building's asphalt, having landed with a crouch and a roll.

Alive. Traveling just a few feet through the air, but it's as if she's arriving on another planet.

She looks up in time to see Conner leap off next, cross those few terrifying feet of Manhattan air, and land next to her.

Her landing had been easy enough, but with his hands cuffed behind him, his is much uglier. Feet, then knees, then his side hit the asphalt, scraping up all of them, his black-hooded face now against the gravel.

He lies there moaning against the roof, reduced to something briefly animal. It is the same sound he makes during sex, she notices, somehow the same primal pain.

Elaine takes a step toward him to help.

An unthinking, intuitive moment of sympathy, of connection, in the wake of the shared leap . . .

A mistake.

He is suddenly up off the asphalt.

Shoulders lowered. Hood down.

Heading toward her in blind fury.

Unleashing in this brief one-on-one opportunity, seizing the moment of clatter and jostle, of confusion, of separation, to go for the phone.

His moaning has stopped, converted to rage and focus.

Elaine starts to back helplessly through the HVAC minefield.

To trip over something in the dark . . .

Or be rammed and crumpled into the low sidewall . . .

Or forced over it . . .

Conner will take any of those options, to free his phone.

Nowhere to go . . .

Bend down and hit "Send"?

God, I don't want to.

He knows I don't.

The unexpected . . .

The unthinkable . . .

As she turns to run—run anywhere, insanely, uselessly—she looks behind her to see Conner crumpled on the asphalt again.

Liv is above him, having tripped the hooded bull in the darkness.

Using his handcuffed arms to force him down, hold him down.

Moans of pain come from Conner once more.

Liv stands over him, her face a fist of suspicion and fury, the adrenaline of the jump clearly pulsing through her.

She bends down to him.

Yanks the black hood violently off his head.

Face puffy, red, and sweaty from the suffocating hood. Eyes raging with fury and frustration. Hair at wild angles. Not the smooth televised CEO of quarterly reports. Or the swaggering sexual adventurer.

"We'd push you off," Liv says, "but we need you alive . . . for our little movie to have box office value."

Liv was waiting for this. Was born for this.

It's Banker Girl.

And her trusty sidekick, Junkie Girl. Slave Girl.

Unmasking villains. Leaping from rooftop to rooftop. Superheroes above Gotham.

Liv takes the cell phone back from Elaine, shoves it down the front of her bikini bottom.

Conner stares with fury. "I don't know that you sent that video *anywhere*. It might be *only* in that phone. I could just walk away."

"Walk away, and we toss it twenty stories. And you'll never know *who's* got that video. You willing to take that risk?"

Conner looks openly at the phone riding in Liv's crotch.

Where all the power resides.

They trot through the odd, otherworldly rooftop garden to the exit door.

They pull on it.

It's locked.

As they pause there, unsure what to do next, the door opens.

• • •

Sarah Sheehan, nearly ninety, in gardening clothes, holding a rake and trowel, shuffles through the doorway.

She blinks several times at two young women in bikini bottoms, and nothing more.

Blinks at a man in front of her, naked except for women's underwear.

She reaches into her housedress. Hands and forearms stuttering with Parkinson's, she brings out her eyeglasses.

She usually doesn't bother with her eyeglasses coming up here to garden at night. After sixty years of tending this roof garden, she can walk it blindfolded. And can't make out anything in the dark even with her glasses, anyway. Only sleeps a few hours a night now, so comes up here when it's nice and quiet. Why not? The plants are happy to have her. They don't feel so lonely.

She fumbles with the eyeglasses, starting to put them on.

Elaine sees how thick they are.

Jesus. She can't see us, Elaine realizes.

"We really shouldn't have left the apartment like this," Liv offers, unnecessarily, as they catch the door before it closes, brush past the old woman, and hustle down the stairs.

It is like turning someone's own pistol against them. As if gently redirecting the barrel to change the dynamics entirely. Carlton Conner's cell phone is the CEO's private sidearm sheathed in his jacket pocket, all-powerful, a weapon deployable in an instant, to mobilize, to respond, to thrust and parry, to attack and defend. And in an unguarded instant, its power has been turned back on him, coolly, cleverly, effectively.

This most modern, latest twist on blackmail. The specific tool of the blackmail has changed, but the emotions, the effect, the ramifications, the other dynamics of it have remained the same for centuries.

It's a building full of the elderly, Elaine is sure. The rooftop garden. The nocturnal rambling of the old gardener. People who bought in years ago when they could afford it. The lucky, the wealthy versions of her own mother. They feel safe, secure, set in their routines. And increasingly fearful of their own forgetfulness. And that is why Elaine heads for the umbrella stand by the elevator. Looks inside it, and as she half expected, she sees something glinting near the bottom. Pulls out a set of apartment keys. Belonging to someone who leaves them hidden there, when they go out. Not to lose them. Not to forget them. Which apartment is it? Only one way to find out.

Three figures stand nearly naked in a penthouse hallway. The topless red-haired young woman moves down the hallway, trying a set of keys in each apartment door. It's two thirty in the morning, and the apartment occupants are asleep and don't hear the wrong key's quick jiggle. The black-haired woman is standing topless next to a man whose hands are cuffed behind him. He is wearing women's panties.

At the fifth doorway, the key turns.

The red-haired woman rings the apartment doorbell as the black-haired woman and the handcuffed man gather behind her.

They wait a moment outside the apartment door, silently. No one answers the door.

The red-haired woman opens the door. All three slip inside.

This is precisely what the surveillance cameras would have recorded. If the dowdy, arrogant old residential building had any.

29

Elaine and Liv riffle through the closets silently and find temporary street clothes—sweatpants and sweatshirts—while Conner, wrists cuffed behind him, waits seated on the edge of a bed.

Elaine tosses an extra sweatshirt and pair of sweatpants at him. Motions for him to stand up.

Wordlessly, unceremoniously, she unclips the handcuffs.

Conner's arms fall forward in relief. He rubs his wrists gratefully.

He silently inspects his scraped-up elbows, knees, and legs before quickly pulling on the sweatshirt and sweatpants.

He can't stride out onto the Upper East Side wearing only handcuffs and women's panties. And they can't risk staying here more than a few minutes.

The phone is still in Liv's crotch, now beneath her gray sweats. The apartment door is double-bolted, and they're watching Conner warily. He won't try anything now. It's two of them again. One of them always free, ready to hit "Send."

In a moment, all three of them are sitting, looking at one another.

They've never seen one another dressed.

Elaine feels enormous relief at the simple sensation of the thick cotton along her thighs and arms and shoulders. She feels close to crying with relief.

It has all been at breakneck speed.

Literally.

No chance to think. Just keep moving. Keep ahead of whatever vague, hovering, ruthless force the two penthouse guards are part of. And oddest of all, Carlton Conner is with them, just as naked, just as terrified. Opponent and teammate. Ally and enemy. Occupying the strange half status of client: the coddled focus of the brothel's operation, and a fickle, careless threat to the brothel as well. Fully aware, apparently, that in the netherworld he patronizes, he is just another paying john, no safer or more valuable than any other, his high profile probably making him riskier and less desirable than most.

The three of them jumping, nearly naked, between two twenty-story rooftops.

Now seated in a Manhattan apartment, like a million other New Yorkers. They silently absorb it for a moment. Regard one another's ill-fitting, roughly matching gray sweats. Temporarily equalized. Inmates at the same prison. Supplicants in the same purgatory. Then . . .

"Let's get this done. Name your price," says Carlton Conner.

Liv is about to respond, but Elaine puts her hand on Liv's arm to gently stop her.

She leans forward toward Conner. "We could ask for anything, couldn't we? You'd give us anything to get your phone back." It comes out of her, somewhere deep and uncontaminated. She feels the power of it. The pharmaceuticals are still coursing through her, the adrenaline of the past few minutes still pumping, but it's something more, too. Some deeper release.

Conner shifts irritably, instantly angry at the challenge. Annoyance itches him into blunt aggression. "I'm not gonna sit here negotiating. We obviously can't stay here"—he checks his wrist, but of course there's no watch there—"and we don't have a lot of time. My corporate staff, my family, will start looking for me."

"Pretty embarrassing if they found you," says Elaine. She sees Liv smile.

He's exasperated. "Look. What do you want?"

"Not a dime."

Which has precisely the predictable effect. Conner looks at her, confused.

So does Liv. Enemies sharing a moment of confusion.

She reads Liv's look: *What are you doing? What are you pulling here?*

And then Elaine answers. "One phone call," she tells him.

His eyebrow arches with question and suspicion.

"One phone call from you," she says. *One bullet fired from that powerful wireless weapon of yours.* "I've got money sitting in a Federated reverse mortgage account. I can't get at it until my house sells. But with one call you can have it shifted into a favored assets account . . . the kind we . . . you . . . give your best customers."

Conner allows himself a grim little resentful smile. A smile of recognition, of unexpected connection. "Well, well . . . a banker." He waits, feasts a moment on the irony. Contemplates and calculates it for another moment that makes Elaine nervous. "I can't do that," he says finally. "It's drug money. We both know that. Working at that penthouse wasn't *your* idea. You were there because you crossed them."

He smiles coldly: "Clever of you to park it in an account like that. No oversight. No sweeps. But that's drug money and if they know I helped you get at it, we're all dead. To say nothing of what the government would eventually do to me. So I can't." Which he seems decidedly pleased about.

"You can, and you don't have a choice," says Elaine, calm but adamant. Where is the wallflower? Where is the dutiful employee?

Is this who has been waiting all these years, waiting for the right circumstance to unleash?

"Yes, I do. I can just refuse to do it. Simply refuse. Let this be the ending. You send out your little movie, and I apologize. Resign. Retire. I've got plenty of money, a wonderful family. Take this opportunity to reset my life . . . do something new . . . maybe even something useful . . ." As if he is already rehearsing the script, taking on the tone, of the interviews he'll give.

Elaine doesn't fall for it. She leans in close to Conner. Looks him hard in the eyes. "You won't. You can't. I've seen close up exactly what power means to you, and you'd never give it up. Power you can keep with one phone call. I get the money, you get your phone back . . . and the video."

He sits up ramrod straight on the bed. Regards her for a moment as if from a haughty higher perch, looking down his nose at her silently, like a hawk regarding scurrying prey. *How dare she . . .*

Then nods okay. Deal. Good enough. He reaches for his phone to make the call. But Liv dangles it out of his reach.

"I dial it, and hold it, till we know this is going to work. What's the number?"

He recites an international number, adding at the end, "London opens any minute now. They can do it from there. Then I walk out with my phone. I have to be at work by morning. Big day for me."

"You'll be a little delayed," Elaine informs him, like a functionary, a disinterested official communicating an immutable fact of natural catastrophe or weather conditions, of fate that can't be shifted or changed. "Until I know I can access the money. Figure out something to tell them. You lie to your shareholders, your board, your wife," she says with fluent disdain. "You'll come up with something."

30

At Elaine's old bank branch in Queens, Vicki, the older teller with the smoker's voice, is smiling to herself at the coincidence.

An attractive woman is standing across the service counter from her, opening an account, and when Vicki asks for ID, the woman passes over her New York State driver's license, and what do you think her name is? *Look at that. Huh.*

As Vicki shuffles through the woman's documentation, she smiles at the woman and tells her, "We used to have an Elaine Kelly who worked here."

The attractive new Elaine Kelly smiles back. "Yeah, I've met a couple myself over the years."

Vicki looks at the new account forms the woman has filled in and types the necessary information into her terminal. *Opening accounts is so streamlined now*, she thinks. *The bank wants to make it easy to get new business—and it is.*

"You're all set, Elaine Kelly," Vicki says with a twinkle in her eye. "You making an initial deposit to open the account with?"

"Yes. First paycheck," the woman says, with a hint of pride.

Hautmann Financial, the check says, Vicki notices.

"New in the neighborhood?" she asks Elaine.

"I am, yes."

"Here for a job?"

"Yes. A job."

"Elaine Kelly, how 'bout that?" Vicki says to flamboyant Sam at lunch.

Sam shrugs. "Ten million New Yorkers and still plenty of them Irish, breeding irresponsibly."

"Oh, Sam." And after a moment. "It was a little weird to see a second Elaine Kelly after that whole thing with two Antonio Desirios. Of course, this was different." After a pause, quieter, to Sam. "You miss Elaine?"

"Adorable creature," Sam admits.

"I miss her," says Vicki. "Her quiet class. Wonder where she is. And why she quit like that."

"A little fragile, that one. Easily rattled, I guess. Questionable survival skills." Sam sniffs. "It's a tough city. You gotta be tougher."

Vicki doesn't want to argue with Sam.

"Just up and disappearing like that," says Vicki. "And then the awful thing with Bob. At least she didn't have to deal with that. Might have sent her over the edge. It's been a weird time for our little branch, hasn't it?"

. . .

The tall, attractive, tailored Elaine Kelly is—very strangely, but quite appropriately—sitting in the living room of the Kelly row house.

Crisply stylish, fresh and cool, she looks uncomfortable on the sagging sofa, amid the frayed dinginess.

John Ellis sits across from her.

"So?"

"Smooth. Nothing to it."

He hands her an envelope. "First portion. Hoping the rest is as smooth."

"As it will be." Adding, "They remember Elaine."

"As do I," says Ellis, smiling.

31

Nussbaum enters the lobby of a midtown Manhattan office building. He's neatly dressed in blazer, dark slacks, and tie. His Yom Kippur outfit, as it happens. He heads to the elevator.

He gets out on the fifteenth floor, takes in the serene cool transformation. Gleaming glass and chrome furniture. Thick carpeting. Dark paneling. Original artwork. It could be a law firm.

"Can I help you?" the receptionist asks.

"Here to see Mr. Desirio."

"Do you have an appointment?" A little ruffle of frown crosses the smooth, calm, Connecticut face.

Nussbaum flashes his badge. "Let him know I'm here about his Federated accounts. Remind him we spoke at court. I was assigned to look into it for him. He'll remember."

Nussbaum had the foresight to approach the Desirio party as they were leaving court, introduce himself, and say he was on the team assigned to help them sort out their account issues. On their side. All done to create some name recognition and good will to get him in the door today.

The receptionist gestures Nussbaum to sit in the comfortable waiting area so she can, he knows, dial the phone and speak out of Nussbaum's earshot.

He hardly even gets seated before she turns to him. "He can see you now."

A short hallway.

An open door.

The silver-haired mane. A smoothly professional and unrevealing expression. Nussbaum shakes hands with Desirio as he sits.

"So what have you got, Detective?" The unplaceable Eastern European accent seems to slink around the words.

Nussbaum opens his briefcase, slides across the picture of the blonde high school girl from Arthur Holden's apartment. "I've got this."

The smooth exterior fractures only slightly. "What is this?" Nussbaum watches Desirio look at the picture and then look away. *Too quick, Antonio, you looked away too quick. My guess is because you know her.*

"Know who it is?"

"I thought this was about my money."

"It is, Mr. Desirio. I'm pretty sure if I can find her, I can learn a lot more about your money."

Desirio is starting to get the idea. He stands up instinctively, the fury gathering.

Nussbaum pushes him down.

Desirio reaches for the telephone on his desk.

Nussbaum pushes the receiver button down to disconnect it.

Nussbaum tosses another picture in front of Desirio—a passport-style picture of Elaine. "What about her?"

Desirio looks at the photo. Looks up at Nussbaum.

"Why do you ask?"

"Ever seen her?"

"You know the answer. You're about to show me lots of grainy pictures of the two of us together."

Nussbaum tosses a fan of photos in front of Desirio: bank security photos of Desirio at the teller counter with Elaine. Then of

Desirio confronting Glen, the branch manager, causing a commotion while Elaine looks on. Then staring at Elaine.

"Any idea where she is, Mr. Desirio? She's been missing for several days . . ."

"I don't even know her name."

Two "associates" enter Desirio's office now—one with shoulders like a fireplace mantel—and if they are Desirio's business partners, the stratum of business they oversee and the manner in which they oversee it is immediately apparent to Detective Nussbaum. They head aggressively and eagerly toward him.

Desirio subtly signals them off. Well-trained dogs with excellent hearing and obedience to commands.

Nussbaum regards the two associates openly, as he inquires, sardonically, "What kind of work do you do, Mr. Desirio?"

Desirio, equally sardonic in return, says, "Technology." He shrugs. "I'm a tough negotiator. Some people don't like it"—he gestures to the two men—"so I protect myself."

Technology. The catchall phrase to imply, *Something you'll never understand.* A business you won't question for its international flavor. One in which you'll accept the vision of a level, lively playing field where educated, aggressive Israeli, Russian, Bulgarian, Pakistani, and Taiwanese engineering types all compete, all come to thrive and succeed here in America. Technology. Thousands of firms in thousands of obscure little niches, making lots of money. The new front organization. Nussbaum could almost believe it.

The code is clear. The battle lines are drawn. Nussbaum knew he would never intimidate someone like Antonio Desirio. But there is the chance he can force some action, some error in judgment, some unmeasured response, as a result of today's visit.

• • •

Nussbaum and Dominguez stand in an apartment hallway of an expensive residential building with the building manager.

Nussbaum signals the manager to open the door.

The manager protests a little, politely, gently squirming. "Look, you don't have a search warrant. I feel funny doing this. I told you, it's owned by a corporation . . ."

Nussbaum cuts him off impatiently. "You know as well as I do what goes on here. Don't make me go back and get a warrant. Open the goddamn door."

The manager unlocks it, and Nussbaum and Dominguez enter.

An empty penthouse duplex. Office-like, with a desk in the foyer. Bright and cheerful, sunlight flooding in from the sliding glass doors on the second floor. "Those lead out to the pool," says the building manager proudly, like a realtor showing it off.

It is immaculate. Swept clean. *Carefully, consciously so*, thinks Nussbaum. He moves down the hallway respectfully, as if in a temple—a recently abandoned temple, whose ghosts and prayers still hover in the suspiciously cheerful light.

He opens the door to an interior bedroom that is empty, but paneled, and has no windows.

He feels along its long wall, to a crack, which he pushes, and a closet door opens to a sizable walk-in closet. His pulse jumps a little at the discovery of this bit of trompe-l'oeil. He walks into it but finds nothing hanging on its various brass hooks and bars. His disappointment is palpable.

He goes to the sill of the little bedroom's windowless alcove. Squints down. Frowns. Looks closely. Picks something up.

A strand of red hair.

While Dominguez waits, Nussbaum stands alone at the pool's edge for a moment. Looks down into the water and out over the city.

32

At three in the morning, a taxi cruises slowly through Elaine Kelly's old neighborhood, which is now dark and unlit. It crawls slowly past the Kelly row house.

Inside the cab, squeezed into the backseat are two prostitutes running for their lives and the chairman of Federated Bank, the celebrated deal maker, impatient to consummate a fairly straightforward arrangement that will allow him to remain chairman. A strange contingent, but the streets of Queens have undoubtedly seen stranger.

"Jesus, Elaine, it's the one place they know to look for us," Liv said nervously to Elaine.

"We've got no choice. Without a wallet, I need what's in my desk to put together enough ID for the bank."

"But your bank knows you."

Elaine shook her head. "Have to have ID for this kind of transaction. Computers can't process it without it."

"Can't we just get him to step in? Throw his weight around?"

"That might work for a rent check or a car payment. But a verbal assurance over the phone is not gonna cut it for 1.3 million dollars. And he's not gonna sit in a branch for some kind of formal cosigning, and we don't have the time anyway . . ."

As the taxi slides silently through her neighborhood, Elaine searches the street and the driveways carefully. "I don't see that silver sedan," she says. "I know all the cars I see."

Liv looks doubtful at such a claim on a populated street in New York.

"I've been on this street my whole life," Elaine explains. Startling even herself with the fact.

Lisbon. Johannesburg. Milan. Venice. Those magical images hazy, receded now, faded into mist. Places farther away than ever.

She hadn't gotten very far. Yes, she had squeezed a lifetime of terror and anxiety and violence and debasement into the past few days, yet she was back where she started. When she jumped into the cab escaping to Bob's loft, featureless numberless days ago, she had known she was seeing the row house for the last time. Yet here she was again. She'd lived a lifetime since. And had not progressed at all.

Elaine, Liv, and Conner crouch silently in the row house's tiny backyard.

Elaine reaches under one of the cat bowls at the edge of the back patio, pulls out a key.

The house is dark inside. No lights on. Elaine looks in a couple of windows. Then carefully opens the back door.

Elaine flips the lights on in the living room.

She, Liv, and Conner immediately see the chaos of opened mail, riffled papers, bank statements, and empty coffee mugs and cups all strewn across Elaine's space.

Elaine's computer is on.

She stands there taking it in.

On the desk is Elaine's purse, wide open. Her wallet is next to it.

Elaine picks up the wallet and examines it anxiously. Fans a few credit cards. The way she had financed her mother's illness. Several of the cards are gone. Along with her license. She realizes what that could mean.

Maybe petty theft. Maybe more.

"I have to be at my old branch the second it opens," she says to Liv. "At that point, you'll have to keep him here yourself."

They look at each other evenly, both silently wondering if Liv will be able to do that.

And until then? They'll have to wait here together, the three of them, counting minutes, marking time. Keeping all the lights out, watching out the window for anyone who comes looking for them. Keeping just as close a watch on Conner.

They have the invisible leash of his phone, and his need for it.

And a further assurance of his cooperation, as well.

Elaine touches the bulging pocket of her sweatpants.

Pulls the black hood and the cuffs out of it.

All they owned in the world, virtually their only worldly possessions, it occurs to her, as they scrambled across the roof, as they leaped across Manhattan.

"Put them back on," Elaine says to him.

"What?"

"The handcuffs. The hood."

"That's not necessary," he says. "This is not the place, the situation . . ."

Exactly. "Put them on . . . or I hit "Send."" Tossing the handcuffs and hood at him.

"Look, it's just not . . ."

"Now!"

Elaine and Liv watch him clip the handcuffs on his own wrists, hands in front this time.

"Is this really—"

"Now!"

She is shocked by the strength and fury of her feeling, the vehemence in her, the insistence, the utter command she feels. The rage bounces from the familiar row house's living room walls, a directness of feeling never expressed within these walls before. She is surprised, embarrassed by it. Experiences for a moment only a bare edge of control. But she *will* send the video if he doesn't put them on, she realizes. No matter the consequences to Conner, Liv, or herself. In that moment, she will send it, absolutely, unquestionably. And Conner must sense that.

The hood and cuffs were practical, precautionary, to discourage him from trying anything, from suddenly walking away with some ingenious path out of the blackmail, some way to survive or head off the embarrassment and effect of that video that hadn't occurred to them before. Practical, precautionary, but there was much more in it for her. Putting him at her command. Making him feel the humiliation. Taking away the charge of those items for her and taunting him with their meaning, defusing their meaning for her.

He pulls the hood down over his face. The eyeholes frame the whites of his eyes.

The three of them sit in silence a moment, absorbing the strangeness, the shame of it, until Elaine breaks the silence. Smiling. Coldly.

"We just want you to feel comfortable, Carlton."

33

Of the 310 Federated Bank branches spread throughout the five boroughs, 304 of them look largely indistinguishable from one another. The same cheerfully neutral color scheme, the same rigid unwelcoming furniture, and the same unsigned prints and photographs, purchased in bulk through the corporate art department.

Three are "novelty" branches that are individually, whimsically designed to fit the neighborhood: one masquerades as an open-air vegetable market, one mimics a Mideast bazaar, a third is a floating "tugboat" branch that cruises out to Ellis Island, Governors Island, and the small islands and inlets off the coast of Queens.

And the three remaining branches are regal icons, architectural marvels from a glorious financial past.

Like this one: an elegant Park Avenue showcase, a centerpiece of the Federated brand. With its dark-paneled interior, marble floors, vaulted ceiling, Palladian windows that majestically diffuse the morning light three stories above the tellers and officers, it exudes power and station.

The beautiful antique clock set halfway to the ceiling vaults reads 9:02.

An elegantly dressed woman enters the branch—heels, Hermès scarf, and a tastefully cut, plum-colored designer suit.

She approaches a crisply dressed, perfectly coiffed male teller, who is dressed as attentively as she.

He is immediately and visibly impressed with his stylish customer.

"Good morning," she says with a quick smile that she reserves for the servant class.

The teller is smitten.

"I need to transfer funds from one account to another. But there's something very odd going on with my account numbers." The word *odd* rings and lingers in the high vaults and puts the woman's heritage somewhere offshore and exotic and overprivileged. "I brought all my most recent statements . . . Perhaps you can help me sort it out?"

"Happy to." A little too eager. "Primary account number?"

The elegant woman recites familiarly, "Four five six four four two four nine three seven," and without needing to be asked, she slips her ID, along with her paperwork, across the counter to him.

Elaine Kelly, the teller reads.

"We'll get this worked out for you in a moment, Miss Kelly."

• • •

The plastic, generic, black-and-white clock high on the cork wall says 9:02 when Elaine walks tentatively, anxiously, into her old bank branch on Northern Boulevard.

She looks around quickly, anxiously for other customers. She half expects to run into one—a silver-haired one.

But there are no other customers.

Sam is the first to spot Elaine. And can hardly be expected to keep the discovery to himself. "Look who's here!" he says exuberantly.

The tellers eagerly gather around her to say hello. Elaine greets them nervously, checking the clock.

"We've missed you."

"How *are* you?"

"Where have you been?"

"What have you been up to?"

"You look . . . exhausted."

"Elaine, did you hear about Bob?"

"Oh my god, Elaine . . . Prepare yourself . . ."

"Elaine Kelly," says Vicki, in the thick of all the good feelings, "I was just thinking about you. This attractive young woman came in—"

Alertly, Elaine turns to Vicki to ask more, but Glen joins them, and instead Elaine addresses Glen urgently.

"Glen, can I . . . Can I speak to you in private for a moment?"

"She wants to come back, Glen. Give her a raise. We want her," Sam shouts out gleefully.

• • •

At 9:05 in the paneled Park Avenue branch, the crisply dressed male teller is finishing his review of Elaine Kelly's paperwork.

"Real estate closing, I presume?"

"Exactly," Miss Kelly confirms.

The teller studies his monitor. Thumbs once more, wordlessly, through the pile of statements Miss Kelly has brought him.

He studies his monitor for another moment, then stands up, stretches victoriously.

"Okay, I see what happened. It went into your mortgage account. Normally you can't move money out of that kind of account without special approvals . . ." But he is already squinting at the screen, redirecting the thought. "Ah, but I see you got the approval. And you've been put into a favored assets account." He looks up at her with frank admiration. "Nice to have friends in high places." And then, realizing, a little sheepish and ashamed for not having quite followed, he says, "Now I understand, Miss Kelly . . . That's why you're here this morning."

And if the elegant Miss Kelly looks momentarily confused, she covers it so smoothly it is never even noticed. "Yes. Sorry. I should have been clearer."

"I can switch it for you now," the teller says.

A few keystrokes.

"All set." A note of satisfaction in his voice.

"Terrific. Thank you for sorting it all out," she says graciously.

"I assume the next step is a wire transfer?"

"Yes. To this account." She hands him a slip of paper.

• • •

"Elaine, it's so good to see you," Glen gushes. "We've all missed you."

"Glen, I'm making a . . . a sizable transaction this morning . . . I . . . don't want the other tellers to know . . ."

Glen looks puzzled. *Sizable transaction?* But she has surprised him before.

Elaine presents a withdrawal slip. Glen reads it, looks up at Elaine surprised after seeing the amount.

"My mother's house sale," Elaine explains. "Just closed."

"Wow. Forty-five years of real estate inflation, huh?" He smiles a little. "Now I understand your quitting."

"You won't say anything?"

"Course not. So what kind of transaction? You want to set up a new account for it?"

"No, no. I want to withdraw it."

He looks at her. "Really?"

"Really."

He is surprised but professional. Showing her he can take it in stride. He can be trusted.

"Sure. Cashier's check?"

"Yes, please."

As he squints at the monitor and taps the keys, he speaks to her. "I always assumed you got your mom a reverse mortgage," he admits. "I mean, with, you know . . . your salary and your mom's medical bills. But I guess you never really know about people's financial status." Smiling mildly. Shrugging. "Or anything else about them."

Then Glen frowns at the monitor. Keystrokes several more times. Shakes his head in frustration.

Elaine sees it. A clammy cold shoots through her. *What? No.*

"Ah, Christ, Elaine. There's some system error." He keystrokes some more. "Big surprise, huh?" he says sarcastically.

No. No.

"According to this, you just made this transaction two minutes ago"—Glen is squinting now—"on Park Avenue." He shakes his head. "Which is impossible, of course, since you're sitting right here." Shaking his head again. "I'll find out what the hell's going on."

He looks up at her from his terminal sympathetically. "You seem to have the worst luck."

Eight thousand five hundred branches of Federated on the planet.

A Federated customer is welcome at any one of them, thinks Elaine.

Whoever helped themselves to all her paperwork and her license has waltzed into one of the other branches—Park Avenue, apparently—and helped themselves to Elaine's account balance, with the lucky assistance and endorsement of the bank's chairman himself, in an earlier phone call on her behalf.

Glen was right. The worst luck.

34

Elaine stares down again at her riffled desk. Her riffled wallet. Her riffled life.

They took over my house. They got my statements. They took over my identity. They got their money back. It's over.

She looks over at Conner, on the far side of the room. The chairman of Federated Bank. Seated on a threadbare couch, its sat-out springs pushing through the fabric in the dark, dingy, still-cluttered, already-sold Kelly row house on undoubtedly his first and final visit to the borough of Queens.

A visit made more indelible, she hopes, by the black hood over his head and the cuffs back on his wrists.

Certainly, he needs that phone. And a single phone call to London to help her shift accounts must have seemed an easy way to get his phone back, a pretty good deal. And allowing her the ten minutes she needed once the branch opened to get the money, to confirm the transfer before they handed the phone back to him. That must have seemed a good deal, too.

Now that she'd come back without success, without transferring and gaining access to the money—either some glitch or somehow beaten to the punch—now it would no longer be a simple, straight-forward deal for any of them.

Yet she couldn't help feeling, all through these last hours—picking up the sense, irrationally, intuitively—that the phone was disguising something else about Conner's being here. Something further that she started to feel on the tense cab ride over and feel even more once they were here in her house. Something still smoldering at the back of her mind as she rushed from the house to the branch, greeted the other tellers, and dealt with Glen, all the while anxiously picturing Conner and Liv waiting for her.

Much of this began, after all, when he selected her. Violated her, devirginated her, yes, but first, selected her. And however dark and perverted and tainted, it is connection. Connection that perversely, startlingly, she senses he wants to retain.

Connection. She shudders physically. Feels a little churn of nausea. Tries to dislodge from her head the whole line of thinking. But she can't. It has grabbed on and won't let go. Is there an element of curiosity for him? About where she lives, where she comes from, a glimpse into the past of the red-haired lightly freckled girl who for whatever reasons stirs his imagination? Or is it an element of guilt that holds him here? Guilt at who she has turned out to be—not an imported professional prostitute, but a young, innocent Catholic girl, a dutiful former Federated employee, no less, caught up in something, in over her head.

She has the nagging, unshakeable sense that he has leaped that building, come with them to Queens, and waited here in her living room for something more than his phone. For some reason that darkly accompanies the rational excuse of the phone. His perversion, his sexuality, gets the better of him, after all. It motivates him. In a perverse way she doesn't understand—and maybe he doesn't, either—is it continuing to?

Or is this sense only something that *she* is putting on the interaction? Is it nothing beyond his cell phone that he wants? Pure, simple, transactional. Is it a connection that *she* is trying to build in order to justify, to make sense somehow, of what has happened to her? Because he already made the cold calculation, made the leap across a building, demonstrating to Elaine the phone's estimable value to him. The estimable threat of the video it contains. He risked the leap. He is a risk-taker. You didn't risk coupling a daylight life like his to a nighttime life like his if you weren't a risk-taker.

He has waited quietly on the couch, cuffed and hooded, with Zen-like patience, even shutting his eyes at dawn for a little while until the bank opened. Maybe contemplating the altered, shifting meaning of the hood and cuffs. Maybe contemplating, as Elaine is, how she had first thought of these props as representing his power over them, and now, here, their power over him, but realizing—once the hood and cuffs were on him again—that it isn't so simple. In the penthouse, yes, he had power over them, but it originated in, was born of, their sexual power and hold over him. Here in the row house, he is powerless to their blackmail, yet it is only his power that can make the blackmail work. The hood and cuffs seem to represent not power or powerlessness, one or the other, but instead, how they operate together. How power and powerlessness are inextricably tied, how they dance with each other, need each other, seem even, in some way, the same. That is the meaning lurking in these props, a meaning itching at her, a meaning she can't yet fully fathom. *Connection.* A subtler, deeper sense of it. *Connection.* Limbs, thoughts, lives entwined . . .

And maybe, for Conner, these small hours passed without any contemplation at all. Because he is so sure of the power of his phone call on her behalf. Because he is confident of the power and order of the bank he runs. *Maybe only the powerless brood about power*, Elaine thinks, *while the truly powerful never ponder or doubt it.* Maybe power is fated, contained, embedded in personality. And powerlessness is her fate, her natural state, her stasis, while power and dominance are his to such a depth and degree, so relentlessly and unforgivingly, that he craves their opposite. Craves relief and release.

She would never know, of course. They would never, could never, simply talk to each other. Only trouble, only accusation and hostility and deception, would come out of it. So no words. They are beyond words. The gulf is too wide, and they both know it. So there is silence—both enforced and self-imposed—and silently, mutually agreed. As if the row house were occupied only by ghosts. Presences in transit. Staying silently alert. Hewing to the tentative, fragile atmosphere of a deal, each party waiting to escape the other.

In these last hours, in the quiet waiting, she has finally felt the ebb of the pharmaceuticals. The racy, pulsing feeling wearing off, the hyperintense color normalizing, her own lost home starting to look like itself once more. Maybe it's the one good side effect of being here, surrounded by the completely familiar, the mundane, helping return her to her former self.

But in the end it came down to this: he had bought into her plan. They all had. And her plan let them down.

Conner stands up now from the threadbare couch at the far end of the room, squints out the window as if catching a glimpse of his approaching freedom. Somberly and with a sense of ceremony he removes the black hood and says reasonably, plaintively, honestly, "I'm out of time . . ."

• • •

"We've still got his cell phone," Liv whispers urgently. "Let's just ask for money. Hell, he's *expecting* it."

"Take money from Conner?" Elaine looks at Liv. He would never transfer the money until he had all copies of the video. And then the CEO could simply say he was kidnapped and taken to Queens, held up for ransom. His bank account debit and payment would prove it—and prove it was them he paid. Returning his phone, they'd lose their leverage. Their own version of events, without video evidence, would sound far-fetched to say the least. *Steal again?* thinks Elaine. *Look where it got me the first time.*

She shakes her head no, resolutely.

"So what then?" says Liv, frustrated. "We hand Conner back his phone and run for our lives? Now that they've got their money, maybe they'll leave *you* alone," she says, "but they won't stop coming after me."

"And you still won't tell me why," says Elaine resentfully.

Liv is starting to fidget anxiously. Elaine knew this was coming. She knew the clock was ticking. Her own frustration with no license, no official ID, credit cards taken, the identity she relied on gone—her own *missingness*. But Liv is missing something even more critical, that her daily life is even more dependent on.

"Look Elaine. I'm running out of time, too. We've got no money, and . . . I'm gonna need a fix real soon." Elaine sees the jumpiness entering Liv's muscles, hears it in her voice.

"Or a clinic, Liv. You just walk right in. I'll take you."

In response: a silent sullenness. A turning away. A fury swallowed into silence.

The pain inches up Liv slowly from her bowels, beginning to spread out from the center of her. She concentrates closely on Elaine as a trick to distract herself from the creeping pain.

She watches Elaine sit down at the computer.

She sees Elaine hit some keys. Regard the screen with a frown.

She sees her pull a desk drawer open. Riffle around in it for something.

She sees a stricken look cross Elaine's face.

"Conner, you better come look at this," she hears Elaine say.

Elaine can hardly believe she's in the position of confiding in him. Of revealing anything. But she sees no choice. She is cornered.

The worst luck.

She points to her e-mail screen. "One of the places I sent the video link was to my home computer. Looks like whoever was here opened it and, I'm guessing, made a copy on to a backup drive that's always in this drawer . . . and isn't anymore. Neither one of us wants that video in any other hands. Liv and I lose our leverage. You lose everything. Whoever this is probably has my account information *and* the video. Maybe they're going to be loyal Boy Scouts and deliver both to you and collect a gold star on the forehead, but I doubt it."

Conner narrows his eyes. She has leveled with him, and he knows it. "I need to play my phone messages," he says.

"Only if we listen," says Elaine.

Conner pauses, looking at Elaine carefully. Then nods his assent.

Liv holds Conner's cell phone between the three of them.

She hits the speakerphone setting, and they start listening to the messages.

Conner signals to skip ahead on several straightforward business messages.

And in a moment, there is a voice that Elaine recognizes in just a few syllables—perhaps mostly for their blandness, for their very lack of distinctiveness or memorability.

"Hey, Carlton . . ."

Ellis, thinks Elaine. Or whatever his name really is.

When Conner hears the voice, he holds up his index finger. *Wait.*

He signals Liv to let it play by twirling his finger in a loop.

"In the course of business I saw an interesting video," the flat voice continues,

"Interesting enough to change the course of our business arrangement . . . so I've made new plans."

"I know that voice," says Elaine, quietly bewildered. She looks at him. "Ellis?"

"Not his real name," says Conner gruffly. "I made a call for you. Now, *I* need one."

"Okay. But we dial it together."

"No need. Just hit seven."

Through the speaker, they hear the phone ringing.

A deeply accented voice answers, street noise behind him. "Yes?"

"Alton crossed me," says Conner. Apparently explanation enough, in a mere three words.

"Not to worry," the deep voice assures. "We take care." His own three-word mantras.

Click.

Elaine looks at Conner, startled.

Because she immediately recognizes the voice of the truck driver.

The truck driver is on Conner's speed dial. Client Seven's own number seven, oddly enough.

The truck driver. Ellis's partner in the horror of Bob's loft. Ellis, whose real name is Alton. But here, the driver is turned against his partner by a few words from Conner. Conner, Desirio, Ellis/Alton, the truck driver. Elaine is trying to sort through the sudden maze of connection, the elusive, shadowy hierarchy.

Liv's understanding is much simpler and more direct. She looks in fresh terror at Conner. "My god," she says frantically, "you could do that to us!" She shuts off the cell phone violently, regards it, horrified. The weapon they've been brandishing is suddenly pointed at them.

Conner had been a figure of perverted sexuality. A classic sado-masochist. A smooth corporate titan with a venal double life. Now, unimaginably, he is suddenly something worse.

Elaine regards Conner evenly, blankly, as she explains it to Liv. "No, he can't do that to us. Because we're *in* the video *with* him. Anything happens to us, it's too obvious who had a motive to get rid of us. Being in that video with him was disgusting and demeaning. But now, it's keeping us alive."

She looks again around at her invaded house. The house that she and her mother occupied—unchanged, inviolate—for years, with rarely even a guest crossing its threshold. And now, it has been totally violated, trashed, inhabited by people she knows enough to hate and fear.

She paces around the small living room, thinking, assessing. She looks out the window into the expanding morning. It is becoming clearer to her. The connections, the interrelationships, are slowly coalescing in her mind.

She says it to Liv, but her speech is really for Conner's benefit. She says it to Liv as if ignoring Conner's presence, as if he is suddenly of no consequence, no bearing, no standing. The most frustrating thing you can do to a narcissistic power addict, she senses, is ignore him, pretend he doesn't exist.

"Here's the thing, Liv. He tells us they're going to come after us. But nobody has. We're in my house—the first place they'd look for us, wait for us—and they left it before we got here. Pretty clear they knew we were coming. I looked back when we were running. That guard didn't fire at us, didn't even run toward us. Those guards, *somebody*, would have gotten to us by now. But they called their bosses and their bosses called them off. Don't you see, Liv? They're not coming after us. Because they're not coming after *him*. They're not going to hurt him. He says we could all be killed? Not Client Seven. Because, see, I think *they're* actually *his* clients."

Conner doesn't acknowledge anything she is saying. Impatiently cuts to the chase. "Your money is gone. You've had your chance. Give me my phone."

Elaine continues to ignore him, talk past him. Continues to explain, with Conner listening, she can see. "You know how much drug money there is in this borough, Liv? Someone once told me that the sums are incomprehensible. That it's a whole economy. Well, that money doesn't sit in mattresses. It goes to work: gets laundered, earns more money, goes legitimate as fast as it can." Looking at Conner. "And it does that through a bank. Through one bank in particular, as it turns out. Millions of dollars, laundered through hundreds of transactions at who knows what branches of Federated. But they don't own him, these dealers. And he doesn't own them. It's subtler, more complicated. They own each other. They need each other. It's business. It's a deal."

Conner smirks, remains silent.

"And where do you hide huge amounts of cash in New York where no one will even think twice about it? You can't bury it," she laughs bitterly, "it's all concrete. So where can you make huge deposits and transfers and no one questions it? New York real estate transactions, that's where."

Where I did, she thinks. *Like any drug dealer. That's how they do it, why they do it, where they do it.*

Just added my own twist to it. A mortgage escrow account. An account that's supposed *to have large inflows and outflows of unpredictable sizes and amounts, so a computer sweep is useless.*

Conner and Elaine are looking at each other.

"We're talking hundreds of millions. That's what Arthur Holden knew." She pauses, pictures the long black coat, the black hat. "Yes, as long as we're nobodies, he can have us killed with no consequence once he's back at the bank." She smiles thinly. "But there's a lesson in our little movie: if we're in the spotlight, front and center, nobody's gonna risk coming out of the shadows for us."

She looks around her again. "This place is sold. I've got nowhere to live. We've got no money. So we've got absolutely nothing to lose." Elaine holds up Conner's phone. "Which, oddly, gives us all the power."

Conner is more desperate now. "What . . . what do you want? Just say what you *want* to get rid of that video."

Turning to him, as if suddenly remembering him, suddenly returning to the bargaining table. "So you want to make a deal?" She leans in toward him, says it with dreamy speculation but hard menace arcing behind it. "What if, this time, there is no deal?"

Conner looks at her with impotent fury. Curt, forceful. "I've got to be at work in less than ninety minutes."

Elaine understands. If he doesn't show, it will be the police, an investigation, an all-points bulletin out of the hands of any of them. No controlling it. All doomed together. A slow motion steamroll of doom . . .

"Oh, you will be," says Elaine. "You'll be back at work. And I'll be with you."

"What?"

"Federated just rehired me," she says. She unclips the cuffs from his wrists.

He can't take it. Can't envision it. Just wants to be done with this. His face flexes with frustration. "Name your price," says Conner.

"Jesus, Elaine," Liv cuts in, jumpy, sweating now. "He'll pay us anything."

He will, Elaine realizes. He'll pay them whatever it takes. Anything to get them to disappear, which was, after all, Elaine's goal from the beginning. So why is she resisting? Because it's wrong to take his money? Because it's blackmail? A moral offense?

Hardly. It's something bigger now, more fundamental, more radical than that. It's as if, after seeing the deep well of human depravity, of dark capacity, money is suddenly meaningless. If he is so quickly, casually willing to pay, then the money is meaningless to him. And if the money is meaningless, then money—no matter how much—is not enough. Mere money is too low a price. Too small a settlement. The price must be higher. More fitting with the personalities, the emotions involved. More commensurate to the tenor and actions of the past twenty-four hours, to the upheaval and transformations of the past few days. Elaine is now playing for higher stakes: some mix of morality, lessons learned, and rough justice. Higher stakes that she has a hard time sorting out. She isn't clear on exactly what those stakes are.

She is shocked to realize it: she is no longer interested in the money. Money is too practical. Too obvious. Too inadequate. She wants something . . . else. Something . . . more.

Something has come loose in her. Is jangling around in her. Something new.

Stealing 1.3 million dollars.

Being drugged and locked naked in a dark room.

Losing your virginity at a brothel.

To the chairman of Federated.

Jumping nearly naked from one building to another.

Maybe these things change you.

She holds up Conner's cell phone. It's suddenly clear to her. She knows what she wants. It's power. The power has seized her. The solution, the settlement, is power over him. Continued control. Nothing else matters. And power will only accrue if she remains with him. If she is by his side like a needle, a pinprick, a thorn. Power that he can feel. That he can cower from. That he can look in the face of and feel the terror of uniquely.

She realizes, as she experiences it, that this is what Conner feels. This power addiction. This scent of it. This warmth of it. This coating in it. She has become Conner. But the realization doesn't make her recoil or retreat from it as it would have a week ago, a lifetime ago. *How power and powerlessness are inextricably tied, how they dance with each other, need each other . . .*

"Here's how it'll work," she says. "You buy a duplicate cell phone. I program this one to forward your calls to it. While I use this one." Dangling his. She leans in toward him once again. "See, I don't want the money." Smiling. Mocking. "I want the power." And then another smile, more knowing, almost close, friendly, conspiratorial. "You understand."

Liv whispers furiously. Confused, disoriented, unglued. "What the hell are you doing Elaine?"

Excellent question.

Impulse.
Getting the better of her?
Or just a better impulse?
"I'm not sure," Elaine says. "We shall see."

35

In the same diner where Elaine watched through the window a week ago, curious and terrified, a couple occupies the same booth, at the same odd hour of the night. In the same booth where Antonio Desirio and the truck driver huddled before, this time it is not a crooked businessman and a henchman thug. This time, it's an elegant woman and a blond-haired, innocuous-looking cipher. A first date? Celebration of a job well done?

Something like that. "John Ellis" is passing the elegant "Elaine Kelly" an envelope under the table.

But this time, it isn't Elaine who's watching through the window from the shadows, unobserved.

This time it's the truck driver watching through the same plate-glass window, shielded by the same huge old tree. He can't see the envelope being passed. But he can see the sudden slight hunch forward of the man's shoulders, the shift forward of his biceps, and the matching lean and arm movements of the woman. Their eyes lock, he sees, and in that moment no mouths move. There is silence between them. A signal to him, a confirmation, of the amateurish transfer of funds beneath the table.

The hulking truck driver frowns, flips open his cell phone, makes a call, speaks animatedly in the same guttural, forceful foreign language. Reporting it thoroughly, or sufficiently, or excitedly. Hanging up, he shakes his head at this turn of events, at his partner who mastered the language, even many of its subtleties, but did not master loyalty or trustworthiness.

The truck driver follows the elegant woman down the street.

He watches her go into an apartment building.

He stands outside, eyes patiently watching the face of the building until a light goes on.

His eyes and his attention travel unerringly, with intense focus, to a fire escape now lit by the window, framing it.

When the truck driver flips open his phone again, and speaks the rich, thick, molten syllables into it, an observer would make out only two words of English: *Elaine Kelly*.

It is the name on the New York State driver's license that he is holding in his bear-paw hands, next to the picture of the elegant woman. Words he is speaking awkwardly, sounding out carefully for whoever is on the other end of the phone.

It is also, presumably, the name of the woman now lying dead at his feet.

He wipes off the license, puts it back carefully in her wallet.

Once he is off the phone, he reaches carefully inside the lapel of her overcoat, feels around, and withdraws a folded manila envelope.

He opens it enough to see the stack of cash. Shoves the envelope deep into his own lapel pocket.

No reason to leave it.

36

Nussbaum is talking with a uniformed CSI as they ride the elevator up.

"Had bank receipts, statements, ID," the CSI reports cheerfully. "Statements show she was just at a bank a few hours earlier. Huge transfer. Nothing else in the purse. Seemed suspicious. On a hunch, I checked the missing-persons wall, saw your post, and called you. You been looking for her long? You don't seem real surprised."

Elaine Kelly. Dead on a floor in an anonymous apartment in Brooklyn belonging to no one they can find.

No, not surprised.

Inside the apartment, Nussbaum stands over the covered body. He pulls back the sheet.

Nussbaum stares at the body of Elaine Kelly.

Suppresses the elation that it is not *his* Elaine Kelly. Because it is someone, after all. Someone somehow tangled up in this.

"Now, Detective, you *do* look a little surprised," says the CSI.

"Yeah, well, I guess I am."

"Sorry about this," says the CSI.

"Yeah, well, thanks."

He suppresses the urge to skip down the stairs. To celebrate some poor woman's death.

What is her relationship to the other Elaine Kelly? The missing Elaine Kelly?

First, two Antonio Desirios.

Now, two Elaine Kellys.

And only one Evan Nussbaum. Which is not enough Nussbaums, apparently, to figure this out.

37

Madrid. *Rome. Buenos Aires.*

The man who called himself John Ellis, who Conner called Alton, is sitting in a window seat of a commercial jet's business class cabin, smiling to himself.

Lisbon.

Auckland.

Shanghai.

He has seen Elaine Kelly's fantasies and plans on her home computer's search history.

He could have chosen any of them. She had done all the research for him. He smiles again. He is taking her plan.

First inhabiting her home. Now inhabiting her escape.

His own fantasy, though, is not so exotic or imaginative. More predictable, but more practical regarding extradition treaties, prosecutorial jurisdictions, etc.

He holds a tropical drink in his hand and looks out the window to see, thirty-five thousand feet below them, a little chain of islands and atolls, licked and cosseted by the glistening Caribbean. He breathes deeply.

A flight attendant brings him another drink. He takes a big, satisfied swig.

He blinks. Presumably at the spectacular scenery.

He gasps. Presumably at something he's just remembered . . . or suddenly realized.

He looks down at the drink. Perhaps about to ask for a refill.

Then he slumps forward.

The flight attendants come running.

An Eastern European businessman in a brown suit is seated in the second row of coach.

He leans forward toward the commotion in business class, along with the other passengers in his row. Frowns full of concern.

Then leans back, slips a packet of powder back into his jacket pocket, and pats it unobtrusively before returning to his in-flight magazine. The chemical is only reactive with alcohol, so he's had to presume quiet celebration from the business class passenger, but he has presumed correctly. Waiting for him to nap. Brushing past him to the lavatory at the business class bulkhead. Now he can relax.

When the passenger next to him asks, he says he's in the "transportation business." Which a truck driver is.

He'll take a day in Grand Cayman when they land, then hop a flight to England, switch for a flight to Bulgaria, then switch again for a prop plane to Slovenia, where he'll spend some time with his extended family, and go back to work at the hospital where they're always glad to have as skilled an anesthesiologist as he. It's the work he loves and excels at. If only it paid enough to support his extended family. So many of the males in his family have been victims of war and displacement, he is the sole means of support for nearly twenty people now. The contract work in the United States is dangerous, and is hardly proper work for a doctor, but it pays enormously well, and the tools are simple and elementary—a few syringes, some packets of various fast- and slow-acting compounds and poisons—and his employers always do their part in keeping him unidentified, helping him slip in and out of jobs and the country. It's work they only want him for occasionally. They didn't want him to, couldn't have him, work continuously. He would become recognizable, a target. He's more valuable this way.

He does the work only when he needs the money. As for the morality of the work itself? The drug world. Junkies, thieves, double-crossers, scam artists, the desperate. All life is precious, has value, but these lives have let themselves go awry, have less value than others. It's a challenge to his Catholicism. The priests would object strenuously if they knew. But what can he do? He is supporting his family, enabling its next generation to survive in the struggling economy of Slovenia, to thrive in the world beyond it, and no priest will be able to talk him out of that.

PART THREE

38

A corner conference room in downtown Manhattan. Floor-to-ceiling windows on two sides. Breathtaking views across civilization—across a dozen bridges and into neighboring states—as far as the eye can see, trumping what the mind can imagine.

Banking's inner sanctum. Its highest reaches. The New York headquarters of Federated.

A dozen bankers are seated around the huge conference-room table, waiting.

Carlton Conner sweeps in confidently, takes his place at the head of the table.

He appears tan, fit, impeccably dressed and coiffed, as always. The past twelve hours are nowhere on him.

With him are several lieutenants, who take chairs along the perimeter of the room. One of them is a well-dressed, well-turned-out special assistant.

Elaine Kelly, in her charcoal suit and white pearls, is every inch the banker.

She wears a name tag: *Elaine Kelly. NE Operations Special Liaison to Chairman's Office.*

There are 164,000 employees of the bank where she works, and an executive staff of thirty who will today decide their fate.

She's a banker. The kind her mother imagined. Dreamed of.

Well, not quite. A fractured, errant version of the dream.

Dressed primly, elegantly, properly, in a glass corner of sky. At an altitude, with a sweeping view, that only reminds her of jumping through that same sky nearly naked and fully terrified just hours ago, it occurs to her.

She earns a glance or two. Like a wedding guest who each side—bride's and groom's—thinks the other side invited. The more cynical assume she is the chairman's new plaything. That there is something going on between them. Something he needs and gets from her. Something she needs or wants from him. They're right. But what else is new? What does that change? Nothing. There are bigger issues, much bigger issues, preoccupying the large, somber staff.

She would go largely unnoticed under normal circumstances.

But she is doubly invisible—unnoticed, accepted—amid the disruptions and upheavals at this moment of bank crisis.

It's good to be back at the bank.

Once Conner is seated, the conference room lights dim and a senior vice president of operations stands up and launches a PowerPoint presentation.

"We're talking about a six percent global staff attrition. About eight thousand jobs. That's the only way to escape Q3 slaughter from the analysts . . ."

Eight thousand jobs.

She watches the projections in a haze—the parade of graphs, the steady, monotone accretion of logic and justification.

Power, Elaine sees immediately. They are all powerless. Answering blindly to the system, to the imperative of profit, to the machine of business, to quarterly results, to huge faceless masked forces hovering above them all, panting like dogs humping them in the infinite dark.

She focuses again when the vice president of the New York region gets up. Refers to his own projected PowerPoint.

"Eastern metro region . . . We can close these one hundred fifty branches, eliminate one thousand seven hundred jobs . . ."

"Net net?" asks Conner.

"Three hundred mil in payroll," says the VP flatly. An accounting machine.

She sees the Northern Boulevard bank branch in tiny type on the PowerPoint listing. The branch, wiped out with one stroke, one nod of a VP's head. Sam. Vicki. Glen. Sarah. Pam. All jobless. Lives changed. Years and loyalty erased. The branch not even mentioned by name. Gone, with not even a word. She is glad she is here to see how it happened. To at least bear witness for them . . .

Banker Girl. Able to wipe out whole branches with a single Power-Point slide.

Banker Girl. Scaling one of banking's tallest buildings, only to discover she has no superpowers at all.

"Good, good. That's it?"

The older, distinguished vice chairman, sitting to Conner's right, chimes in. "That's everything, Carl. With all regions, eight thousand jobs, and eight hundred fifty million saved."

"Okay," says Conner. "Time to face the music."

• • •

Carlton Conner and his "crisis staff" from the corporate boardroom file somberly into the front of the bank's intimate, well-appointed, private auditorium, and if it usually hosts an orderly, obedient audience of correctly dressed employees, hushed and attentive and predictable, today's audience is anything but.

TV cameras on tripods. Camera operators in baseball jackets and T-shirts. Wires and cables crossing the seats and floors like slouching teenagers. Financial reporters seated in the front row, waiting for the press conference to begin. Raucous, skeptical, impatient.

As Conner takes his seat along with other senior officers, the remaining staff—Elaine included—fill in behind him. The TV camera lights ignite suddenly, blindingly bright.

At the moment they do, Elaine's right hand is bumped hard from behind.

She drops her cell phone.

Conner's cell phone.

She spins around to see who bumped her, but all the surrounding staffers are staring straight into the unfamiliar, disconcerting glare of the cameras.

Carlton Conner, the chairman and CEO of Federated Bank, her boss, cynosure, center of attention, seated directly in front of her, graciously reaches down to retrieve the dropped phone off the floor for her.

The TV lights shine white and blinding. The TV cameras are running.

Conner straightens, hands the dropped phone to Elaine.

"Your phone, Miss . . . Kelly." Squinting at her name tag.

A brief bit of chivalry caught on camera before the onslaught of questions, the shouted war of numbers and spin.

What a gentleman the chairman is.

What a decent, regular guy.

Twenty seconds of video—offhand, accidental—captured by the media.

It will make a graphic, compelling piece of evidence.

She knows immediately.

How, as he reached for the cell phone, he put his replacement phone down next to it, scooping up the one she dropped.

Elaine blinks in the television glare, disoriented.

Mumbling anxiously, weakly, in front of the bright lights, "No, I . . . I don't think that's mine . . ."

A couple of the bankers standing beside her look down briefly.

Conner turns the phone over.

It says *E. Kelly* on a tape label on the back.

Deft little touch, Carlton. To erase any doubt.

Confidently, graciously, "No, it's yours, Miss Kelly."

His own phone, she knows, is already back in his own pocket.

Holstered before firing.

He looks up at the TV cameras and begins. "A complex operating environment calls for swift and substantial response, and today, Federated is announcing significant layoffs. Unfortunately, a total of eight thousand jobs will be eliminated . . ."

Make that 8,001.

Her leverage is suddenly gone with Conner's quick scoop of the cell phone, a hawk swooping down on brushed-steel prey.

Her superpowers neutralized.

He'll quickly see where the video was sent. Have it retrieved and destroyed. And issue a sufficiently vague-sounding, utterly clear directive like "*Tie up the loose pieces.*"

Loose pieces, as in whores.

Tie up, as in much worse than tie up.

"*My god, he could do that to us!*"

Liv's words echo in her.

She can barely hear what Conner is saying through her panic.

39

Nussbaum is kicking back with a beer in his living room. For the moment, the kids are quiet, occupied with Legos and video games in the next room, for a few minutes anyway. The *Post* is spread out in front of him.

The television is tuned to CNN, which is covering some press conference. He'd turn to a more interesting channel, but he can't find the remote.

Carlton Conner, a smooth-talking CEO, is speaking to reporters. The chairman of Federated Bank, says the crawl below. The bank where Elaine Kelly worked. Plus that kid who was killed downtown.

Several of the executives arrayed behind Conner are visible on camera.

The shock is as sudden and complete as a jolt to his whole body. In retrospect, he realizes that he probably stopped breathing.

There she is. Elaine Kelly. Missing. Then found. On television. On the news. That's where the missing end up, yes. But not like this.

He's been looking for days. And here she is, in his living room.

He jumps up from the couch, knocking the newspaper fluttering away, searches the toy-piled coffee table and couch frantically for the remote control. There! Christ! He punches up the volume frantically.

". . . a complex operating environment calls for swift and substantial response . . . significant layoffs . . . eight thousand jobs . . ."

He sees Elaine. She seems to be paying little attention, merely frowning at her cell phone.

Nussbaum leaps forward to the TV screen, as if hoping to jump inside it.

He sees her pushing buttons on her phone.

His cell phone rings on the coffee table.

He leaps for it.

A text message appears.

Rather pithy, complete and accurate, he will reflect someday: *In trble. Lf & dth.*

In the auditorium hallway, as camera operators and reporters are exiting after the press conference, Elaine can see Conner talking intently, privately into his cell phone, ten yards away from everyone.

His back is turned. Clearly the chairman does not want to be disturbed or interrupted on this important call.

At one point in his unheard conversation, he glances over at Elaine.

Their eyes meet as Elaine frantically dials her own phone, looking back at Conner.

Their intense mutual phoning is completely unremarkable amid two dozen bankers and staffers all on their own smartphones and BlackBerry devices, catching up, plugging back in, post–press conference.

"Liv, it's me," she whispers urgently into her phone. "He's got his phone. You're no longer safe. Get out of there. Stay away from me, they'll be watching me. Stay away from everyone . . ." Elaine looks over at Conner in time to see him hand his cell phone to a staffer with a crew cut. Unsmiling, military looking.

She recognizes him as the one standing behind her during the press conference.

The unsmiling staffer exits quickly through a side door, and is gone.

Christ.

Elaine frantically dials another number. Thinks about the path and speed of the electronic pulse, the path, the invisible waves, of e-mail and video, of their terminus.

She says a name she had not expected to. One that reminds her of games in the dark growing up—when games in the dark were innocent—when she wanted her sister to emerge from hiding to end the game. But now it is no game.

"Annelle? . . . Annelle?"

40

In a sunny garden apartment in an undistinguished but immaculate complex in downtown Atlanta, a place that acknowledges no past and no future, only a bland prefab-pressboard present, Annelle Kelly lounges on a cheap IKEA couch. The apartment is cheerful and bright. Framed music posters. Potted plants. The TV is on in the background.

Between drags on a cigarette, Annelle is registering a grievance and confusion she has been nursing for a while but has not had the heart nor energy to pursue, though she does so now. "My god, Elaine, I've been trying you since I got that . . . that horrible . . . that filth! My god! My own sister . . ." When Annelle had first seen the familiar number just now, she'd refused to pick up. She didn't know what she would say. She let the machine answer, and listened back, and heard the desperation in her sister's voice. It happened a second time; she listened again to her sister's panicky plea to call. When the familiar number appeared a third time, Annelle had calmed herself enough with a cigarette, and, inhaling deeply once more, picked up the receiver.

In the Federated hallway, the whisper is urgent. "Annelle, they took my cell phone, my wallet, I had no way to reach you . . ."

"And then there you are on the news," Annelle continues, ignoring her, "with the *same* guy . . . Is that how much you wanted success? I don't know you anymore . . ."

"Listen to me." Elaine's jaw is clenched, trying to remain calm in the face of her sister's blithe stubbornness, trying to deliver the information coherently, and quickly, and usefully, and above all, believably. "Some very dangerous people now know you've got that video, and they've probably already got someone coming for it, and they're going to delete the video, erase your hard drive, and—" Her voice catches on the word, on the thought. "*Kill* you, Annelle, and no one will know who did it or why. There's only one thing you can do to save yourself . . ."

And something in her tone, something in the ancient immutable sisterly connection gets through to Annelle, who is beginning to understand, to experience the appropriate frantic response . . .

"What?"

"Post the video to YouTube."

"What?!"

"Once it's up, they won't risk hurting you. He'll be exposed. It'll be over. It'll be too obvious who did it if anything happens to you. Post it. Post it now."

But with that ancient immutable sisterly connection, there is a sisterly protectiveness, too. "I won't do it," says Annelle. "Your life will be over. I won't do that to you . . . or Mom's memory . . . or our family . . . I just won't . . ."

"You have to. They forced me. It's your only chance."

At that moment, there is a knock on Annelle's apartment door. Annelle spins in shock toward it.

Elaine can hear the knock through the phone receiver. "Don't answer! Post the video! Post it now!"

Annelle hurries over to sit down at her computer.

She opens the video file, looks at its first frame again, getting ready to post it.

"I can't! I just can't!"

Another knock.

When Annelle doesn't answer, whoever is on the other side starts to jimmy the lock.

Annelle panics.

She jumps up.

Flees across the apartment . . .

Out her sliding back door . . .

Across the garden apartment's tiny wooden back porch . . .

Down the wooden stairs and out the back gate . . .

Running away again.

• • •

Elaine can't see any of it. All Elaine knows is the confusion of sounds she can hear over the phone. The drama she must construct in her head. And Elaine Kelly, once again, is the sister left behind.

Because Annelle Kelly's cell phone is still open next to Annelle's computer, Elaine's voice emanating from it, whispering, urgent, plaintive, over and over, "Did you post it?! Did you?!" And when she pauses, she hears footsteps, the scrape of a chair, the sounds of a presence at the other end.

Someone is there, in the apartment, at Annelle's desk, where Annelle had just been sitting, about to send, forward, or delete the video.

And while Elaine listens intently, hears the shuffling at the desk, suddenly there is a dial tone.

Whoever it is has ended Elaine's eavesdropping, cut off the call. Whoever it is can see what number was calling, and now has Elaine's cell phone number.

Standing frustrated, impotent, in the auditorium hallway of Federated Bank, Elaine can't see the front door handle turning in Atlanta.

She can't see the door opened carefully. Or the hulking, intimidating male figure who enters and sits down quickly at Annelle's computer.

She doesn't know that the opening frame of the video is still on the computer screen.

Or that now the male figure takes out his own cell phone, makes his own call.

Reporting to the man who retained his services, the man he knows is waiting eagerly, impatiently, cell phone in hand.

"Nobody here," the hulking male says into his cell phone, authoritative, sounding pleased, relieved. "But like you said, Detective, there's a pretty interesting piece of video on the girl's computer screen . . ."

• • •

In Evan Nussbaum's living room, he doesn't even notice the kids climbing on his lap. He isn't aware of the toys and newspapers spread around him. His wife hears him speak into his cell phone—focused, urgent, police business. "Can you forward it to me?" Nussbaum says.

"It's your missing person," the male voice on the other end informs him. "Plus the girl in the photo you sent down. Plus—get this—Carlton Conner of Federated Bank. I recognize him. All of them . . . uh, interacting . . ."

"I owe you big, Ronaldson. And your fair city. Thanks."

• • •

There is another knock on Annelle Kelly's apartment door.

Detective Ronaldson draws his gun.

Pulls back into the kitchen and out of sight.

There's someone fiddling with the lock. Just as he had fiddled with it a minute ago.

The door opens.

A man enters.

Sits down at the computer.

Looks at the first frame of video on-screen.

Quickly dials a phone number on his cell phone. "Got it."

There is suddenly a gun held to the side of the man's head.

Detective Ronaldson pulls the cell phone out of the man's hand, and as he does, he can hear the arrogant, confident voice of authority on the other end, instructing the man to "Get rid of it. Take care of it. Now."

Ronaldson can't resist. "Oh, we'll take care of it, all right," he says into the cell phone before hanging up. He immediately checks the cell phone display, to record what number Mr. Get Rid of It is calling from, and forwards the information to Nussbaum in New York.

• • •

With an open beer, a TV remote, a cell phone, and a two-year-old climbing all over him, Detective Evan Nussbaum has saved a woman's life—maybe two women's lives—and cracked a case without getting up from his living room couch.

Two Antonio Desirios.

Two Elaine Kellys.

Which needed, in the end, two Evan Nussbaums.

The second one named Ronaldson, who had left for Atlanta and a lifestyle change over a year ago, but missed the thrill of the 114th and couldn't have been happier to help out.

Nussbaum loves police work.

41

"Oh, we'll take care of it, all right." Carlton Conner stares at his phone. Still hears the unfamiliar voice, the surprising, arrogant response, ringing in his head. And knows, by its tone of confidence, by its note of victory and sneer, that it is a law enforcement officer of some sort.

He hangs up the phone, looks down the hallway toward NE Operations Special Liaison Elaine Kelly.

Hanging up her phone. Looking back at him.

A duel with modern, matching weapons of telemetry . . . and she has won. The combatants in charcoal suits and polished shoes and perfectly coiffed hair, but still a duel. A duel of life and death. And somehow she has won. Somehow, she was quicker, smarter on the draw. The Master, the feared overlord of thousands, recovering his gleaming weapon, brandishing it again to strike awe and fear. And yet, she was quicker.

It's obvious the piece of video has fallen into other hands. That it is the authorities, or some other competing party, that will "take care of it."

And that will be the end of it all: His chairmanship. His public life. His career. His marriage and family life. His power.

He will have nothing. With the benefit of his intelligence, his dispassionate business acumen and vision, he can see he'll have nothing.

He smiles. Because he sees at once that she was right. When you have nothing, you have nothing to lose, and oddly, you have all the power. A different kind of power. A dangerous, unchecked power.

He feels it fill him, this sense of power. A power he has waited to feel all his life. A power of rage and revenge that he has had to concoct artificially, approach obliquely, in seedy staged settings late at night with actors for hire. A show that always falls short.

But now the rage and revenge are real. After a lifetime, they will have their moment.

Carlton Conner—unleashed, transformed—moves toward Elaine. In full recognition of his impending undoing. Bent on a little undoing of his own.

There are a handful of bankers and journalists still left in the hallway. They see the chairman of Federated moving forcefully down the hallway, focused, intent, attending to important business, clearly not to be interrupted. Some of them notice a young assistant hurrying away on some important business of her own.

Elaine has been quick, clever, sharp. Under stress, she has calculated well. Devising a blackmail plan using someone else's smartphone. Executing an escape across rooftops that worked because it was so unexpected. Insinuating herself into the halls of power to stall for time and keep her enemy close. Reacting quickly when Conner swapped the phones. Texting a police detective at exactly the right moment.

She has saved her sister. Her actions have recovered the digital file.

But after such admirable calculation, she has miscalculated slightly. And in this league, at this lofty altitude, miscalculating slightly means miscalculating badly.

Because if the video file is now in other hands, and not hers, then she has lost her leverage.

Maybe it was the consuming effort to save her sister Annelle that made her miss that point.

She watches Carlton Conner coming down the hallway toward her.

Having been there herself just hours ago, she recognizes by merely the nature of his movement, his posture, his expression, his speed, that this is someone who has nothing left to lose.

Nothing but the power of the moment. The power of action. A final exercise of power. What will he do with it? In what ultimate way will a man like Carlton Conner expend it?

He is accelerating down the hallway at her.

Jaw set. Eyes blank. Unleashed. Unbound. Fury and rage finally pure and unadorned. Heading toward the woman who has engineered his ruin.

Elaine turns and runs.

She pushes the elevator button and realizes as she does it—*old thinking, charcoal-gray suited, high-heeled thinking*—she can't wait that long and has no choice but to barge into the stairwell next to the elevator bank.

She rushes down the first flight, no time to think, to plan . . .

He explodes into the stairwell above her as she rounds the first landing. Their eyes meet for only an instant.

Fifty floors to go.

A spiral descent into the void, into oblivion, staying a few steps ahead of him.

She knows she will never make it.

He'll catch her—leap down on top of her—in another few flights.

Which is why she suddenly ducks back out of the stairwell, onto another floor, at the next stairwell door two floors below.

Empty. No one here.

Chairs, desks, computers, the dizzying panoramic views out the floor-to-ceiling windows, but no people. Lights off. Not even the electric hum of the overhead fluorescents. No employees. Not a soul.

She had assumed it would be another floor of Federated.

Suddenly she realizes, it is.

A floor where the jobs have already been cut. An earlier round of layoffs. Carlton Conner's budgetary handiwork, his vision, already instituted, decisively begun.

The complete, eerie silence lasts only a few seconds.

Until Conner bursts out of the stairwell behind her.

Panting. Staring. Possessed.

Carlton Conner, Elaine Kelly, on an empty floor of a downtown skyscraper. Alone.

She reaches for her cell phone.

It is ripped from her hand, flung across the floor, and she is on her back on the floor, too, Conner on top of her, his fists tight around her wrists, and then around her throat.

It is all instantaneous. With an unthinking swiftness fueled by rage, and an imbalance of power and control that is complete and inarguable.

The constriction around her throat is all she can feel. All she knows. All she is. Her own fists are up frantically against it. Futilely.

The light beyond the panoramic windows—the light and life of the city of her brightest dreams—now darken into shadow . . .

Now darken further toward black . . .

The brothel room comes back to her. The pitch-black cell. The dizziness.

The sensory memory overwhelms her. And with some small final clarity of mind she realizes this is the last thing she will know, feel, remember. The nightmare she awoke into is the nightmare to which she is being returned. Coming full circle to that cold hard womb. It has the feel of inevitability, as she drifts darker, drifts down . . .

Caught, no escape.

And then the constriction suddenly eases. Light floods in again. She draws a breath from some previously unknown, sacred place in her lungs.

And is now aware of the shifting of his body above her. Aware of his groin against her. And then realizes, feels, his cock hard, insistent, angry, eager.

Power.

Genuine, ultimate power of life and death over her.

Of course it turns him on.

Deters him, defers him, distracts him momentarily from strangling her, into an activity even more compelling, even less conscious or controllable, even more *impulsive*.

No cuffs. No mattress. No mask. No props.

None of it needed. Raw encounter. Raw revelation.

Just the empty floor of his domain. The floor he has cleared out, commandeered, emptied but for him and her, as if for him and her. As if for this last encounter. This culmination.

No words. They are beyond words.

Connection . . . limbs, thoughts, lives entwined . . . Connection . . .

Panting, wild, unconscious, merely muscle and motion, he rips her skirt and panties aside. Unzips his fly.

Brandishes his hard-on like a weapon.

For whatever reasons of association, through whatever mysterious methods the mind employs to protect itself in times of extreme duress, she is suddenly picturing his other weapon: his phone.

The weapon he just swapped and recovered in the press briefing.

Its power interchangeable, from him, to her, to him.

A weapon's power, interchangeable . . .

The weapon she first reached for in the brothel's blue light.

To save herself.

She reaches for a weapon now.

Again, to save herself.

Grabs his hard-on in her fist.

Yanks it furiously in one direction.

A gasp and a scream.

Yanks it hard again the other way.

The scream exploding, multiplying . . .

Shifting it into neutral.

Taking it out of gear.

In the ten seconds of his unanswered cry of intense writhing pain, his scream echoing across the empty floor of Federated, she is up off the floor, scooping up her cell phone, pulling her ripped skirt back up, running for the elevator, and dialing Evan Nussbaum once more.

Live by the sword. Die by the sword.

There are 164,000 employees at Federated. And here at global headquarters, not one can hear the chairman screaming.

42

Elaine and Nussbaum sit across from each other in a small quiet room in the 114th Precinct.

The door is closed.

There's an old, scarred wooden table between them. A witness to decades of interrogation, to a thousand attempts at the truth.

There's a small window that looks out on to the side street. A window in the interrogation room . . . it tells how archaic and out-of-date this end of the stationhouse is. The window, like the table, bears silent witness, but adds perspective, like a wistful, dreamy good cop to the scarred table's bad cop. Nussbaum has had that odd thought before.

"So by then," Nussbaum is explaining to her, "after what happened to your friend Bob and the fake Elaine, I knew what we were dealing with. And by your panicked text, that you might be next. I had them trace the next call you made. Annelle Kelly. A sister, presumably. Atlanta area code. I didn't know how exactly, but I figured it was a call to protect her." He smiles. "When you only got her machine at first, you must have been terrified. But of course, for a trace, her machine was all we needed."

All he needed to launch Ronaldson like a rocket toward Annelle Kelly's apartment. Nussbaum doesn't bother to explain how they all teased Ronaldson mercilessly when he said he was moving his family to Atlanta, a "cost of living" and "quality of life" decision. Atlanta PD had made him a nice offer. Atlanta! And how it was just a phone call to Ronaldson to do Nussbaum a solid, and how Ronaldson said it was the most action he'd had in the two years he'd been there.

Elaine looks across the table at Nussbaum. Those same warm, swimming eyes, a still place amid the inordinate chaos of her life. "So what's going to happen to me?" she asks.

She lifts her hands and sets them on the wooden table. The handcuffs she's wearing are now between them, so there's no pretending she doesn't have them on—by either one of them. Handcuffs that are the protocol in any arrest. How every suspect is safely moved through the 114th.

Once again, she thinks, *handcuffs and their mixed meaning*. Nussbaum has saved her, but Nussbaum has captured her. Has caught a thief.

The dance of power. The mixed meaning lurking in the props.

Nussbaum's partner Dominguez is in the room with them, sitting in the corner, listening silently.

Nussbaum nods to him. Dominguez gets up, walks over, uncuffs her, returns quietly to his corner.

Nussbaum looks at her somberly, ruefully. "Elaine, you stole one million three hundred thousand dollars." It seems to her that he simply wants to hear the fact aloud. To put it out into the little room, out into the universe. Let both of them hear how it sounds.

He squints at her. "And by the way, why a million three?"

She is confused. "What do you mean? That's what was in the account."

"Well, no. You left about fifty-five grand in there."

"I wanted to leave something. Look, it happened fast. The exact sum was just . . . impulsive." She is trying to be as honest as she can. She figures that's her only chance at mercy.

He nods. "It's just that, one point three million is . . . you know . . ."

"What?"

"A multiple of thirteen. Like in, you know . . . unlucky . . ."

Unlucky thirteen. Multiplied.

Unlucky times a hundred thousand.

Unlucky, and if you keep moving the decimal point over . . . unluckier and unluckier.

He crosses his arms, cocks his head. "You also managed to bring down a corrupt bank chairman, reveal hundreds of millions in money laundering, and help bust a white-slavery ring. And you and your partner across time, Arthur Holden"—he gives her a knowing, little smile—"even drew a drug kingpin out of the shadows when he couldn't get to his money. Not a bad week's work."

Nussbaum gets up, wanders over to the window, looks out on the side street. Shares for a moment the window's perspective, its ancient witness. "I feel sure the scales of justice will tip in your favor. Or *should*, anyway." He smirks a little, then turns to her anew, and smiles. "But I think you've learned it's wrong to steal."

"Very wrong."

Nussbaum sees something out the window and silently gestures Elaine to come look out the window with him.

On the street below them, Liv stands smoking a cigarette. Waiting for Elaine. Nowhere else to be.

Nussbaum smiles, pleased. "And she's free."

"No, not free," Elaine corrects him. "Getting free. I was there a few days. She was there who knows how long. You don't emerge from that so fast. If ever."

As they watch Liv smoke, Elaine tells Nussbaum what she's finally learned. "She was Desirio's girlfriend. Aborted his child without his permission. That was it. The Bulgarian patriarchal types don't go for that. He made her a slave. Sold her nightly. The greatest degradation he could think of."

"And Arthur Holden?"

As mysterious as ever, she thinks. No relationship to Liv. Not even friends, Liv had told her. Just someone from the neighborhood. Someone who knew what had happened to her. Someone who decided to care.

Nussbaum has explained by now the outline of Arthur Holden's plan: trying to turn the dealers against one another. Make them think, amid the tangle of accounts, that they are stealing from one another. A plan that didn't work because the bank, at a high level that Arthur Holden had no access to or knowledge of, was serving several of them directly, attending to their financial needs, overseeing their accounts, treating them as legitimate customers in a way he might never have imagined.

She tells him everything she knows about Arthur Holden. Maybe everything there is to know. "A bank teller," she says. "A bank teller who cared what happened." Sounds crazy. Incomplete. Before she realizes that's what she is, too.

But now Nussbaum adds to the picture of Arthur Holden, carefully, ruefully. "Maybe Arthur Holden realized exactly what he was up against. Realized that criminals at this level might be too smart to attack each other, might be insiders, bank clients, their financial interests watched out for, protected. Meaning they would only be found out in an official investigation when the accounts were opened and examined, meaning, in the wake of Arthur Holden's own death." Nussbaum grows quieter, shakes his head. "So all his frantic bank activity, his busy transferring of assets, was only to make the irregularities more obvious, harder for anyone to eventually hide or gloss over. Maybe he knew exactly what he was doing, and if he did, he knew he was doomed. And he was just making sure his doom meant something. Stuffing in more powder to make sure the explosion was big enough."

That black coat. That black hat. That black sense of mission.

"And Liv?" she asks.

Nussbaum shrugs. "She's . . . the reason." Pausing. "We all need our reasons. Our motivation. We all need our saints, Elaine." He gives a quick, grim smile.

Which just as quickly evaporates. Nussbaum regards her expressionlessly. "You'll be arraigned this afternoon." He continues looking at her, and promises, "But I'll be there."

He'd promised to look into the case. He'd promised to follow through. Elaine smiles appreciatively. "I know you will, Detective Nussbaum."

She would hug him in appreciation—maybe in something more than appreciation—if Dominguez weren't there.

A knock on the door. Two suited men enter, and she remembers them immediately—the burly precinct captain, Hanratty, and the police lawyer Elaine saw days ago in the captain's office, arguing with Desirio and his lawyer.

Captain Hanratty says quietly, seriously, to Nussbaum, "Detective, we need a little privacy with Miss Kelly."

Nussbaum looks down at the windowsill. The chipped paint. The divots of age. The deep channels of its old-fashioned sash. He thinks of his odd metaphor again. The scarred table like the bad cop, burrowed deep with the worst of human behavior. The old window like the good cop, looking out, hopefully, beyond it. Silent witnesses to the margins of human interaction, the good, the bad, and the very beautiful blend of both seated and handcuffed before him. Her red hair like a beacon to the complexity of human choices. Her foolishness, her impulsiveness, her morality, her bravery.

Rabbi Akiba comes back to him, a medieval figure in the Yom Kippur service. *If not me, then who? If not now, then when?* The Yom

Kippur service comes flooding at him again—his children against his shoulders, his young son on his lap. And with it all, one more Akiba-like question, but more practical, grounded in the reality of the 114th Precinct: *Hey, what can one man do?*

Nussbaum, Elaine sees, is about to protest being suddenly shut out but swallows his pride, slaps the windowsill with an indication of finality, and he and Dominguez exit, abruptly, dutifully, and without another word.

43

The lawyer closes the door behind him. The captain sits down opposite Elaine, spreads his thick hands on the old wooden table, looking for exactly where to put them. As if to brace himself. Steady himself. Then begins.

"You may or may not realize it, but your little adventure has set in motion a lot of accusation and posturing and politics. Federated's lawyers are already putting distance between Conner and the company, denying any corporate wrongdoing. Regulatory agencies are already closing ranks, saying it wasn't their failing but proposing new controls. There'll be new scrutiny on all the banks." He lifts his thick hands for a moment, spreads them, holds them out, to symbolize the scope of what has happened, before dropping them to the table again.

He tilts his big, square head. Scratches at his ear for a moment as if to chase away all the noise of politics, all the distraction of institutional issues that have lodged inside it. He looks at her. "Miss Kelly, that money that you took from them and they took back from you . . . you know it's drug money. So it can't simply be transferred into some new squeaky-clean Federated account. And it can't be shifted to some other bank or financial institution. That would be directly contrary to the money-laundering laws and fiduciary regulations of the State of New York."

The lawyer now chimes in. "Plus, our office doesn't want to undertake the difficult and expensive international prosecution of a criminal who's already dead." She knew what he was referring to. Nussbaum had mentioned to her the fate of Ellis/Alton.

But she is confused. *What does this have to do with me?*

"Let me cut to the chase," says the captain. "I can waive prosecution this afternoon, if you'll do something for me."

Waive prosecution. Elaine sees a light, a thin narrow light, opening in the sky above her.

"Do what?" *I'll do anything.* That's what she would have said, if it felt appropriate, if she knew these men. If she could throw her arms around them in gratitude at the chance, the second chance, she felt was coming.

"Elaine, we want you to take the money."

What?!

"Wait. I don't under—"

"Elaine, our forensic accountants traced exactly what you did. Your mom's house sale . . ." Hanratty looks at her, smiles. "Elaine, that house sale, your plan . . . the thing is, it still works for us. And solves a huge financial headache." The lawyer nods in accord. The captain continues. "The money will be back in your account in a few hours." He's smiling warmly, generously, knowingly, at this bit of serendipity, at this turn of events, but now frowns, becomes a little firmer. "Frankly, there's no other choice, Elaine. You have to take it."

My god.

He's serious.

Elaine sits back in the chair, stunned, amazed . . . starting to smile at the absurdity and irony, and to get used to the idea of the money coming back to her.

"The worst luck."

Glen's words echo in her head.

"The worst luck."

Maybe not. In the end, maybe not.

"I . . . I can't believe it . . ."

The captain keeps smiling at her. "Believe it," he says as he struggles his big frame up out of the chair and to his feet. "Oh, and one more thing, Elaine." Leaning forward now so the full bulk and heft and consequence of him is part of what he tells her next. "You can't touch it."

You can't touch it. There's something entirely new now, fierce, in Hanratty's blue eyes.

"You do and we prosecute you," says the lawyer, enthusiastically, eager, she notices. "You have to leave it there."

Slowly comprehending, "So . . . I'm parking it for you." *Like a criminal would.* "For . . . for how long?"

"Forever."

Confused. Utterly confused. "Forever?"

Hanratty's eyes move openly along Elaine's body. He studies her curves. He examines her red hair. Her green eyes. He inhales slowly, deeply. "Although, if you, uh"—and here he pauses, searching the scarred table for just the right term—"*cooperate* with us"— clearly pleased with himself that he's found it—"*cooperate* with each of us, individually"—he gestures to the lawyer—"you can have the money." He looks at her, smiling warmly, grandfatherly, eyes twinkling. "A little at a time."

She is startled into comprehension.

Once a hooker . . .

Once a whore . . .

The captain and lawyer steal a complicit glance at each other. Seal their pact with quick, perverse, tight little smiles.

Elaine looks back at them with shock . . . and defeat.

Grandly, heartily, and seeping with irony as the hulking Hanratty exits, he says, "So, Elaine Kelly, how does it feel to have over a million bucks in the bank?"

Elaine stares back. Silent. Speechless. Enslaved again.

44

In a methadone clinic in a former elementary school just off Queens Boulevard, Liv is lined up to get her dose.

The attendant matches her freshly issued New York State ID with the approved state prescription with her name on it. Breaks the seal, hands her the two pills.

She frowns at the pills.

They look a little different today. The color is a little lighter. Oh well. New batch.

She shrugs and swallows them. Chases them with the paper cup of fruit juice they always give her.

A wiry Kurd in thick glasses stands in the clinic doorway and watches her swallow the pills, then turns and disappears onto the bright, sun-soaked street.

Not much to it, he reflects. And they said if it went well, they'd have more assignments like it. He looks like a student. In fact, he is a teacher, a professor of molecular biochemistry in Kurdistan. He's pretty sure no one even looked at him. *That's a frightening and yet exhilarating thing about New York*, he thinks. No one even looks. He's going to like it here, he realizes. The big Slovenian anesthesiologist who had explained the assignment, who had given him the pills to use, promised him he would.

He skips down the street, and at the corner, before crossing, dials the phone number they gave him to report in.

The other pedestrians waiting around him at the crosswalk hear only a harsh, guttural, aggressive-sounding foreign language. Not one of them can say exactly what language it is.

• • •

In a maximum-security federal prison in western Pennsylvania, a guard comes up to Desirio's cell.

Nods to him.

It's done.

Desirio nods back.

He lies back on his bunk.

Stares up.

Smiles with coarse satisfaction.

Degradation. Slavery.

That was only when he was feeling generous.

Sometimes, you had to be more decisive than that.

45

Elaine Kelly is lying on a beach in the sun.

She's wearing sunglasses. There's a cold drink by her side. She squints toward the water, where the waves break modestly, predictably, each with a moment of hollow pause and then a deeper pounding sound, like a pulse against the sand, a steady heartbeat of the earth.

It's not an exotic shore of the Mediterranean or a balmy, languid, palm-shaded inlet on the Indian Ocean that she had once imagined herself lying on, that she had carefully planned to lie on. It is, instead, a strip of sand packed all summer with chaises, blankets, and colorful humanity. A beach at the very edge of Rockaway, Queens.

It's well after beach season. An older Indian couple strolls the shore. A gaggle of die-hard high school girls lie on towels in their halter tops. A couple of joggers come huffing by. Two bums sleep curled on benches at the beach's edge. And Elaine Kelly.

She dragged her beach chair and little cooler on and off two buses to get here.

To feel the familiar Rockaway beach beneath her.

The only beach she's ever known.

The only beach she'll ever know, she realizes.

When her cell phone had rung the night before, she had answered it, listened to the news, and put her head in her hands. She only had to hear the first name—Olivia—the somber formality of it, and she knew.

"You don't emerge from that so fast. If ever." Her offhand comment to Nussbaum as they watched Liv from the window, the prescience of her words now haunting her.

So she came out here. To look at the water. To look at the sky. It was all she could think to do.

In the summer, the beach is filled with splashing kids and water toys—toys and kids of every shape and color. Mothers and fathers with them, laughing, floating, stretching and swimming a stroke or two, abandoning themselves happily to the scene. Aunts and uncles and cousins, fat and lean, diving like sleek slippery fish, floating like colorful whales. It's the beach she knew as a kid. That her mother first brought her to, sitting so regally and stiffly on the sand. The beach she came to later with high school friends.

During summer, a literal sea of humanity—extending well beyond the buoyed swim area—would fill the sandy beach and the busy street that runs alongside it. Vendors, families with strollers, couples holding hands, the sizzle of grills, and the scent of dishes of a dozen national cuisines.

The same diverse, colorful bustling crowd that surges noisily every weekday down the hot, bright sidewalk in front of the cool, silent, serene Federated branch.

The branch now empty. Raw, unrented commercial space.

The branch where she stood at the computer terminal, rooted to the branch's cool high silence, looking out the huge windows at the humanity flowing by.

Not part of it.

Separated from it.

As separated as she is today, sitting by herself on the sand.

There were 164,000 employees of the bank where she worked. And Elaine Kelly is alone.

Some time later, when even the afternoon walkers and runners and dads and their little sons with baseball gloves have abandoned the beach, when the sun has made its way closer to the horizon, a figure looms over her suddenly, silhouetted by the sun's angled glare.

She blinks, blinded momentarily as she tries to look up, reaching for her sunglasses.

"Not easy to find you," says the voice, warm as always. "But hey, I am a detective."

She is startled. Confused. "What . . . what are you doing here?"

"Mind if I sit?" And before she can answer, he is down on the sand alongside her, dark-gray twill pants planted comfortably, looking out at the water and the sun still lingering above it.

"Not the Mediterranean," Nussbaum says.

She can't help smiling. "No."

They watch in silence. Not looking at each other. But she is waiting for an explanation, and he must know that.

"You'd have been a pretty good detective, Elaine," he tells her, cocking his head a little. "Maybe even better than me." He smiles briefly, then squints at the water and pauses before he says, in a different tone, "You reminded me about some things, Elaine. About perseverance. Curiosity. The will to survive. The quest for truth."

He kicks a rock by his shoe. "I never did watch the video, but nevertheless, it inspired me," he says.

Meaning what?

"And your impulsiveness, Elaine. I guess that inspired me, too."

He takes his cell phone out of his jacket pocket, holds it up in the light, studying it like an object of mystery. "When Hanratty and that police lawyer came in to talk to you, I set my cell phone on audio record, put it on the window out of sight behind the sill, and pressed 'Play.' I recorded everything they said to you."

The old interrogation room window. The scarred table. *Good cop. Bad cop.* He'll never know what role the odd metaphor played in his impulse.

She stares at Nussbaum's cell phone.

Stares at him.

"It's not admissible in a court of law," he says, still looking at the cell phone, "but it's highly admissible, and extremely interesting, to Internal Affairs. That's where I was going to take it. I was headed down the hall with it. It would finish them both."

He looks out at the water. "Then I stopped. Thought about it. Thought about you. And instead, I went and told Hanratty and the lawyer about it."

Good cop. Bad cop.

She stares at him. Stunned. Speechless.

Not understanding.

Waiting.

"They know I've got it. And they know I won't do anything with it if they leave you alone." He puts the cell phone back in his jacket pocket. "They know me. I know them. They know I keep my word. And they know they've got no choice. They won't fire me. They won't try anything. And I won't report them." He shrugs. "It's a stalemate."

And at last she says something, asking him because she can't hold back anymore. "But what made you record them? What made you suspect anything?"

What was behind . . . your impulse?

"See?" he says with an affectionate smile. "You're still curious. Still the detective." He looks out again over the water. "Remember when we were leaving the precinct and you stopped us to listen to the argument inside the captain's office?" Yes, she remembered. Her fingers on his forearm to hold him there. She'd been so surprised to hear Desirio practically threatening the captain outright. "I only realized it later," Nussbaum says. "Replaying it in my head.

The tone of the exchange, of what we overheard—they *knew* one another. Those four people in that room, Hanratty and Desirio and the two lawyers, *they already knew one another.* Had obviously met somewhere before. Knew one another well enough to speak to one another that way. You don't talk to a police captain or a police lawyer quite like that unless you've got a prior acquaintance. And if they did, then I knew the context of that acquaintance—some long-standing agreement or arrangement, no doubt." The tone of familiarity, the sense of threat—he'd heard it, too. Who knew how deep the captain's complicity was in the drug-money laundering. Taking a cut, or just turning the other way, or simply doing his own boss's bidding?

"If you hadn't stopped us at that door, Elaine"—Nussbaum shakes his head somberly—"you'd be prosecuted like any other white-collar thief. You'd be headed to prison. I would have walked you right by that argument. Just another argument in a police station. Your curiosity, your alertness . . . It saved you."

Nussbaum looks over at her now. Fully. Unblinking. "I came to tell you, Elaine, that you can spend the money. However you want. Wherever you want. Me, I would never have offered it to you. Unethical. Way wrong. But that was their offer to you, and I'm just making them stick to their deal." He smiles.

Lisbon. Johannesburg. Barcelona. Rio. The Internet images appear in her mind, and instantly recede.

1.3 million.

Lucky.

Unlucky.

She doesn't know what to say. Or even, what to think.

The number appears to her: *1,300,000.00.* A green figure on a terminal screen. Nothing attached to it.

"I also came to tell you"—his look turns suddenly serious, pained, as he traces his fingers in the sand beside him—"that you should use the money to travel." He squints out at the water. "Liv's death . . . We both know Desirio had her killed. Prison apparently doesn't stop him. And who can say where his taste for revenge will end? He might know by now that it wasn't you lying dead in that apartment with an Elaine Kelly license." He punches the sand gently with the back of his hand. A gesture of decision, of finality. "So you need to cut and dye your distinctive red hair"—he smiles sadly—"and take off. Go . . . I don't know"—his eyes light up a little—"somewhere exotic you've always wanted to go." *Lisbon. Johannesburg. Barcelona. Rio.* "Start a new life. Become a new you." He is trying to put the best light on it, but the message is obvious: *You have the money, and now you must run.* Elaine shakes her head in amazement. A New York police captain could be controlled; a man in federal prison could not.

"You read about Conner, I'm sure," Nussbaum says.

"Oh yes."

Suicide. The only way for the disgraced former chairman to retain power over his fate. Jumping naked from a building while awaiting trial. Drama, the limelight—a power junkie to the end. And it was an echo of that night, of course, of that bizarre moment when they had jumped nearly naked from building to building together. She will always wonder if his manner of suicide was meant as a message for her. A perverse, twisted valentine.

The sun is descending now, starting its daily, dramatic dive into the sea. Beginning to turn the sky pink around it. The beach has emptied. He looks down at the sand, scoops up a handful, watches it run through his fingers.

"Nice Jewish boys, nice Catholic girls, we've got a lot in common, you know. We operate by the work ethic, never question responsibility and duty, worry about doing the right thing versus the wrong thing, probably a little more than the next person." He smiles.

The pink is spreading across the sky. A last gasp of day. A last chance.

If not me, then who? If not now, then when? Rabbi Akiba comes back to him.

He looks at her face once more in the fading light.

And leaning toward her, comes to the second point of his visit.

Impulse?

Premeditated?

Good cop?

Bad cop?

He has no such questions, no questions at all, right now.

It is their first kiss, and their last kiss, and both of them know it.

It is a kiss long in coming.

A kiss long in ending.

A kiss that envelops her, that travels down through her, that slices and sunders her. That finds every corner of her. Plunges deep. Sweeps her insides.

She has been ambushed, attacked, drugged, devirginated. She has been degraded, abused, stripped of clothing and of identity. She has been a slave. A sex worker. An orifice and receptacle. An object of male dominion, and submission, and perversity, and obsession.

And through it all, she has never been kissed.

Not like this.

A kiss that is restoration and destruction, cruelty and kindness. That she has waited a lifetime for—without knowing it and knowing it full well.

A kiss of things unfinished—and things unstarted.

A kiss that lasts forever.

And will have to. Because he is married. With three young children.

It is their first, last, and only kiss.

A kiss that is nothing.

And everything.

And truly something.

When they pull apart, she has tears in her eyes.

And through her tears, in the fading afternoon light, she can see Nussbaum's tears, too.

Despite her tears, she can feel her own smile.

Uncontrollable. Warm. Irrepressible.

As warm and irrepressible as his.

Lucky.

Unlucky.

The two words wrestling again in her head, dancing in the waning light.

There are 164,000 employees at the bank where she worked.

Not one could feel the way she does at this moment.

This ordinary, extraordinary moment of beach and sunset, spent with Detective Nussbaum from the 114th.

Acknowledgments

My thanks to my agent Jill Marr, my editor Anh Schluep, my developmental editor Kevin Smith, and the entire Thomas & Mercer team. Book lovers all!

About the Author

Jonathan Stone writes his books on the commuter train between his home in Connecticut and his advertising job in midtown Manhattan, where he has honed his writing skills by creating smart and classic campaigns for high-level brands such as Mercedes-Benz, Microsoft, and Mitsubishi. Stone's first mystery-thriller series, the Julian Palmer books, won critical acclaim and was hailed as "stunning" and "risk-taking" in starred reviews by *Publishers Weekly*. He earned glowing praise for his novel *The Cold Truth* from the *New York Times*, who called it "bone-chilling." He is also the recipient of a Claymore Award for Best Unpublished Crime Novel and a graduate of Yale University, where he was a Scholar of the House in fiction writing.